The Time Thief

By Jacqueline Richardson

Also by Jacqueline Richardson:

The Burning Side
Dream Jumper
Beyond Reason
The Time Thief: A Change of Face

Trent chuckled. "No worries. I'm not here to talk religion. I do fear it may seem a bit stranger, though. Have you noticed anything odd going on around here?"

"Odd like what?"

"Like strange time discrepancies, namely."

Was he mad? "No, I don't think so. I've only been here a couple of weeks." I tried to shift my body as much behind the partially opened door as I could without being obvious. I wondered if I was going to have to shut the door in his face.

"Ah. All right. Say, did you ever meet the previous occupants of this house?"

"No, I didn't."

"Do you by chance know their names?"

"I don't recall off-hand," I replied, feeling uneasy. "Is this conversation going somewhere, or are we done here?"

"My apologies. I know this all seems a bit bizarre. I'll be off then." He held out a business card to me. "If you notice anything out of the ordinary, please give me a ring. I have a sneaking suspicion that something is afoot, and I'm rarely wrong about these things."

I hesitantly took the card from him. I knew I must've been giving him the most obvious look of disbelief, but he just smiled again at me and bowed his head slightly before turning on his heel and walking down the driveway. I shut and locked my door and watched him from the window, peeking from behind the curtain. He had a confident gait, but it was almost amusing how disproportionately large his feet were and the way his legs bowed slightly when he walked. He walked a short distance down the driveway and then stopped. He turned and looked back at the house, a look of puzzlement contorting his face. His brows drew together and he looked down at his watch. He glanced back at the house one more time before he walked to the end of the drive and headed up the road to the north. The trees around my house and along the road quickly obscured my view of him and I lost him. He had appeared to be on foot, but who walked around on foot in a tweed suit down an old dirt road out in the middle of nowhere? My closest neighbor was three miles to the south of me, and there was nothing but state forest in the direction he was headed. Where was he going? Where had he come from?

I looked at the card he had given me, which I was still clutching in my now clammy hands. It was only a phone number – or at least I assumed it was supposed to be, but it had too many digits. No name, no explanation. I ran around the house locking all the windows and the basement and back door. I took my handgun from my purse and holstered it at my hip. I was a strong, athletic woman with some martial arts training, and I could hold my own if I had to – but no one was a match for a gun. I looked out the window again, where my fluffy white cat, Cattiel, was now sitting on the sill. He looked up at me with palpable contempt for invading his space, and it was then that I realized just how much I wished I had a big, intimidating dog.

I was on high alert all afternoon and evening. I checked my windows every few minutes. Had that man been sent by my ex-husband? It was possible. He had always been a bit off mentally, but the divorce had really brought out the worst in him. Psychological warfare was his specialty, and after being married to him and enduring his abuse for over two years, I had come to expect that everything out of the ordinary was either a trick or a test. I may have had a restraining order against him, but he was maliciously inventive and I couldn't rule anything out at this point. I was prepared for the worst.

That night, everything was quiet. I had turned on every outside light I had, including the light on the detached garage, but nothing crossed a single beam. By 2AM, I was barely able to keep my eyes open, and I grabbed Cattiel and crawled into bed. All the lights in the house were on save for my bedroom and hallway light, and I had my door closed, my .45 near my bedside, and my phone under my pillow. I wished I had a burglar alarm, but the tripwire I rigged up in the hallway outside my door would have to do for tonight.

Some time later, I awoke with a start. I lay frozen in my bed, listening, trying to gain my senses and figure out what had awakened me. I turned my eyes toward the clock, trying not to move, and saw that it was a little after 3AM. Then I heard it. It sounded like voices talking, but it was faint and muffled. I sat up in bed and looked around, reaching for my .45. I racked a bullet into the chamber and slipped carefully out of bed, keeping the gun pointed at the ground, safety on. The sound of Cattiel growling caught my attention. In the darkness, I could make out only the outline of his body, but it appeared that his ears were back and he was flattening himself against the bed. It was clear something was upsetting him. I tip-toed closer to the door, hoping to be able to hear what the voices were saying. As I listened, however, it became apparent that the voices weren't coming from a particular place. They were all around. They were muffled, like listening to a dinner party from under a pool. It was like a hundred conversations going on all at once all throughout the house, inside and out.

I didn't know what to do. I stood in the darkness with my sidearm, feeling fairly certain that it would do me no good in this situation. The voices didn't seem to grow or wane in volume, but they did seem to move and change, like people mingling about. I heard laughter. I heard excitement. I heard arguing. But none of it was quite loud enough to make out what was being said. I only got tones and pitches and syllables, and I stood and listened for what felt like an eternity.

Finally, I gathered up enough courage to open my bedroom door. I peeked out into the hallway, and it was empty. I stepped out of my room and sneaked down the hallway, being careful to avoid the tripwire. I investigated the living room. Nothing. The kitchen was clear, too. Everywhere in the house was empty, but the voices emanated throughout the entire place.

"I bought a goddamned haunted house," I whispered shakily under my breath.

Everything went instantly and eerily silent. It felt like a thousand eyes had just turned their attention to me.

"Oh, hell no," I declared, suddenly panicked. I ran to my room to get Cattiel and my car keys, and in my haste, I forgot about the tripwire. It sent me sprawling over the floor in what I can only imagine was the most graceful tumble nobody ever saw. I felt a sharp jolt in my wrist when I landed on it, but the adrenaline coursing through my veins helped to dull the pain. I scrambled to my feet, forgetting about the gun I'd left laying on the floor, and ran into my room. I clumsily fumbled with my keys and snatched my phone from under my pillow. As I reached for Cattiel, he bolted.

"Dammit, cat! I will leave you! I'll do it!" I dropped down and looked under the bed, but it was too dark to see the cat. "Fine, fend for yourself, butthole," I said in exasperation as I stood up. I took the keys and my phone and hurried out of my room – and hit the tripwire one more time. With a slurry of swear words and self-deprecation, I finally made it down the hallway, through the living room, and out the front door. I rushed down the front porch and ran to my car, diving in and locking the doors behind me. I jammed the key into the ignition and started it up.

Just then, my phone started ringing. Surprised, I looked at the screen. It was a jumble of numbers and symbols on the caller ID.

The ghosts are calling! I thought to myself in horror.

I juggled with what to do briefly, but ultimately my curiosity won out. I answered the phone.

"Hello?" My voice sounded higher pitched than usual.

"Has something odd happened?" an English (or Nohkean?) accent asked from the other line. "I feel like something odd has happened."

"Who is this? What kind of sick joke is this?!" I demanded.

"Oh, where are my manners? This is Trent Morgan. I take it something did happen, then? What happened?"

"How did you get my number?" I asked in disbelief.

"Roselyn, we can ask each other silly questions all night or you can just get to the point and tell me what has happened. I can't help you if I don't know what I'm dealing with."

I was taken aback. I stammered, "Voices…voices everywhere. I…I think it's haunted." I noticed that my fear had somewhat dissipated with this distraction, and I realized how crazy what I just said sounded.

"Voices? Oh! Well that's interesting. I wasn't expecting that. Give me a moment. I need to check this out."

"…What?" The call ended before I could give any more of a response. I looked down at my phone, perplexed, and then set it aside.

While the car idled and I sat with my hand on the shifter, I contemplated where exactly I was going to go. I didn't really

11

know anyone around here yet, and my family members were all hours away from me. What on Earth had made me decide moving out to the middle of nowhere would be a smart life choice?

I jumped out of my skin and shrieked when I heard a tapping on the car window next to my head. I continued to shriek until my widened eyes registered what they were seeing outside the car. It was Trent.

…Wait, Trent?!

"Where the hell did you come from?!" I shouted through the closed window.

"I was out and about," he shouted to be heard over the car engine and the closed window. "I told you I was coming to check things out."

"You didn't say you were coming! How did you get here so fast? It's three o'clock in the morning! Who the hell are you?!"

"Can we maybe do this with the window down? Or the car off? I'm afraid I'm not terribly fond of shouting my conversations if it isn't absolutely necessary."

"Go away!" I commanded. I threw the shifter into reverse and hit the accelerator. The car rocketed backward down the driveway, and I saw Trent Morgan throw his hands into the air in exasperation. I slammed on the brakes at the end of the drive and watched him in my headlights. He put his hands on his hips and hung his head slightly, like a parent who has just about had it with his kid's nonsense. He looked at his watch and then looked up at the car. He raised his hands to me as if to say *fine, you win,* and then started walking toward the house.

What was he doing?

I drove the car back up the drive and jammed it in park, rolling down the window to yell, "Hey! I'm calling the cops!"

His pace didn't falter as he replied, "I wouldn't bother. They really won't be of much assistance to us. Now, quit messing around and come on."

I was beyond frustrated. I wasn't even scared anymore. I turned off the car and jumped out. "Trent! You stop right there!"

"Are you coming?" he asked as he stopped in front of the basement door.

"You can't go in there!" I said defiantly.

He started walking toward me again, and I retreated back to the car.

"For the love of…" he said as he stopped and rubbed his forehead in annoyance. "Roselyn. I'm not here to hurt you. There is something infinitely interesting going on in that house, and I'm dying to figure out what it is. It's kind of my thing. Now, you can come with me and help me to help you, or you can get in the way and be a big old annoying nag. I'll let you in on a little secret: the first option is way more fun." Despite his obvious irritation with me, he smiled and held his hand out to me invitingly.

"What do you even want?" I asked contemptuously.

"I'm sorry, I thought I had made that fairly clear. I want to know what is going on in that house," he said, pointing behind him. He stood and looked at me with a pleasant smile on his face.

"Who *are* you?" I asked in wonderment. He was unlike anyone I had ever met.

"I feel like we are going in circles again. I am Trent, you are Roselyn, and together we are going to figure out the mystery of this house!" he declared, jutting a finger into the air excitedly.

"No," I said, approaching him finally. "Who are you, really? I know your name, but where did you come from? How did you get here so fast? Have you been watching me? How did you get my phone number?"

Trent gave me a tight smile and looked away. "These are all things that will be answered in due time, but there are more pressing matters at hand. Please just trust me. I'm here to help."

"Tell me now," I demanded.

"You wouldn't believe me if I did."

"Try me."

Trent sighed. He walked away from me toward the basement door.

"Hey, where are you going? Answer me!" I shouted.

He stood in front of the basement door and turned to look back at me. He then pressed a button on his watch and disappeared in an instant.

Chapter 2

I blinked several times, expecting him to still be there, but he wasn't. He was gone. I looked around me, thinking he had performed some kind of illusion and was going to pop out from behind a tree. That was when I heard a rapping coming from one of my living room windows. I looked up and saw Trent standing in the window, waving to me.

…How?

I ran up my front porch steps, knowing that I had failed to lock my front door in my haste to escape the house earlier, and burst through the door. There was Trent, standing in my living room.

"How did you do that?"

"I have a thing that does a thing. You said there were voices. I don't hear voices."

"You didn't—"

Trent shushed me mid-sentence. He tilted his head and moved around the living room. "No, I definitely don't hear voices. Are you sure you aren't going mad?" he asked me as he climbed onto the couch and stuck his ear to the wall.

"*Me?!* You're asking *me* that?! You're the one listening to walls right now!"

"Because you told me they were talking."

"I never said the walls were talking!"

He stopped and turned to me, still standing with his shoes on my couch. "Well, when you said 'voices everywhere,' I assumed that walls were part of 'everywhere.' Where exactly were the voices coming from, then?" He hopped down with the energy of a five-year old.

"Just…I don't know…everywhere. The air, I suppose. Inside and outside the house it seemed."

"But they aren't talking now. What were they saying?"

"I couldn't make out the words. As soon as I spoke out loud, though, it all stopped."

Trent furrowed his brow. "No, that's wrong. That's not supposed to happen."

"Don't tell me I'm wrong. You weren't even there," I said defensively.

He stepped uncomfortably close to me and looked me in the eye. "Are you sure it wasn't in your head?"

"I'm not crazy!"

"No, that's not what I mean. I'm wondering if the voices you were hearing were coming through telepathically."

"You're nuts, aren't you? This is one hell of an elaborate joke."

"You know this isn't a joke, and I wish you would find a better coping mechanism because this is getting tiresome." Trent looked over toward the hallway and his face lit up with a smile. "Oh, who's this?"

I followed his gaze and saw Cattiel sauntering out of the bedroom.

"There you are, you jerk," I said to the cat. "That's Cattiel. He ran off on me when I tried to rescue him from the voices."

"So he heard them too?"

"He must have. He was growling and seemed scared."

"Hm." Trent rested his chin in his hand, covering his mouth with his fingers. He crossed the other arm over his chest and rested his elbow on it, standing in contemplation.

"Hm? That's all you have is 'hm'?"

"At the moment, yes."

"Should I be worried?"

"Not unless you hear me say something colorful." He looked at me and pointed. "Did something hurt you? I notice you seem to be favoring your wrist."

I looked down and realized I was holding my wrist in my other hand. I must've sprained it when I fell, but I had been mentally blocking the pain. Now that someone had brought attention to it, I felt the ache of it.

"Oh, this. This was just me being clumsy," I said as I inspected my hand and arm for further damage.

I suddenly heard a loud crash and felt the floor shake. My head snapped up and I saw that Trent was no longer in the room. I whipped around just in time to see him scrambling to his feet in the hallway, his hair going every which way and a look of surprise on his face.

"It was that, wasn't it," he stated rather than questioned as he pointed down to the tripwire at his feet. "That's what happened to your wrist." He smoothed his hair and straightened his tie, trying not to look embarrassed.

"It's rather effective, though, isn't it? Got me twice."

17

Trent bent down to pick something up. It was my gun. As soon as I saw he had possession of it, my heart jumped into my throat and I became conscious of the fact that I was in a situation that didn't warrant the level of comfort I had allowed myself to fall into. I took an instinctive step away from Trent.

He wasn't looking at me, though. He was giving the gun a distasteful look as he held it away from him like it was a dirty diaper. He brought it to me and held it out for me to take it.

"You shouldn't leave these things lying around loaded like that. That was incredibly irresponsible."

I took the gun and stared at him as he turned away from me and started pressing buttons on his watch. Was he for real?

Trent pulled a pair of thick-framed glasses from his jacket pocket and slid them onto his face. I watched as a holographic interface appeared, projected above the watch. Trent was using his other hand to manipulate the images and quickly sort through what looked like a whole lot of nonsense to me.

"What is that?" I asked, dumbfounded.

"Data," he replied without looking at me.

"What does it mean?"

"I don't know yet. It doesn't become information until it is interpreted, and that could take me a bit." He pressed a button and the holographic display disappeared back into his watch.

I couldn't help myself. I had to ask one more time. "*Who are you?!*"

Trent gave me a smile that seemed to be hiding a thousand secrets and the kind of wisdom only time can bequeath. "I'll see you again, Roselyn." He pressed another button on his watch and was gone.

It was like he'd never even been there. I looked at the clock on the wall. It was 4AM. Was I dreaming? Was this some kind of convoluted sleep walking hallucination? I looked out at the driveway and saw the tire tracks and agitated dirt and gravel from when I was in the car earlier. The couch was still in a state of minor disarray after having giant feet walking all over it. Cattiel was rubbing against my legs, assuming that it must be time for breakfast. This didn't *feel* like a dream. But then again, when did dreams ever feel like dreams while you were in them? I went back to the bedroom to try to sleep away whatever this was, but not before catching the tripwire just *one* more time.

I didn't wake up until noon. Thank god for Sundays. Cattiel and I investigated the house, and it was obvious to me that whatever it was that had happened last night had really happened. I started a pot of coffee and took down the tripwire before I could trip over it again and break my face. It wasn't going to do any good against disembodied voices anyway.

I sat down on the couch with a hot cup of black coffee and a warm, fuzzy, grumpy cat and turned on the television. As I flipped through the channels, however, I began to notice that the television was playing shows for 3PM. That couldn't be right. I looked over at the ticking clock on the wall. It said 12:24. I pulled out my phone and checked the time. I frowned when I saw it showed 3:06PM. I jumped up and checked all the clocks in the house, and every other clock showed 12:24   even the atomic clock at my bedside.

Were these the "time discrepancies" Trent had mentioned upon our first encounter? What did it mean? Had I really slept until 3PM in the afternoon? I went outside and looked up at the sky. The warm summer sun was hanging high in the western sky. It wasn't noon. I had lost a big chunk of my day somehow…or had I lost a chunk of my night? Or morning? When did this happen?

I went back inside and looked at my phone again. I should call Trent...shouldn't I? He was weird and mysterious and I had no idea what his story was, but he seemed to want to help. This whole situation was absurd, and he seemed to be ok with absurd. Besides, I had to work tomorrow and I wanted to make sure I had my time correct. I had just started on as a trainer at the fitness center in town, and I didn't want to show up three hours late and lose clients or my job. I was going to call him.

No. No I wasn't. He was basically a stranger! A strange stranger, at that! This house had been completely normal until he showed up on my doorstep – maybe he was the one causing this! Maybe it *was* some kind of elaborate trick orchestrated by the psychopath I was trying so hard to leave in my past. Trent could have switched my clocks when he was in the house last night. The voices could have been some kind of sound system he rigged up before he knocked on my door. That would explain why he was at my house so quickly, and how he knew that something had happened last night. I glanced up at my ceiling and light fixtures suspiciously. He could be watching me right now.

But what about the teleporting? How did he get from outside my locked basement door to inside my living room? Where did he go when he disappeared from my living room? There was still something about the whole situation that didn't add up. Perhaps I did need to call him. Keep your friends close and your enemies closer, right? I would pretend I believed this was all real until I could figure out how he was doing it.

I looked at my call log. The number Trent called from last night appeared to have been scrambled. I tried to call it anyway, and I wasn't surprised when it wouldn't go through. I found his card sitting on the table where I had left it when I'd gone around barricading the house, and I entered the oddly long series of numbers into my phone. When I put the phone to my ear while it was dialing, I heard strange sounds on the line. It wasn't the typical "ringing" you hear on the other end, but rather a crackling and beeping.

"Yes! Hello! Who's there?" I heard an out-of-breath English voice answer the other line impatiently.

"Trent? Is this Trent Morgan?"

"Last I checked, but I've been wrong before. Who might this be?"

"It's Roselyn."

"Roselyn? I don't know a Roselyn. Are you from housekeeping?"

"Seriously?"

"No, I'm just having you on," Trent said with a chuckle. "It's Roselyn with the voices in her head. But, for future reference, if you ever do run into me and I don't seem to know who you are, don't be cross with me. It happens occasionally."

"…What? That doesn't make any sense."

"It makes perfect sense, you just aren't quite there yet. What can I do for you, Roselyn?"

I had to take a second to remember why I called. He kept my brain moving in all different directions when he spoke and it was hard to maintain my train of thought.

"Are you there? Did I lose you?" he asked.

"I'm here. The time. Something is weird about the time," I said vaguely. I didn't mean to be vague, but those were the words that came out of my mouth.

"Time's gone wonky, has it? That was what I was waiting for. Tell me about it."

"Well, I noticed this afternoon that my phone and my TV were about three hours ahead of the rest of the clocks in my house."

"That makes sense. Your telly and smart phone get time updates from a source outside the bubble. The clocks in the house are inside of it and therefore only advance according to the passage of time experienced in the bubble."

"Excuse me? Bubble? What do you mean bubble?"

"I'm not sure yet. But after looking at the data I gathered last night, it appears there is some kind of weird gravitational force in the vicinity of your house. The gravity is affecting time, but only time inside a certain space. Namely, your house."

My disbelief took a brief hiatus as I was drawn into his explanation. "Why only my house? What kind of gravitational force?"

"I don't know. Isn't that exciting? I love it when I have to figure it out."

"Does that mean I weigh more when I'm in my house?"

"Strangely, no. The gravity doesn't seem to be affecting objects in our three dimensions. It's coming from somewhere else."

"Where?"

I heard a knock on my front door. My brows snapped together and I walked to the door, parting the blinds over the window on the door to see who was out there.

Trent smiled at me through the window. "I don't know where!" he exclaimed excitedly. He wasn't holding a phone to his ear, but I could still hear him on the other line as though he was talking to me through the phone as well. I quickly hit the button to end the call on my phone. I inspected him through the window. No Bluetooth device in his ear, no visible microphone on his suit. It could be under his tie, I supposed. He was wearing another tweed suit today, and there were a lot of places one could hide a microphone or Bluetooth device on a suit.

"Why are you here?" I demanded.

"You rang me. I thought you wanted me here," he said loudly through the window. "Are you going to let me in?"

I paused. "I don't know yet."

"Well that's rude," he said.

"How did you get here so fast?"

"You've seen it. I have a thing that does a thing, remember?"

"Not good enough."

"You wouldn't understand. It's…classified."

"Are you just making that up?"

"Nnnoooo," he said unconvincingly.

"You're a terrible liar," I said.

He smiled with amusement. "Yeah, well, it isn't my favorite thing to do."

"Ok, enough is enough, Trent," I said, fed up. "I know you must be working with Barry. The jig is up. You can go home now." I had intended to play along until I figured out what he was up to, but this was just getting too weird.

Trent looked at me through the window with genuine bewilderment. "Who?"

"It's obvious he set this all up to mess with me and try to scare me. I'm not going to lie, it worked for a minute. But I'm over it. You can tell him to screw off."

"I'd rather not tell anyone to screw off. Who is Barry? Is he a friend of yours?"

"My ex-husband. Barry Schmidt. I know you're working for or with him. You can quit with the act now."

23

Trent stared at me. After a long pause, he said, "I'm sorry, what? I'm not sure what you're talking about. I don't know Barry Smith."

"Schmidt."

"I don't know Schmidt either."

Despite my current mood, I still had to suppress the snicker that threatened to bubble up my throat. It seemed that he might have been being truthful, but what was he up to? "You obviously don't know Schmidt," I said, unable to resist the joke.

Trent raised an eyebrow at me, my pun apparently going right over his head. "Are you having a laugh?" he asked in confusion, an expression of mild irritation on his face.

"A small one, yes."

"Well, are you done now? Can I come in yet?"

"No."

"What do you mean no?"

"No."

"Why not?"

"Because you're weird and I barely know you and this could all be a trick."

"Not with the trick thing again," Trent said, running his hands through his hair in exasperation. "It's not a trick! What reason would I have to trick you?"

"I don't know! That's what people do! They play games and trick each other and hurt each other. I don't know what you're playing at, but you can count me out."

Trent's face became somber. He gave me a sad, empathic look. "I'm sorry." He shoved his hands in his trouser pockets and leaned his shoulder against the door.

I took a step back from the door. "'I'm sorry'?" I questioned.

"I know this level of mistrust doesn't just happen overnight. Someone made you this way. Jerry, was it?"

"Barry. And I'm behaving perfectly rationally. Why won't you just go away? Your persistence is raising all kinds of red flags."

"Why did you ring me if you don't want my help?"

"I *called* you. I didn't ask you to show up at my *door*."

"You know what? Fine. Fine! Have fun dealing with this yourself. I'm not going to beg."

I watched him straighten his tie and walk away from the door. He looked down at his watch and stopped as he was on his way down the porch steps. He turned around and came back to the door.

"Ok, I might beg a little," he amended, looking at me through the window with pleading eyes.

"No."

"Ugh. Fine." He threw his hands into the air and walked away.

I went to the window and watched him walk down the driveway. I threw open the window as a thought occurred to me.

"Hey!" I yelled to him.

He stopped and turned toward the house. "Change your mind?" he asked, a hopeful smile spreading across his face.

I ignored his question. "If you have a 'thing that does a thing,' then why didn't you use it to get in the house again?"

"You told me no."

"It didn't seem to matter to you last time."

"You weren't inside the house last time. It wasn't the same."

"What, are you like a vampire or something? You can only enter when invited?" I challenged.

He looked up at me like I had said the most ridiculous thing. "No. I just have manners."

"Why aren't you using it to disappear out of here? Why are you walking to the road?" I asked, thinking I had caught an inconsistency in his game.

He shook his head. "I was hoping to give you time to change your mind, but it appears you have no intention of doing so. I'm sorry you have chosen to be a big annoying nag. I'll be off now," he said curtly. Before I could scold him for calling me an annoying nag, he touched his watch and disappeared, much to my surprise.

And there I was, alone again. I thought about what Trent had told me about the gravitational field and how it affected time, and I wondered if it were possible that this *wasn't* all a hoax. Had there been weird things going on before now, and that's why the house was for sale? I picked up the phone and called my realtor. I hoped she accepted calls on Sundays.

When she picked up, I introduced myself. "Hi, it's Roselyn Schmidt…excuse me, I mean Wolff. Roselyn Wolff. I bought a house through you a few weeks ago—"

"Oh yes! How are you Roselyn? Are you enjoying your new home?"

"Yes, thank you. I was just wondering if you had any information about the previous owners, or if you had heard anything…strange…about the house."

"Oh dear, is something wrong?"

"No, no. Some things have just come to my attention and I was hoping I could find out more about the house."

"With foreclosures I have very little information about the previous owners or the house itself, really. I can probably find you a name, but that's about all I can do."

26

"That's all right," I said. "I recall seeing the name on some of the forms. I was just wondering if you'd heard anything, being a small community and all."

"No, nothing of the sort, I assure you. It's a perfectly lovely home."

I thanked the realtor for her time and hung up the phone. It seemed that if there was something wrong with this house, and people had been living here before me, surely someone would know something.

I went rummaging through my papers from when I closed on the house, and eventually I found a name. The home had been foreclosed on a woman named Tilda Titus. I got online and did a search on her. It didn't take me long to find her. My address was listed as her previous address, and her current address was at some retirement home about forty-five minutes away.

What was I doing? I wasn't actually going to go bother some old woman about a house she lost to the bank, was I? And spouting nonsense about voices and lost time and a strange man at my doorstep, no less! No, I couldn't do that. I wouldn't do that. Everything was fine. I'd sent Trent away, this was all a hoax, and it was over. *This will be the end of it*, I convinced myself.

For the next week, everything was quiet. Trent Morgan had disappeared, I heard no voices, and my clocks all stayed perfectly in sync...sort of. The house clocks did seem to run a little slow for some reason, but they were only off by a minute or two each day by the time I got home from work. Admittedly, it was odd, but nothing I couldn't deal with. I adjusted them and went on with my day.

I should've been perfectly happy, but I wasn't. I found myself thinking about Trent on a daily basis, and I wished I hadn't run him off. It was probably just my loneliness affecting my logic, but I kind of missed the excitement of having him show up. He was weird and he never said what you thought he should say, but...I realized I kind of liked that about him. If I hadn't been so suspicious of him, I might've become friends with him, even if he was a complete mystery. But now, the more I thought about him, the more I wanted to know who he was. I worried that I might never find out, and I knew it would always bother me if I never saw him again.

Suddenly, as I sat absent-mindedly petting Cattiel on the couch next to me while I day-dreamed with the television on in the background, the house was filled with the low murmur of voices. As I froze and listened, I caught movement out of the corner of my eye. My head swiveled around just in time to see a shadowy figure glide across the kitchen and disappear into a wall, and the voices were silenced in an instant.

Chapter 3

I sprang from the couch almost as quickly as my heart had leapt into my throat.

"Hey!" I yelled at the vanished entity, because…well, that's just what you do when something like that happens.

I watched the kitchen and hallway for several minutes, expecting something more to happen. But that was it. There wasn't anything else. I glanced over at Cattiel, and he seemed perfectly unperturbed. I looked over at the front door, wondering if Trent was going to magically show up. I wouldn't have minded if he did.

I sat back down and took a few deep breaths, trying to calm my nerves. In an attempt to distract myself from my racing heart, I returned my attention to the television show I had been half-watching earlier, but it was over already. I checked the channel guide, but it was on the five o'clock block of shows. That wasn't right. It was only supposed to be 2:30PM.

"No, no, no! Not again!" I cried. I looked at my phone and felt an overwhelming uneasiness when I saw it said it was

5:26PM. It hit me right in the gut to finally accept that this time it absolutely wasn't a trick. This was real.

I quickly scrolled through my phone log and called the ridiculous number that I knew would connect me to Trent. The line crackled and beeped for a while, and just as I was beginning to think maybe he wasn't going to answer, I was greeted by his jovial voice.

"It happened again, didn't it?"

"Yes. Well, kind of. Did you know I was going to call? I feel like you were expecting this."

"I knew you'd need my help eventually. What happened this time?"

"There were voices and an apparition in my kitchen, just for a moment, and then the time changed by almost three hours. Are ghosts causing the time changes?"

"Time 'change' isn't really what's going on. The *rate* at which time passes in relation to the rest of the world is what is changing. It isn't that the time on the clock just suddenly 'changed.' You do understand that, right?"

"I don't care about the semantics. All I know is that I've lost three hours of my life in an instant and I want this to stop!"

"Oh, no, you haven't lost those hours. Well, you did lose them from today, I suppose. But you aren't 'out' that time in the biological sense. Actually, you're three hours younger than you should be now."

"I'm sorry, what?"

"Do try to keep up, will you? You only age as quickly as the time you experience. If you experience a twenty-one-hour day, then you have only aged twenty-one hours rather than twenty-four. In other words, you've discovered the fountain of youth."

"Why, though? Why is this happening?" I asked.

"Gravity."

"Yes, but gravity from what?"

"I don't know," he said simply.

"I thought you were going to figure it out!"

"You told me to go away!"

"I thought you were the one responsible for the things happening!"

"Obviously I'm not!"

"I know that now!"

"Then why are you yelling at me?!"

"I don't know! You're yelling at me!"

"You started yelling first!"

I stopped and took a deep breath. "Ok. Ok. I'm sorry," I said calmly.

"You should be. You've been quite cross with me, and I've done very little to deserve it."

"You're right."

"I beg your pardon?"

"I said you were right."

Trent chuckled from the other end of the line. "I know. I just wanted to hear you say it again. I do enjoy being right. I mean, I am most of the time, but it's still nice to hear it once in a while."

"So are you coming or not?" I asked impatiently.

I heard him gasp. "Are you actually *inviting* me to come help? But you usually get angry with me when I do that."

I sighed. "You've made your point. Just come help me."

"Be there in a jiff."

I ended the call and turned around – and Trent was standing in my living room.

I gave a quick gasp of surprise and threw my hand over my startled heart. "Good lord, I cannot get used to that."

"The fact that you aren't shouting at me right now indicates that perhaps you are starting to get used to it." Trent smiled slyly.

"How do you do that? How?"

"Let's wait until we know each other a little better before we start divulging our secrets, eh?" he suggested as he looked at his watch and walked to the kitchen. He walked through the path the apparition had taken through the kitchen and stopped, backing up again until he was right in the middle of it. "It was here, wasn't it?"

"The ghost? Yes. It floated through the wall over there and disappeared," I said, pointing.

"Disappeared? Or did it pass through the wall and go into…" Trent glanced around, then walked down the hall and looked into the door to his right. "…The loo? And then right through the loo to the next room, and so on? I don't think these walls exist to whatever came through here. Or perhaps it just doesn't have enough solid form to be affected by the walls." Trent pulled his glasses from his pocket and put them on. "Is this a dimensional overlap or a parallel problem?" he muttered to himself as he activated the holographic display on his watch. The fingers of his right hand flitted through images and numbers and symbols as he looked at the display pensively. He stopped for a moment to turn and look at the clock on the wall, then the clocks on the appliances in the kitchen. "Parallel. Definitely parallel," he said as he returned his attention to the watch.

"Do you know what it is?" I asked. "Is there anything I can do?" I felt completely useless standing in the living room just watching him. I wasn't accustomed to feeling useless.

He held his finger up in the air to quiet me. "I'm thinking."

I frowned at him but kept my mouth shut.

He stared at the display before him and scowled. "I know I fix this eventually, but I can't seem to crack it!" he complained.

I gave him a puzzled look. "How do you know you fix this eventually?"

He looked at me with raised eyebrows, like he had just remembered I was still in the room. "Oh! Well...I fix everything eventually. Usually. Most of the time. I've had a lot of time to ponder this query, so I should have figured it out by now!"

"It doesn't seem like that long to me. You've had, what, a week?"

He smirked mysteriously. "Something like that."

"Is there something you aren't telling me?"

He glanced over at me, still smirking, and winked at me through his glasses without saying a word. In that moment, I realized he no longer seemed "plain" to me. I felt the corners of my mouth lifting slightly, wanting to smile back at him.

Stop it. He's weird, remember?

"Shall we go see what Tilda Titus has to tell us?" Trent said cheerily as he deactivated the holographic display on his watch. He tilted his head to the side and raised his eyebrows. "That was oddly satisfying to say. 'What Tilda Titus has to tell us.' Tilda Titus. That's quite a name," he mused.

"How did you know about Tilda Titus?"

"I'm very clever," he said simply. He took off his glasses and slid them back into the inside breast pocket of his jacket. "Come along now. Grab on," Trent instructed, gesturing for me to come to him.

"What? No. Why?"

"If you want to take the long way 'round, be my guest. Last chance." He tinkered with his watch briefly, then looked at me expectantly. "You can't tell me you don't want to give it a go."

"Are you serious? You're going to zap us there, just like that?"

He cringed at my terminology. "Zap, no. No zapping. We're going to teleport."

"Using the thing that does a thing."

"Yes! Now you're getting it," he exclaimed, pointing at me approvingly. "Let's go!"

I approached him somewhat timidly and stood next to him. I was afraid of what this was going to feel like. Did it hurt to teleport? Was there a flying sensation?

"Do you have an aversion to physical contact with strange men?" Trent asked, looking down at me.

"I think I can give a universal yes to that statement on behalf of all women everywhere."

"Well, time to get over it," he said as he put his arm around me and pulled me to him. He was stronger than I had expected. "Hold on tight! Here we go!"

I squeezed my eyes shut and shamelessly threw my arms around Trent's torso, hanging on for dear life. Adrenaline shot through my veins and my heart raced and…nothing happened.

"You can let go now," I heard Trent whisper with amusement.

I opened my eyes. We were outside. I quickly released Trent and took three steps back, looking around. We were around the side of a large building.

"Was that it?" I asked, confused.

"That was it," he replied with a big smile.

"But…it didn't feel like anything. I thought it would be…exciting," I said with disappointment.

"That weirdly hurts my feelings," Trent said, looking a little surprised.

"Why?" I asked with a short laugh.

"You think my thing that does a thing is inadequate. I thought you'd be impressed." He looked down at his watch and frowned. He gave me a disgruntled look and waved for me to follow him. "Come on, let's meet Tilda," he said flatly as he started to walk away.

I laughed unapologetically for a moment and then followed him around to the front of the building.

We went inside and approached the receptionist.

"Hello," Trent said. "We were hoping to visit with Tilda Titus today. Would that be possible?"

The man behind the counter looked at us sympathetically. "I'm sorry to be the one to tell you this, but Tilda is no longer with us. She passed a few days ago. Are you family? You were here just last week, weren't you?"

"Oh, dear!" Trent said in surprise. "Oh, I'm sorry to hear that. We were acquaintances. When is the funeral?"

The receptionist gave us details on the wake and funeral, and we left quickly after that. Trent headed around to the side of the building where we had arrived.

"Why did you ask about the funeral? Are we going?" I asked.

"No, of course not. But it would've seemed callous to not ask about it, now wouldn't it?"

I scrunched my face. "Really? Well, I suppose, maybe."

"Do you *have* feelings?" Trent asked me sardonically.

"Of course I do. I'm not a sociopath."

"I do wonder," Trent muttered.

I ignored him and asked, "Were you there the other day, like the receptionist said? Is that how you knew about Tilda?" I asked Trent.

"Apparently I was, but I figured out who she was before that."

"What did she say to you?"

"I don't know yet."

I stopped and crossed my arms. "Excuse me? How do you not know yet?"

"I haven't done it yet."

"But you did it just the other day."

"Correct." He looked at me blankly. "...Is there a problem?"

I waved my arms dramatically. "Yes! How does any of this make sense to you?! If you did it the other day, how can you not have done it yet?!"

"Oh," Trent said, realization washing over his face. "I forgot that you don't know yet. All right, off we pop to the past. Grab on."

Before I could protest, Trent pulled me to him and pressed a button on his watch. It was almost like watching a single frame change of a time lapse video. We were in the same spot, and things looked *mostly* the same, but minor things like cars parked in the street and the wind speed had changed in an instant.

"Did we just time travel?" I asked in awe.

Trent ruffled my hair as though I was a child. "Sure did!" He started to walk away.

I scowled and quickly combed my fingers through my long, straight hair to fix whatever mess he had made of it. I hurried after him.

We followed the same procedure as last time, only now we were able to visit with Tilda. As we were being led by a nurse through the corridors to the sitting room where we were told Tilda was drawing, I felt strangely. I knew she would be dead soon. Trent knew she would be dead soon. But no one else knew. This felt wrong.

"Aren't you bothered by this?" I whispered to Trent. "We know when she's going to die."

"But she doesn't, and it needs to stay that way," he warned.

"You and I have a lot to talk about when we are done here."

"I suspect we do."

The nurse led us into a large room with a television, comfortable chairs, a bookshelf, and tables. There were only about five people in the room at the time.

"Where is everyone?" I asked the nurse.

"You came at a relatively quiet hour. Many of our residents like to rest in their rooms around this time," he said.

He took us over to a woman who looked entirely too young to be in a retirement home. She had very little gray mixed in her saffron hair, and her skin was fairly smooth still. She only looked to be in her early sixties, but she was supposed to be close to eighty. She was sitting at a table with paper and pencils scattered about her, her attention completely focused on the artwork she was creating.

"Tilly," the nurse said in a soft voice as he rested his hand gently on her shoulder. Her head shot up and she looked around wildly, eyes wide with fright. "Tilly, these nice people are here to visit with you. Are you all right with that? Is it ok if they sit and visit with you?"

Tilda looked at Trent and squinted her eyes. "Are you one of...*them*?" she asked in a hushed whisper.

Trent pulled out the chair next to Tilda and sat down. "No. But I'm here to figure out who they are," he replied calmly. "I just need your help in understanding when they first showed up."

I was already lost. Who were "they"?

The nurse came to me and said quietly, "I'll be around the corner if you need me. Tilly is prone to delusions, but she's harmless. I'll come check on you in a little while." He turned and walked away.

I pulled out a chair next to Trent and sat down, feeling uneasy. What did he mean she was "prone to delusions"? Did she have dementia? Alzheimer's? I looked down at the pictures she was drawing, and I immediately recognized what she was depicting – shadow figures, like the one I'd seen earlier today. Or, not today, but whatever day I had come from. One of them, however, was more frightening than the others. The one that particularly drew my attention was the drawing of a tall, broad-bodied shadow figure with long arms and long, gnarly fingers, red eyes, and a wide, gaping mouth. Was this something she had seen in that house? In *my* house?

"When did you start seeing them, Tilly?" Trent asked, indicating the figures in the pictures she had drawn.

"Oh, right from the get go," she said. "I bought that house back in 1971 after my husband died in an accident. He had been the love of my life. I never did remarry. The house he had built for us just held too many memories for me, and I thought a change would help me move on. At first, I thought the Time Thieves were the ghost of my late husband. I would talk to them when I saw them, and it made me feel like he wasn't really gone. They never spoke back, of course. Never paid any attention to me. None of them but the one," she said ominously. She looked over at the picture she had drawn of the tall, frightening shadow figure. "That one...I still have nightmares about him. The Big Bad, I called him. He wanted something, but I never could figure out what it was. Whatever it is, it ain't good." She was thoughtful for a moment. "No one ever believed me. Truth be told, sometimes I miss the Time Thieves. They kept me young. But I will never miss the Big Bad." Tilda looked over at Trent with a slightly confused, almost suspicious expression. "You know, I spent a long time around them. As I got older, I found I could sense them coming. When you came today, I felt that same feeling."

"Maybe you were just sensing that we have seen them too, Tilly. I assure you, I am not one of them. This young lady here," Trent gestured toward me, "is Roselyn Wolff. She bought your house, and she saw her first Time Thief recently. I'm trying to help her make the Time Thieves go away. I was wondering if you had any suggestions for us?"

It surprised me when Trent used my last name. I was unaware that he knew it.

"They won't go away," Tilda asserted. "They live there. Why would you want them to go away? If I had the choice, I would still be living there too. I probably would've lived forever if the bank hadn't taken the house from me."

I felt a lump in my throat. She was going to die soon, and she had no idea. Not a clue. She looked perfectly healthy, but she was going to die. In fact, in my time, she *is* dead. I'm sitting here talking to a dead woman. It made my skin crawl.

Tilly continued, "Just watch out for the Big Bad. Whenever he shows up, you'll be sick for days. He's going to really hurt someone someday, I just know it."

"Sick? What do you mean sick? What kind of symptoms?" Trent asked.

"Weird symptoms. Throwing up, bloody nose, and just feeling completely wiped out for days. One time he showed up and hung around for longer than usual, and after that I noticed a lot of hair loss when I was in the shower. It all grew back eventually, but that one had me worried."

"That is odd. Very odd. Say, Tilly, can you tell me about the time loss at the house? Did it only happen when the Time Thieves showed up?"

"It was sporadic. All of it was, really. I would have weeks, sometimes months of relative calm, and then the whole house would go haywire for days on end. The most time they ever took from my day in one go was a 16-hour block. I had no night that day. It went from evening to the next morning just like that," Tilda said with a snap of her fingers. "That was the time the Big Bad showed up and made my hair fall out."

"Wow, that's incredible," Trent said. "Now, you said the Time Thieves never paid you any attention or responded to you when you talked to them. Have you ever heard them make any noise, or ever heard any unexplained voices in the house?"

"No, nothing like that. They were always silent."

I heard voices, though. What does that mean? I wondered to myself.

"Tilly, thank you so much for taking time out of your day to share your wisdom with us. You have been such a tremendous help. It was so wonderful to meet you. I'll let you get back to your day and your drawings. Thank you," Trent said as he stood and gently shook Tilda's hand.

I thanked her and shook her hand as well, trying to keep my emotions in check. I didn't want to stay at my house. Tilda's story had terrified me. I could handle Time Thieves if I had to, but the Big Bad scared the hell out of me. I wanted to run home immediately and get Cattiel out of the house. Poor Cattiel was there all by himself in that creepy house!

…But wait, he wasn't, was he? If I was in the past, then I was also at home with Cattiel right at that very moment. I was in two places at one time.

I walked with Trent down the corridor back to the lobby. How could he seem so calm and collected right now? He had a pleasant smile on his face as though he had just visited his grandma and was headed out for a nice walk in the park – when in reality he had just visited with a dead woman in the past and was returning to a house in the present that was full of potential horrors. *Who was this guy*?!

Chapter 4

We walked out the front doors and headed around the side of the building. As soon as we were out of earshot of anyone else, I started in on him.

"How did you know my last name? I never told you that."

"I found Tilda Titus, but you didn't expect me to find out your last name?"

"Most things still have Schmidt as my last name. I just recently changed it back to Wolff. Even I sometimes forget it isn't Schmidt anymore."

"This is what you're hung up on? After all that has happened today, you are upset because I know your last name?" He stood in front of me with his arms hanging at his sides and his head tilted slightly to the side in exasperated disbelief.

"No. I'm not upset. I just don't understand how you just *know* things."

"Get used to it. It's my job to know things."

"What is your job, exactly? Where did you come from? And what's with the tweed suits?" I said, pointing at his outfit.

"Oi!" Trent objected with a look of injury. He looked down at his suit. "What's wrong with my suit? This suit is cool." He tugged at his lapels to help emphasize his point.

"Are you ever going to tell me anything about yourself?"

"I suspect so, but not right now. You've gone and insulted me."

"I didn't say there was anything wrong with your suits. I just asked about them," I countered.

"It was the way you asked about them. 'What's with the tweed suits?'" he said, mimicking me in an exaggerated high-pitched voice. "There's nothing 'with' them. They're fantastic."

"Ok, ok! They're lovely."

He gave me a disgusted face. "They aren't *lovely*! A woman's blouse is *lovely*. A floral summer dress is *lovely*. My manly, cool, stylish suits are not *lovely*."

"You're right. They're horrid."

Trent opened his mouth in brief outrage. "Sociopath," he mumbled as he turned his attention to his watch.

I chuckled to myself, and I saw the corner of his mouth curve upward slightly in the beginnings of a smile. I think he enjoyed the banter almost as much as I did. I really needed to stop finding new ways to like this madman.

"Let's get you home," he said as he held his arm out to me, "…before I decide to leave you here."

I walked up to him and he wrapped his arm around my waist, nestling me next to him snugly. I noticed he smelled pleasant. He had a clean and faintly woodsy scent.

"You'd come back for me," I said.

"I'd have to. Two of you in the same timeline would be a bloody nightmare."

In an instant, I was in my own living room again. I thought I would feel more apprehensive about being home after hearing Tilda's story, but I wasn't. With Trent there, things didn't seem quite as scary. His perpetual ridiculousness kept my mind distracted from the possible dangers we could face.

I slid out from under Trent's arm and walked over to the couch, plopping down next to a slumbering Cattiel. Cattiel opened his eyes and looked at me contemptuously.

"I love you, too," I said to the cat sarcastically.

Out of the corner of my eye I saw Trent – who is normally gesticulating about and fidgeting with his watch and just generally a wiry ball of energy – freeze in his tracks. He glanced over at me with a strangely startled expression, and quickly looked away again.

"What is it?" I asked, concerned.

"Nothing. It's nothing. How has Cattiel fared in our absence?"

"He hasn't budged since we left."

"I wouldn't imagine so. We've been gone less than a minute."

I raised my eyebrows at him. "Really?! But it seemed like half an hour!"

"Well, it has been half an hour for us. You remember when I said that you only age as much as the time you experience? Well, it applies in this case too. In your present time, only a minute has passed, but you have aged half an hour."

I ran my hand through my hair and thought about what that meant. "So, does that mean you're the real Time Thief? Time travelling with you takes time away from me biologically? If I were to go to the past with you repeatedly and be gone for hours at a time, and you always brought me back to the moment after we left, I would age faster than other people, wouldn't I?"

"Yes." He was avoiding my gaze.

"How old are you?" I asked him.

"Don't you know it's rude to ask someone their age?"

"How old are you, Trent?" I repeated firmly.

He gave me a tight smile. I didn't know how he could manage to look so sad with a smile on his face. "Older than I look."

"…how?" I asked.

Trent's demeanor suddenly became more playful. He clapped his hands together. "Here I am, spending all this time talking about myself. What about you? What's your story? You and your," he pointed awkwardly, "cat…Cattiel. How did you end up here?"

He started to wander about the kitchen before I even opened my mouth. "You're trying to avoid my questions," I said.

"Who's doing what?" he asked as he began rummaging through my cupboards.

"You heard me," I said.

"Blimey! What's with all this health food? Where are all your fabulously fatty American essentials? Your snack cakes and cereals and biscuits and crisps?"

"I'm a fitness trainer. I don't buy a lot of that stuff."

He turned to me with his face contorted in disgust. "You only eat *kale*, don't you?"

I laughed. "No. I don't like kale."

"Oh good. I thought for a moment I was going to have to end our friendship."

"We're friends?"

"As long as you don't try to make me eat kale. Kale is rubbish. Oh! Look! You do have treats!" I heard plastic wrappers crinkling and knew immediately he had found my secret stash of chocolate toaster pastries.

Trent came out to the living room and flopped down on the other couch across from me. My living room seemed so much smaller with two people in it. He happily and noisily unwrapped a packet of pastries and took a ridiculously huge bite out of one. He sat there staring at me while he chewed.

"You didn't bring me one?" I asked jokingly.

"Oh." He pulled the second pastry from the crinkly wrapper and tossed it at me. "How convenient. It comes with two so if you're with someone, you can share. And if you're not, you can eat two because you're sad and lonely."

I laughed as I took a bite, and we sat without speaking for several minutes. Usually, when you're first getting to know someone, sitting in silence for any amount of time is uncomfortable. That was oddly not the case with Trent. He was usually talking or ranting or arguing, and I would have thought a moment of silence with him would be awkward, if not insufferable. But it wasn't. It seemed so perfectly, completely bearable.

"Ok, here's the thing, and you aren't going to like it," Trent broke the silence.

"Oh goody."

"I need to stay here."

I furrowed my brow. "What? Why?"

"I need to get measurements from the actual Time Thief events. Since we can't predict when they're going to happen, I need to wait it out. Think of me as a temporary roommate. I'll compensate you."

"Why don't I just call you when it happens, and you can go back in time and show up right before it happens to collect your measurements?" I suggested.

Trent grimaced. "Eh, that's probably not the best idea. The energy used to make the trip may end up affecting my measurements. It might also create a minor paradox and I really hate creating paradoxes."

"I thought a paradox indicated something was impossible."

Trent see-sawed his hand and said, "Well, not quite." He failed to elaborate.

"So you're going to be sleeping on my couch until something happens?"

Trent looked disappointed. "Really? You don't have a guestroom?"

"I have two spare rooms, but there aren't any beds in them."

"That's all right, I don't need a bed. I don't sleep much anyway."

"Can I ask you something?"

"If I say no are you going to ask me anyway?"

"Do you have a home?"

"Yes."

"Oh."

"You sound surprised. You thought I was homeless?!" he said with indignation.

"I don't know!"

"Well, for your information, I have several homes."

"Where do you live?"

"Wherever I want."

"What do you do for money?"

"It depends. How much do you have?" Trent asked with a raised eyebrow.

"You know what I mean," I smirked. "How can you afford several houses? Where do you get your money?"

"I have my ways."

I inhaled sharply. "Are you a criminal?"

"No, I'm not a criminal. But I'm not going to say I've never broken any laws. Say, how is it we always end up talking about me?" Trent wanted to know.

"You are a walking impossibility. Of course I want to talk about you," I replied.

"You have a house enshrouded in an inexplicable mystery. Let's talk about you and this house." Trent held up his index finger. "First thing I need to know, though, is whether I am going to have to be wary of tripwires throughout the house at any point during my stay."

I laughed. "No, I took that down."

"You know what I wonder, now that I'm thinking about it? Why, if you were so suspicious of me at first, you never once threatened me? You have a gun."

"I didn't find you threatening. Not physically, anyway. Plus, you have a way of disarming someone with your delightful weirdness."

"I'm not sure whether you just complimented me or insulted me."

I stood up and went to the fridge. "Do you drink?" I asked.

"Not usually."

"Well, I'm having a glass of wine. You're welcome to a glass if you're interested."

"Thanks, but I'm all right."

"You aren't sitting out there judging me, are you?" I asked as I poured myself a fairly full goblet of Sangria.

"I wouldn't dream of it."

I returned to the couch and sat down, careful not to spill my drink.

Trent leaned forward and rested his elbows on his knees. "I have to ask: why did you think I was working with someone to trick you? What was that all about?"

I took a long drink of my wine. "Have you ever been in a relationship with a toxic person, Trent?" I asked.

"Relationships aren't really my forte."

"Let me paint you a picture, then. I married a man because he made me feel so badly about myself that I thought no one else would ever want me, and after I realized how unhappy I was, I was afraid to leave because I didn't know what he would do. He couldn't hold a job for more than a few months before either causing a scene and walking out or getting fired for being confrontational. When I was sleeping between working or college classes, he would go online and chat with other women. I wasn't allowed to mention the name of any other man, even classmates or coworkers. If I did, suddenly he thought I was having an affair with them. If I was two minutes later than usual getting home from work, he thought I was having an affair. I became obsessive about how I managed my time just to prove to him I wasn't cheating and I wasn't a bad person – trying to prove him wrong. If a man tried to talk to me, regardless of how innocent the exchange was, it made me nervous because then I had to decide whether to tell him about it or not. If I told him, eventually it would turn into 'you're having an affair with him!' If I didn't tell him, I would constantly worry that he was going to find out about it and then accuse me of trying to hide it – because 'you're having an affair with him!'

"I remember one year we had a neighbor living in our apartment complex who went to school with me and was even in the same degree program. He was a nice guy, and I liked him quite well. One day, Barry had taken my car and left me with his crappy one, and of course when I went to start it, the battery was dead. I had class that day, and no way to get there. Luckily for me, though, my neighbor happened to be heading to the same class, and he saw me with the hood up. He asked if I wanted a ride, but heavens no, I knew I couldn't do that. Barry would bring down the whole complex if I accepted a ride from another man. So instead, he jump-started the battery, and I thanked him and was on my way. Well, later that evening, as I waited for Barry to get home from whatever random job he had at the time, I wrung my hands in anticipation of having to tell him about our neighbor helping me. He came home, and I gave him a detailed account of what had transpired earlier that day. It was all completely innocent. You know what he did? He stormed out the door and stomped halfway to our neighbor's building, screaming and shouting about how he was going to kick his ass! I was so embarrassed, and I fought to keep him from ruining anyone else's day aside from my own. I finally managed to get him back to our apartment, but not after a lot of yelling in the parking lot and storming back and forth. I think I got accused of having an affair with that neighbor fairly regularly because of that one incident.

"He didn't just scare me away from other men, though. He cut me off from all of my friends, too, and now no one wants anything to do with me," I continued. "He wanted all of my passwords as proof that I had nothing to hide from him, and he then used them to go online under my social media accounts and pretend he was me, sending hateful or strange messages to people. Most of them didn't realize it *wasn't* me. They all just thought I'd lost my mind and they stopped interacting with me.

"He was so incredibly manipulative. I have no idea how he did it, but he always made me feel like I needed to prove myself to him. Instead of feeling like I needed to get the hell out of there, I just kept trying harder. I cried a lot, yelled and got yelled at a lot, and spent a large portion of every day with a huge knot of anxiety in my chest." I stopped to wipe the tears that were suddenly streaming down my face.

"I'm sorry, I didn't mean to bring up something so obviously painful," Trent said apologetically. "You don't have to talk about it. I understand now why you were so suspicious of me showing up at your doorstep."

"No, I think I need to get it out. I've never told anyone all of this. Everybody knew he was awful, but nobody ever got the full story. I think it's time to get it off my chest."

"Then by all means, please continue," Trent said soberly.

"I think the worst part was wondering what he was going to do next – what trick he was going to pull, or what outlandish story he was going to concoct about me that I was supposed to prove wasn't true in order to clear my name. He called me horrible names and accused me of horrible things. He would change my words around and then repeat them to me, declaring that that was what I had said, even though I knew it wasn't true. He made me question what was real. I remember him calling me 'a pile of dog shit' one Christmas because I had bought him a $20 bag of tobacco. We were dirt poor at the time, and that was all I could afford. He had bought me an $11 necklace from the department store that I apparently didn't deserve. As I recall it got thrown out the window of the car as we drove down the highway. Another Christmas, we had used money I had earned as a waitress to buy a digital camera as my gift. He threw it at me and broke it on Christmas day shortly after I opened it.

"He made me crazy. He changed who I was. I wasn't me anymore, and the longer I was with him, the more I lost myself to his insanity. It started to leach into my brain, and I started thinking like him – not because I wanted to, but as a survival mechanism. I needed to know what he was going to do. I needed to be able to predict the unpredictable, and it drove me to the brink of madness. Sometimes I worry that I've been completely broken and I won't ever be able to have a normal relationship again. I feel like I'll always be in a state of recovery – never completely healed from this," I choked out the words.

Trent came and sat near me on my couch. He leaned over and put his hand on my back and rubbed it gently in a comforting gesture. "I am so sorry you were ever treated that way. But can I tell you something? You aren't broken. From what I have observed, you are strong and independent and absolutely wonderful. If you ask me, I think you are strong as steel."

"That's the thing, though. I don't feel strong. I can't believe how incredibly weak I was for allowing him to keep me under his thumb for so long. Why didn't I just walk away at the first sign that something was off? Why didn't I? Why the hell did I stay so damn long?!" I couldn't stop the full-on snot-spewing sobbing that ensued.

Trent got up and took my wine glass from me, setting it down on the end table near the couch. He stepped in front of me, grabbed my hands, and pulled me to my feet. The next thing I knew, my face was buried in his shoulder and his arms were wrapped tightly around me.

"I'm going to get snot on your tweed suit," I blubbered.

"It's all right. I have other suits. Snot away."

I knew I should restrain myself and find my composure. I knew I had no reason to feel this comfortable with someone I had only just met recently. But, by god, it felt so *good* to be held and let it all out. I didn't feel judged or looked down upon. He held me close and embraced me without reservation. I cried until I felt like I had run out of tears. And snot.

When Trent finally released me from his arms, I immediately checked his jacket.

"Oh, gross, I'm so sorry," I apologized profusely as I looked at the big wet mark my face had left.

"Trust me, I've had worse," he said.

As I settled down, I felt it was important to finish my story. "After all this and I haven't even recounted the horrible things he did when I did finally leave him," I said. "This is the part where my mistrust of you begins to make sense.

"After I found out he had been physically unfaithful, I finally found the courage to leave. It wasn't easy though. He made sure of that. He threw a fit, of course, breaking things and yelling in my face the entire time I was packing things in boxes. He'd stop and cry, trying to make me feel bad, and then he'd turn around and threaten me when that didn't work. He made promises to change, then made promises of revenge against me. He tried to force himself on me, then called me names when I fought him off. It was a nightmare.

"When I finally did get out with whatever belongings I had that he hadn't broken yet, I still wasn't out of the nightmare yet. I moved in with my parents briefly, and at night he'd drive up their driveway just far enough for his headlights to fall on my car so he could see I was there. He'd then back out of the driveway and drive off. He'd call from payphones so the caller

ID wouldn't register that it was him. He'd call and leave long, creepy messages on my parents' answering machine. If by chance you did answer the phone to try to tell him to stop calling, he'd just hang on the line so you couldn't hang up or make any other calls because my parents have a landline. He was relentless.

"Then came the games. He'd show up at my work and put things under or in my car. He posted an ad on the internet that gave out my name and phone number and wrote that I hated certain religious groups. Calls poured in with death threats against me, and of course I had no idea what the hell was going on. Then he went online and signed up everyone I knew for dirty magazine subscriptions. Some of them he even had sent to their places of employment. They were then sent bills for the subscriptions and had to deal with trying to get those cancelled. He just wouldn't let things go. I've spent every moment since I moved out wondering what new hell was coming next.

"So now you know the whole story. Now you can fully understand why I would be so wary of you and why I would believe so whole-heartedly that this was all some kind of trick or game," I said.

"I have no words," Trent said. "I'm sorry I pushed you so hard at first. I had no idea what kind of psychological and emotional torment you had just been through. I didn't fully understand. Now I do. Thank you for sharing with me. I know that couldn't have been easy."

"I feel a lot better right now than I have in a long time. I needed to do that. I needed to talk about it. I'm sorry your jacket had to suffer for it," I said, trying to lighten the mood.

Trent looked down at his jacket. "Yeah...but it was worth it."

"I probably look like a damn train wreck now, though, don't I?"

"Eh, a bit blotchy and puffy, but that's to be expected, isn't it? I don't mind if you don't."

"Honestly, I really don't." I looked over at the clock on the wall and realized I still needed to change all of the clocks ahead almost three hours. Then I mentally calculated the actual time. "Oh shoot, I need to eat," I said as I leapt up from the couch, wiping away the last of the tears from my eyes. "Are you hungry?"

"I could eat. Should I pop out for some takeaway?" he asked as he stood up and jutted his thumb toward the door.

"No, no. I prefer to eat at home."

"Well that's a bit boring, isn't it?"

"Hey, at least I know what goes into my food if I'm the one preparing it. I have a hard time trusting other people with my food. People are disgusting and food poisoning is no joke."

"I suppose you're not wrong," Trent said as he followed me into the kitchen. "What are you making? It isn't kale, is it?" he asked, wrinkling his nose.

"What do you like? It's your first night as my temporary roommate, so I suppose I should try to make you feel at home."

"I like takeaway. Pizza or Chinese, ideally."

I put my hand on my hip and turned to him. "What do you like that *isn't* takeout?"

He pressed his lips together and his brows knitted thoughtfully. "Um...eggs? I like eggs."

"That's not a meal. You said you like Chinese, so what if I made some fried rice and stir fry? Would that be acceptable?"

"You aren't going to put k—"

"No kale!" I shouted.

Trent leaned away from me in mock surprise. "Good grief, what did kale ever do to you?"

I closed my eyes and took a deep breath. "Go sit down. I'll let you know when the food is ready."

"I can help! Probably. Maybe. Well, I don't really cook, but I can hand you things," Trent offered, hovering over my shoulder as I started rummaging through the fridge.

"I can do it by myself, thank you. You'll just be underfoot."

Trent folded his arms and leaned against the wall near the kitchen table where he was out of the way. As I started getting my pans ready and chopping up vegetables, however, he wandered his way back into the main part of the kitchen again.

"So the conversation with Tilda today - we never discussed it. Aren't you curious what I've deduced?" he said, looking over my shoulder.

"What have you deduced?" I asked.

"When Tilda was talking about the Big Bad making her sick, it sounded an awful lot like radiation sickness. I'm guessing that much exposure to radiation is what ended up killing her."

"She was almost eighty. It could've been anything age-related."

"But she wasn't *really* eighty, though, was she? She was much younger than that in actuality."

"I suppose so. But what is the Big Bad, then? Why is it giving off radiation?"

"I haven't the foggiest," Trent confessed.

"What about the Time Thieves?"

"I'll know more after we have another 'event.' Whatever is going on seems to be either getting closer or growing in strength. The fact that you heard voices, but Tilda never did, makes me suspect this isn't just a constant, repetitive occurrence. This is something that's changing. But what is the endgame? Where is it headed? What's the next phase? How dangerous is this going to get?"

That last line made me pause. "Should I even be staying here? Am I in danger by being here?" I asked with concern.

"I won't let anything happen to you," Trent promised. "If the Big Bad is emitting radiation, my gadget will detect it," he said, pointing to his watch, "and I'll protect you from it."

"How are you going to protect me from radiation?"

"I can move us through time and space in an instant, but you doubt my technology can protect you from radiation?"

I put my hands up in submission. "Fair point."

As I stir-fried vegetables in the wok, I realized Trent had been awfully quiet for an abnormally long time. I turned around to see what he was up to just in time to see him walking into the kitchen with Cattiel curled up in his arms.

"How did you do that? He hates strangers," I said.

"I'm not a stranger. I'm your roomie." Trent stood next to me with the cat.

I held my arm up to barricade him from the stove. "You need to get the cat out of here. He's going to get hair in the food!"

"Aw, he just wants to see what you're doing," Trent protested. "Fine. Come on, Cattiel," he whispered to the cat. "She's being cross with us."

Trent managed to stay entertained by the cat while I finished dinner. I called him into the kitchen to set the table while I put the food on.

"This is so domestic," Trent commented as he laid out the utensils. "I thought it would be boring, but I'm rather enjoying it!"

We sat down to eat and I began to serve up my plate. "You act like a night at home is an all new experience. What is normal for you? Don't you ever just chill?"

"There are far too many adventures and excitement out there to waste my time 'chilling.'" Trent took a bite of his rice and stir-fry. "Hey, this is actually good! Well done!"

"I feel strangely insulted by the way you said that, but thank you, I guess?"

"I see you didn't put kale in it," Trent said. When I glowered at him, he flashed a playful smile.

I noticed he was trying to redirect the conversation yet again, like he always did when I tried to talk about him. It wasn't going to work this time. "So what do you do with your time, Trent? You just time travel and be weird?"

"And know things. Remember, it's my job to know things."

"Why? What do you do? You never really got around to explaining that."

Trent hesitated briefly before responding. "This, Roselyn," he said with a sigh as he gestured his arms widely to indicate the house in general. "This is what I do. I fix things and protect people from things they don't even know they need protection from. This is my life." He looked down at his plate as he took his next bite, avoiding my gaze.

"So…you're some kind of hero?"

"No. I'm not a hero," Trent said with a disdainful face and a dismissive wave of his hand.

"Where did you get that watch? Is that where all of your superpowers come from?"

Trent almost spit out his food. "*Superpowers?* Good grief, you've been reading too many comic books. My watch is a piece of technology, not a superpower."

"Where did it come from, though? That's way more advanced than anything we're capable of developing right now."

"I'm a time traveler, remember? That includes both backward and forward."

"But you had to acquire it before you could travel, so you couldn't go to the future to get a watch if you didn't have the wa—" I stopped midsentence as I finally understood.

Chapter 5

"You didn't start out here, did you?" I inquired.

Trent raised an eyebrow at me. "What do you mean by 'here'?"

"Either you aren't from this time, or you aren't from this planet. Or is it both?" I asked as I set my fork down. I couldn't focus on eating and the conversation at the same time. "Are Nohkeans an alien race?!"

"Relax, I'm not an alien," Trent assured me. "But no, I'm not from this time. Nohkea is a country that hasn't been established yet. It includes what you currently call the U.K."

"What time are you from?"

"A long time in the future."

"So why are you here? And why aren't there more of you? If we have time-traveling watches in the future, shouldn't our entire history be riddled with time-traveling tourists?"

"If that technology were made available to the public, then yes, it would be."

"But it isn't. Why?"

"There are several reasons why, but mostly it's because I exist. Oddly enough, that's the same reason the technology exists as well."

"I don't understand."

"I made the watch, Roselyn. They made me, and I made the watch. They wanted it to 'fix' history. To kill Hitler, stop the plagues, take away the nuclear bombs, stop the climate crisis, et cetera. But they didn't understand the implications. They didn't understand that, without the past, the present would change, and they wouldn't even know it because their memories would change to reflect their experiences. The only reason I would know the difference is because traveling through time changes your perception of events. History in my brain is established because I've stepped out of the timeline. I've removed myself from play. Think of it as a simulation. If you change things in it, no one inside the simulation would realize it was different. They'd think it'd always been that way. But if you are on the outside, jumping from simulation to simulation, you'd notice that things had changed. If they changed history, some people would suddenly cease to exist, forever erased. Others would pop into existence, full of memories of a childhood that hadn't happened in the original timeline. It would be utter chaos on Earth, and no one would be any the wiser – but me."

Trent got up from the table and took his plate to the sink. He rinsed it and opened the dishwasher. "What? No, you've packed your dishwasher all wrong!" he complained as he started rearranging my dirty dishes. "They don't get as clean when they are facing that way."

I stared at him in disbelief. "Forget the dishes! Who are 'they'? Who are you?!"

He stopped what he was doing and paused briefly. Then he stood up and faced me, standing rigidly with his heels together. He crossed one arm in front of his stomach and one behind his back and bowed deeply toward me. As he rose, he said, "Trent Morgan: the original Time Thief, at your service."

I stood up quickly, knocking my chair over. "You're one of those shadow things?!"

"No, not like that. I just like the name Tilda gave them and realized when you called me a Time Thief that the name really does apply," he said with a grin. He continued his story, "You see, it wasn't until after I had created the watch for them that I learned what I was and what they were planning to do with the technology. I knew they needed to be stopped, so I nicked the time-warping watch and ran. Do you get it now? Time Thief? It's quite perfect, really," Trent said with a pleased smile.

I wasn't smiling. Every time I felt like I was starting to get to know him, he threw me a curve ball and I was lost again.

Trent continued, "I've been using the watch ever since then to keep them from ever acquiring this technology. Whenever the watch detects a disturbance in the continuum, I investigate. If it's them, I take whatever measures I need to in order to stop them."

I needed to know more. "What do you mean by 'them,' and what do you mean they created you? Are you human, or aren't you?"

"It's not that simple," he said.

"Yes, it is. You either are, or you aren't."

"I am human...but tweaked," he said, demonstrating "tweaked" by twisting his hand with his fingers pressed together like he was turning a screw into the air.

"Explain. Explain all of it," I demanded as I righted my chair and sat back down.

"Can I finish arranging these dishes while I talk? They are truly bothering me," Trent said, pointing to the mess in the dishwasher.

"I don't care! As long as you talk!"

Trent gave me a thumbs-up and bent down to work on the dishes. "'They' are a united force of the global elite - the supremely wealthy and top politicians from the most powerful nations around the world. They call themselves SABER – Sovereign Alliance for the Betterment of Earth's Republic.

"Now, in the time that I come from, genetic engineering is lightyears beyond what is possible in this time period. They use gene therapy to treat disease, and they can grow tissue specifically for an individual to replace parts of the body that have been damaged by age or trauma. People can live longer, but they still hadn't found that fountain of youth. The technology was available to alter human embryos in the same way they altered animals and plants, but ethics had always stood in the way of designing human embryos – until SABER. SABER ran an elaborate, secret experiment on thousands of human zygotes. They used human DNA to create me, but they manipulated it in order to expand my cognitive capabilities and to lengthen and strengthen the telomeres that protect my DNA. In other words, I would be smarter and age more slowly than other humans. But that wasn't all. They also injected an experimental technology into the zygote that would grow into me – self-replicating nanobots that repair damage to my cells and restore my DNA as my telomeres shorten, like telomerase without the associated cancer risks. Of all of those trials, out of thousands of zygotes, I was the only success. So, I suppose you could say I am human, but not exactly a 'normal' one."

"How old are you, Trent?" I asked quietly.

He closed the dishwasher. "Oh, I don't know. I lost track a long time ago," he said as he turned to wash his hands in the sink. I had the feeling he wasn't being entirely truthful.

When he shut off the water, I asked, "Are you going to just keep living forever?"

He turned to me while he dried his hands on the towel hanging from the stove handle and shrugged. "I don't know. I'm sure something will kill me eventually. We all have a weakness, right? Maybe a wooden stake through the heart," he said jokingly.

"That isn't funny."

"But you had compared me to a vampire once, remember? It's a little funny."

"I don't know how to feel about all this," I said.

"You don't have to feel anything about it. It isn't your problem. Feeling sad or angry or glad or worried isn't going to make my situation any different. Trust me – I learned that a long, long time ago," he said cynically.

The air felt heavy as Trent walked out of the kitchen. I was at a loss for words. I had gotten what I wanted, hadn't I? I wanted to know who he was, and now I knew. So why did I feel so much further from him now than I did only moments ago when we were sitting down to our first meal together? It felt like he'd become a complete stranger yet again, and it bothered me.

As I walked into the living room, trying to think of something to say to Trent, he suddenly jumped up from the chair he had just sat in, his eyes fixed on his watch.

"It's still slower," he said. "Not as noticeable as a big event, but it's definitely slower." He walked around the chair and headed to the front door. He was still looking at his watch as he stepped outside to the front porch without explanation.

I started to follow him, but he came right back in and we almost collided in the doorway. I quickly stepped out of his way as he came through, clearly on a mission.

"What are you doing?" I asked, following him into the hallway.

"The time doesn't just move slower here during singular events – it moves slightly slower all the time. You know what that means?" he asked as he turned to me excitedly, looking away from his watch for the first time since he left his chair.

"What does that mean?"

"It means I can use that difference in the rate of time passing in order to roughly map out the borders of the bubble!" Trent looked at me expectantly. When I looked back at him blankly, his face fell. "You don't look impressed. I thought you'd be impressed."

"Oh, sorry. Um, yay!" I said with unconvincing cheer.

"You have zero appreciation for how clever that was," Trent said accusingly.

"I'm sorry, I'm afraid I'm still trying to catch up. Borders of the bubble? Like, physical lines drawn out where we can stand on one side or the other?"

"Yes! See, you were all caught up! Now you can look impressed."

"How are you going to mark the lines?" I asked. "I'm not going to let you draw all over my house."

"Do you want to figure this out or not?"

"Of course I do!"

"Then you're going to have to let me make a bit of a mess."

I looked at him reluctantly. "I don't like a mess," I confessed.

Trent stepped close to me and took my face between his hands suddenly. He touched his forehead to mine. "I'm afraid life is messy, my dear. You're just going to have to trust me that it'll all be worth it." He released me and dashed to the kitchen. I heard him rummaging through the drawers hastily as I tried to ignore the lingering flutter in my chest.

"Chalk!" he shouted to me. "Don't you have chalk?"

"I have no use for chalk," I replied as I followed him to the kitchen.

"You most certainly do! What about a marker? Preferably washable?"

I cringed. "I can get chalk tomorrow, so let's forget the markers, ok?"

Trent turned to me and crossed his arms. "You know, I'm beginning to question your commitment to finding a solution."

"Tomorrow is another day. It's getting late, and I have to work in the morning. I can pick up some chalk on my way home in the afternoon," I reasoned.

Trent sighed and pressed a button on his watch, disappearing instantly. He reappeared only seconds later, holding a stick of chalk.

"Did you just time-travel for chalk?"

"No, I just popped over to my chalkboard and came back."

"Your chalkboard? Where?"

"In one of my houses."

"Why didn't you just do that from the start?" I asked.

"I don't want to be teleporting in and out of here if I can help it. I don't want to be out when something happens."

I cleaned up the table and put the leftover food in the fridge while Trent ran about the house like an over-caffeinated child, marking lines and X's on walls and floors. I brushed my teeth and got ready for bed, hoping he would be done soon so he could retire to his room before I went to bed. He was not.

"Trent, I'm going to put a sleeping bag and a pillow up in your room," I yelled down to him in the basement. "I set out an unopened toothbrush for you in the bathroom and hung a fresh towel for you on the rack."

"Thank you!" he shouted up to me, but I didn't see him.

"What are you going to do for clothes? I don't have any men's clothing other than a pair of athletic pants and a couple of t-shirts. You're welcome to them if you want, but—"

Trent stuck his head around the corner and looked up the stairs at me. "I have clothes, but thank you." He ran off again.

"Where did you get clothes?"

"Same place I got the chalk," he yelled to me.

"But…ugh, I don't even care," I mumbled to myself. I grabbed a sleeping bag and a pillow from the closet and trudged up the stairs to the bedrooms tucked away at the top of the house. There were two of them and they were both identical, so I just picked the room on the left. As I laid out his sleeping bag and pillow on the floor, I heard him galloping up the stairs.

He burst into the room with a smile on his face. "This is most interesting! It appears that there is a small patch of the bubble that extends beyond the walls of the north side of the house! Also, do you have a torch?"

"What? Why would I have a torch?"

Trent looked at me strangely. "It's not that uncommon to have a torch. Most people do."

We stared at each other in confusion for a few moments before realization hit me. "Oh! You mean a flashlight!"

"Flashlight. Torch. Same thing."

"Why do you need a flashlight?"

"It's dark outside."

"You need to go outside?"

"Obviously."

I sighed. "Are you going to be at this much longer?"

"Not terribly."

"Is this spot ok for your sleeping bag?" I asked him.

"Oh! Lovely! Yes, that will do just fine."

I stood up and walked past him, heading out of the room. "The flashlight is in the kitchen drawer nearest the back door. Please shut off the lights when you go to bed."

"Roselyn," Trent said. I stopped halfway down the stairs and turned to look up. He was standing in the doorway of his room, looking down at me with a pleasant smile on his face. "Thank you for trusting me. I know this hasn't been easy for you. I promise I will figure this out as quickly as I can and then I'll get out of your hair."

"That would be great," I lied.

I lay in bed with Cattiel slumbering quietly at the foot of the bed and listened to Trent tromping around the house. Yes, the man did have enormous, clumsy feet, but I think even an elephant could have been quieter. He had a habit of occasionally talking to himself, as well. I couldn't fault him for that, though, because I was notorious for it. I just never realized how oddly it sounded hearing someone else doing it.

I thought about what he had said about figuring things out quickly and leaving. It should've given me some comfort to be reminded that this was just a temporary arrangement, but it did just the opposite. It reminded me of how lonely it was here before he'd shown up. It seemed weird that I would *want* him to stay for any length of time, didn't it? He was a genetically engineered time-traveler from the future. Why didn't that knowledge scare me? I was living in a house that had the potential to unleash a radioactive monster from thin air at any moment, yet I fully trusted that Trent would keep me safe. Why? What reason did I have to trust him so fully and completely after only knowing him for such a short amount of time?

And why did my foolish heart start racing every time he touched me?

I was lonely, that's why. It had been a while since I'd allowed a man to come that physically close to me.

But…there was something about him. I hadn't seen it at first, but it was there. It was there in the way he smiled at me. It was there in the way his eyes lit up when something struck him. It was there in his childish and seemingly endless energy. It was there in the way he put to ease my misgivings with a wave of his hand and a silly grin. He wasn't a particularly tall or masculine man, but he seemed to fill a room with his presence. There was an indescribable appeal to him that I just wished I could ignore.

But I would ignore it. I would ignore the hell out of it. He was going to leave as soon as this was over anyway and move on to another wild adventure and forget all about me, and that was the way it should be.

I woke up in the middle of the night to the sound of a voice whispering my name. I reflexively reached for the gun at my bedside.

"No, don't shoot me! It's me!" Trent cried, throwing his hands into the air and dropping the flashlight.

I exhaled loudly. "Why are you in my room?!"

Trent bent down and picked up the flashlight. He bumped it against the heel of his hand and the light came back on. "You didn't wake up when I knocked. I wasn't up to anything nefarious, if that's what you're thinking. I want to show you something."

Trent walked over to my closet and opened the doors, shining his flashlight in. I climbed out of bed and went to his side. I looked in the closet. "Yeah, it's my closet. Woo. Go to bed." I turned to walk back to my bed.

"No, wait!" he said, and I stopped and turned back around. "Look closer. Look at the paint on the wall in there."

I rubbed my eyes and bent down to get a better look. "It's old paint. Is that a problem?"

"Look at the color, though. It's the same paint that's on these walls, but it looks so much older. Care to venture as to why that is?" Trent was giving me a giddy grin.

"The closet is outside the bubble?" I asked.

"Yes! How brilliant is that?"

I didn't share his same enthusiasm. "That's great. Can we talk about this tomorrow? I don't think you understand the concept of having to work in the morning." I closed the closet door and plodded back to my bed. I slid under the covers and pulled them up to my ear. "You should get some sleep, too." My voice was muffled from under my comforter.

Trent walked to the door. "Sorry. I was just excited to share my discovery with someone. I thought you'd be excited, too. Goodnight, Roselyn."

"Goodnight, Trent."

Over the next few days, I had a hard time walking through my house without feeling overwhelmed. Everywhere I looked there were chalk marks. When I got home from work, they greeted my eyes as soon as I walked in the door. Trent had informed me that there was a small corner in the basement that was outside the bubble, in addition to my closet. Since there were only two small exclusion zones, I was at a loss for why he needed to mark up my entire house. However, he insisted it was necessary.

Aside from Trent being in the house, things were relatively quiet. He and I were beginning to figure out our roles in this new dynamic. He gave me money for food and utilities and I cooked dinner and didn't ask where the money had come from. We got along well enough, except for the times when I came home from work to find Trent had forgotten that he was perfectly capable of picking up after himself. We were fairly comfortable, but it was apparent that Trent was growing restless waiting for a time event.

Then, one night as I was settling down to go to sleep, something happened. Shortly after I closed my eyes and snuggled into my pillow, I noticed some kind bright flash in the room – bright enough to be detectable through closed eyelids – and I heard Cattiel jump down from the bed as though he'd suddenly been disturbed. My initial thought was that Trent had come wandering in with the flashlight to inspect my closet again. I opened my eyes and sat up in bed, ready to give him an earful.

There was a creature at the foot of my bed. I sat frozen in horror. The dark figure was almost as tall as the eight-foot ceiling, and it stared at me menacingly with glowing red eyes. It awkwardly raised its long spindly arms straight out to either side without bending where the elbows should be, splaying wide its seven elongated, gnarled fingers on each hand. The Big Bad had come for me.

Suddenly, Trent burst into the room and dived onto the bed, putting himself between the creature and me. Trent fidgeted furiously with his watch as I witnessed the creature beginning to open its mouth.

Terrified, I finally had the urge to flee. I started to scramble from the bed, but Trent grabbed my arm firmly enough to hurt. "Don't run," he commanded fiercely. It was the first time Trent had ever truly scared me. I sat there with his strong fingers digging uncomfortably into my arm while the creature's mouth gaped open impossibly wide.

"I'm going to let go of you, but you cannot run!" Trent instructed. He released me and returned his attention to his watch.

A shrieking sound accosted my ears suddenly from every direction, and I saw Trent flinch. It sounded like metal scraping violently against metal. I threw my hands over my ears, but as quickly as the sound had begun, it stopped. The creature disappeared along with it.

It was only then that I realized how badly I was trembling. Trent finished up whatever he was doing on his watch and turned to me.

"Are you all right?" he asked, putting his now-gentle hands on either side of my face and looking me over. Even in the dark, I could see his face was lined with worry.

"I...I think so..." I replied, but my voice was barely above a whisper.

"We got lucky that time," he said. "I was able to get here in time to block most of the radiation. I thought there would be more of a warning, but I only had a few seconds to get to you." Trent suddenly leaned over and looked under the bed at Cattiel. "There you are, you little scamp. You're lucky you didn't run." He sat back up and looked at his watch again.

"Five hours. That thing took five hours from tonight," Trent said in amazement.

I turned on him. "Why did you make me stay through that?!" I asked, my voice cracking. "You bruised my arm, and you wouldn't let me leave!" I was furious with him.

He looked at me with genuine bewilderment. "What? No, I was protecting you! I have a device that absorbs radiation, but you need to be close to me for it to work. If I'd let you run, you would've gotten the full dose of radiation from the Big Bad! Cattiel would've too, but he stayed right with us under the bed. I was trying to keep you safe, Roselyn. I wasn't trying to hurt you or traumatize you." He gazed at me with deep concern.

My anger quickly dissipated, but my fear remained. I was still shaken up by the whole incident. "I'm sorry. I...I didn't know," I apologized. "I had listened to Tilda's story about the Big Bad," I said shakily, "but I wasn't at all prepared for *that*." I felt tears welling up. I tried to fight it, but they cascaded down my cheeks anyway. "Great, now I'm crying," I said, embarrassed.

Trent scooted closer to me on the bed and pulled me to him. He leaned his back against the headboard and put his arm around me as I rested my head on his shoulder.

"If there were ever a good reason to cry, I would say that was right up there," Trent said.

I wiped my eyes and tried to gather my composure. "You weren't scared at all," I said. "How did that not terrify you?"

"I was scared. But you needed me, and that took precedence. It's easier to be brave when you have someone to be brave for."

I turned my head and looked up at Trent. I wanted to thank him for being there with me tonight. I wanted to thank him for keeping me safe. I wanted to thank him for helping me through this weird, impossible situation in which I found myself. I wanted to say all those things, but I couldn't, because Trent's lips suddenly pressed down against mine, stealing my words.

Chapter 6

It started out gentle and tentative, as though he were testing my willingness. When I didn't protest or pull away, his kiss became more urgent and needful. His fingers raked into my hair, holding me to him as his tongue found mine, and they engaged in a sensual dance.

As quickly as it had begun, Trent abruptly ended it, leaving me breathless. He leapt out of my bed and took a step away, toward the door.

"I'm sorry. I'm so sorry," he apologized profusely. "I just…forgive me. I shouldn't have done that." He hurried from the room before I could say a word, shutting the door behind him.

I had never been kissed quite like that before. I'd been kissed many times, of course, but this was different. It conveyed a desire and need of a magnitude to which I was unaccustomed. I had felt his longing, and it had lit a fire inside me. I sat and stared at the door, butterflies still fluttering in my abdomen, and wondered if I should go after him or if I should just lie down and pretend this never happened.

As much as I wanted to run down that hall and demand that he finish what he started, or at least make him explain why he ran off so suddenly, I knew I wouldn't. I would do what I always did – swallow these feelings and pretend nothing ever happened. My heart was safer that way. I straightened my bedding and lay down, my mind replaying everything that had happened tonight over and over in a loop.

It felt like I had finally just started to doze off when my phone alarm sounded. I had forgotten about the five-hour loss until I looked at my bedside clock and saw that it showed 2AM. It was a good thing I had decided to use my phone for my alarms or I would have slept in and been late for work. I dragged myself out of bed and trudged to the kitchen to make some coffee.

As I filled the pot with water, I noticed the chalk marks were gone from the walls. Had Trent spent the night cleaning? I looked over and noticed a note on the table and a simple gold-chain necklace with a small electronic device attached to it. I set the pot down in the sink and went over to investigate.

Dear Roselyn,

I have collected the data I need. I am working on finding a solution for your problem, and it should be resolved shortly. Thank you for your hospitality and for being a good friend. I'll be in touch. In the meantime, please keep this device on your person at all times while within the house. It will protect you from the Big Bad if he comes again, but I'm hoping I will have this taken care of before he has an opportunity.

- TM

My heart sank into my stomach. He'd left me? Just like that? No heartfelt goodbye, no hug, no explanation for last night

76

– just a cold, initialed note? It was so unlike the Trent I'd come to know. How could he do that me?

I took the note and ripped it into tiny shreds. I picked up my phone and called him. He owed me a proper goodbye. The phone beeped and crackled for what seemed an eternity, but the cheery English-like voice I was waiting to hear never answered. He was ghosting me.

I bit back the tears, cleared my throat, and told myself that none of this mattered. This is what was always going to happen anyway, wasn't it? Right from the start, this was the endgame. He was always going to leave, and I shouldn't have been surprised. I tossed the shredded letter into the garbage can, picked up my coffee pot, and resumed my morning routine.

It wasn't until I was in the car heading to the fitness center that I lost the battle with my tears. All it took was a mediocre sappy song and the flood works began. I quickly changed the radio station and chastised myself for being so ridiculous. I wasn't in *love*. I didn't get *dumped*. There was no reason for me to cry! Regardless, my heart was of a different opinion and I showed up to work with puffy eyes and a blotchy face.

I got through the workday without incident. I was feeling much better after having interacted with other people all day, and I even sang along with the radio on my way home. When I walked through the door, however, it felt like walking into solitary confinement. Loneliness descended upon me, and I felt those blasted tears trying to make an encore appearance. I scooped up Cattiel and buried my face in his soft fur. He growled and tried to squirm away from me.

"Love me, dammit!"

Cattiel stopped fighting me and let me hug him for about ten seconds before resuming his tantrum. I released him, but not before warning him that I was going to start dog shopping.

That night, as I was getting dinner ready, I absent-mindedly set the table for two. I didn't even notice I had done it until I sat down and looked over at the empty seat across from me. I pulled out my phone and tried to dial him again. I just wanted to hear his voice, but I still didn't get an answer. I set my phone on the table and looked at the empty chair.

"Why am I so stuck on you?" I asked aloud to a man who wasn't there. "You weren't that great. You were weird as hell. And obnoxious. And annoying. And you had giant feet and bowed legs. And you moved your hands too much when you talked. And you made weird faces. And you had no concept of personal space. And your hair was always dangling *just* near the corner of your right eye and it bugged me. And you kept me up at night because you somehow never slept. And you kissed me and then *apologized*. And worst of all, you went and made me care about you and then you left. You just *left*. So screw you, Trent Morgan."

As I picked at my food, my eyes kept returning to the device he had left on the table. I hadn't touched it since this morning. It looked similar to an oval-shaped jump drive. It was metallic and ugly. And it reminded me of him, so I hated it. I grabbed it and stuck it in my pocket anyway, though. I might need it, and it made me hate it even more to know that because it was like still needing *him*.

The weeks passed, and life slowly went back to the way it was before Trent. I was still lonely, but I was used to being lonely now. The house had been quiet. There hadn't been any strange time events, and I had noticed recently that I no longer had to adjust my home clocks. But I always kept Trent's device on me, just in case. I had been wearing it around my neck as a daily accessory. Everything was…bearable.

Then, about a month after Trent left, the calm was broken. Autumn was beginning to tinge the leaves of the trees and the air had a chill to it. I came home from work on a blustery Wednesday afternoon and immediately made myself a pot of coffee. I went to my bedroom to change out of my fitness training clothes and into something warmer. When I came back out to the kitchen to pour a hot cup of coffee, I saw something in the kitchen that made me freeze in my tracks.

There was a Time Thief standing near my table. Just standing there. Even though it was only a faint, shadowy figure, I felt like there was something oddly familiar about this one. It appeared to be looking down and picking at something on its wrist.

No. No, it can't be…

"…Trent?"

The Time Thief moved its head. It looked like it was looking around.

"Trent, is that *you*?"

It looked back down at its wrist and started walking toward me. I stepped aside as it walked past me and disappeared into the hallway wall.

"Trent!" I ran to the office on the other side of that wall, but no one was in there. I ran around the house frantically seeking any sign of Trent, but I was alone.

It had been him. I knew those movements. It was Trent. But…how?! I grabbed my phone and dialed his number. I waited with bated breath as the line made its strange noises, but he didn't answer. I frowned. What was he up to? How had he ended up as a Time Thief?

I did a quick time check to find out how much of my day I had lost. I was perplexed when I realized my wall clocks still matched the phone. Same day, same time. Nothing had happened to the time. What the hell was going on?!

There was a knock at the front door. My heart leapt into my throat and I ran to answer it. I was certain it was Trent. I flung the door open without checking, and…it was a stranger. He wore a beige trench coat that looked like he had just quickly thrown it on and forgotten to button it, and beneath it he was dressed in a black suit with a blue tie. He was about 6ft tall and of average build. He had a somewhat round face and bright blue eyes that turned downward at the outside corners. It made him look mournful. His dark brown, almost black hair was cut short, and he wore it gelled in a spikey, bed-head style. He looked to be around thirty years old.

"Oh, hello!" he said with a big welcoming smile…and an English-like accent. "I'm Trent. Trent Morgan."

I panicked and slammed the door in his face. I didn't know what else to do. I stood there, staring through the door window at this man who couldn't possibly be Trent Morgan as a look of pure bafflement crossed his face. That was *not* Trent. This man was slightly taller and not as skinny and his eyes were the wrong color and his face was all wrong and…it *wasn't him.* Not even a well-executed disguise could change someone's appearance this much.

"I know Trent Morgan, and you, sir, are not him!" I yelled through the closed door.

The man on the porch furrowed his forehead and looked down at his watch. I pressed my face against the window to get a better look at that watch – and saw that it was Trent's watch.

"Where did you get that watch?! That isn't yours!" I shouted through the door.

"I'm sorry, who do you think I am?" he asked with his hands turned upward in a questioning manner.

"I don't know who you are, but you aren't Trent!"

"Listen, I just need to know something. Has there been anything strange going on around here? I received a distress signal from this area."

Why did he talk so much like Trent? "I didn't call you."

The man looked down at his watch again and started pressing buttons. As he turned away from the door, I saw him pull out a pair of glasses and slip them on before bringing up the watch's holographic display. It looked similar to the interface from Trent's watch, but there was something slightly different about it – but I couldn't quite put my finger on it. He flicked through the images just as quickly as Trent always did. Was it possible that this *was* Trent?

I opened the door a crack, and the potential imposter turned to me. "How old are you?" I asked.

"Don't you know it's rude to ask someone their age?"

"What is SABER?" I asked, watching for his reaction.

He gave me startled look. "How do you know about SABER?" he asked suspiciously.

"I told you. I know Trent Morgan. Why are you calling yourself Trent Morgan?"

"I've been Trent Morgan for as long as I can remember. It's the one thing I always remember."

I stepped outside onto the porch and walked around him, looking him up and down. "This is all wrong," I said.

"I feel strangely insulted. Is it the coat?" He looked down at it and swayed around in it. "It looks silly, doesn't it? I wanted to try something new, but it doesn't feel like *me*, you know?"

I gave him a deadpan expression. "Are you trying to be funny?"

"I wasn't. Am I?"

"Are you what?"

"Being funny."

I put my hand over my mouth. "Good lord, it is you, isn't it?"

"Well I certainly hope so. If not, I'm not sure who else to be."

"Why don't you look like *you*?" I asked, still suspicious. "And why don't you know me?"

He gave me a raised eyebrow. "You must not know your Trent Morgan all that well if you haven't figured that out by now."

I felt injured by that assessment. "What do you mean by that?"

"I swear I haven't met you before today. I don't know you. What does that tell you?"

I suddenly remembered an off-hand comment Trent made to me way back when I first called him. He'd said that if I ever ran into him and he didn't know me, not to be cross with him because it happens sometimes. Is this what he meant? Did that mean that this version of himself was from his past?

"You're his past," I guessed.

"The Ghost of Christmas Past!" he joked. Then he nodded. "Probably. Or I suppose I could be in his future. Memories get fuzzy when the change occurs."

I was still confused. "What 'change' are you talking about? Why are you different?"

"Didn't your Trent tell you how he came about?"

"Yes. He talked about SABER and genetic engineering and telomeres and robots—"

"Experimental nanobots."

"Yes, to keep him from aging."

"But he didn't tell you the side effects?"

"No."

"Well, let me enlighten you, then. See, there was a problem with the nanobots that didn't present itself until I was about 32 years old. I was working on the time-warping device, as that was my sole purpose at SABER, when I suddenly lost consciousness. When I awoke in the infirmary, I had changed. The nanobots had done their job, but not the way they were supposed to have done it. They weren't supposed to activate until my telomeres had shortened to a level when my aging would start causing damage to my system, but they activated much sooner. Instead of repairing the telomeres, they 'repaired' entire DNA strands in every cell. I was essentially a different person. It affected my brain – I retained some memories of my previous 32 years, but large chunks of information were missing. I knew what my purpose was, but I had 'forgotten' certain aspects of my research. These changes have continued to happen throughout my life at random intervals. I never know when it's coming. It just happens, and I wake up as someone else with only about half of my memories. That's why I say I could be from your Trent's future. It's possible I may have just forgotten you."

It broke my heart to hear those words.

It must've been written all over my face, because Trent looked at me with concern and asked, "Did I say something wrong?"

"No, it's nothing," I lied. I moved the conversation along with, "So how many times have you changed?"

"Eight times."

"*Eight?* In any of those phases were you ever a five-foot-eleven, skinny, bow-legged, swoopy-haired madman with an odd penchant for tweed suits?" I asked.

Trent crinkled his nose. "No." Then his face took on a look of utter displeasure. "Oh, you've got to be kidding me. Is that what I turn into?"

"So you haven't just forgotten me, then?" I said hopefully.

"Apparently not. Although I must say that I would find it rather difficult to forget a face like that. You're quite lovely," he said with a charming smile.

I gave him a half-smile, feeling flattered, but it quickly faded as a thought occurred to me.

"Wait. If you are Trent from the past, then why didn't *he* know me when he came knocking on my door? Shouldn't he have remembered something about me or something about this encounter?"

Trent grimaced. "…Yeah, I was hoping to distract you from that point since you seemed to be bothered that I would forget you."

"You did forget me! How could you forget me?!"

"Like I said, when I change, my memories don't always make it. It isn't as though I do it on purpose."

"It's still insulting," I pouted.

Trent sighed and looked around. "So why am I here? It can't just be to stand outside and listen to you yell at me."

I crossed my arms. "I don't know. You tell me. I didn't call you." I stopped and held my hand up. "Oh, wait! Maybe I did call you. I was trying to call Trent – *my* Trent – but he wasn't answering. I suppose if you're Trent, you must have the same number, right? Was I calling you?"

"No, it wasn't that. Even if it were, my calls get directed to me based on a chronological algorithm I programmed into my device. This was a distress signal that came from somewhere…else." Trent looked at his watch again. "Say, when was the last time you saw your Trent? Is he likely to pop back around anytime soon?"

"Why, is it a problem if he does?"

"Not for short periods of time, but it does add to my memory problem when I cross my own timeline. It does a funny thing to your brain when it tries to remember two different memories from the same place and point in time."

"So if you run into yourself, you don't remember it?"

"Not really, no."

We stood in uncomfortable silence for a moment as he stared at me.

"What?"

"You never answered my question."

"What question?"

"Has my future self been here recently? Am I coming back?"

"Oh. Um…I don't know how to answer that. You were here, yes. You came because—"

Trent quickly stuck his finger over my lips to shush me as he cried, "No no no! No! No spoilers! I don't want to know what happens or what I do in the future. I just want to know if I was here and if I am coming back."

"Wow, ok," I said, taking a step back from his reach. "Yes, you were here, but it's been a while. I thought I saw you in the kitchen a few minutes ago, but as a Time Thief."

"Time Thief? Wait, never mind. Don't explain that. I don't want to know. Actually, I really do. Time Thief?" He looked at me with heightened interest. When I started to open my mouth, however, he shouted, "No, no, don't tell me. It's better if I don't know."

"I was just going to suggest that maybe it was *him* that sent you the distress signal."

Trent raised his eyebrows. "Oh. Yes, it could be that. Can I come in and have a look in your kitchen?"

I nodded and led him inside. He walked through the kitchen looking at his watch. He suddenly stopped, as though he'd found something, and then started slowly following the same path I'd seen shadow Trent walk earlier that afternoon.

"I left a trail," he said as he stopped at the wall where shadow Trent disappeared, "but I'm not getting the entire message. I think I'm trapped somewhere."

I was instantly concerned. "What are we going to do?" I asked, wringing my hands worriedly.

Trent ignored me and walked around the house for a few more minutes before he gave up. "I don't know what to do yet. I need more information."

"What can I do to help? There has to be something we can do!"

"Relax," Trent said, holding his hands up. "If I know me, and I'm quite certain I do, I'll be just fine. I'll leave more clues and messages. We just have to wait for them." Trent pressed a few buttons on his watch. "When I get another distress signal, I'll teleport over here. If I don't show up, ring me. I've programmed this location in so your call will now be directed to me instead of him. I get the feeling he's probably not receiving calls wherever he is right now anyway." Trent held his watch up as though he was about to teleport out.

"Is that it?" I asked. "You're just going to leave?"

He turned to me with a puzzled look. "I told you, we'll have to wait. What more can I do?"

"You aren't going to stay and wait here?"

"It could be weeks before we get another message. What would I do here?"

"Wouldn't it be better if you were here when he showed up? You might be too late if you teleport. And wouldn't it screw up your data if you had to time travel to get here when the distress signal came?"

"I did have to time travel to get here today, and the message was still there. I'm very clever... – wait, what's your name again?"

"Roselyn. Roselyn Wolff."

"I'm very clever, Roselyn Wolff, so you can trust that future me is going to make sure that the message will get to me one way or another."

"Oh. Well, all right, then," I said, feeling a bit dejected. My Trent was a lot more fun than this one.

"Why are you doing that? Why are you making your face look so forlorn? What have I done now?" Trent asked, his brows drawn together in confusion.

"I was just hoping you might stay for a little while. It's been a while since I saw my Trent last and...well, truth be told, I kind of miss the weirdo. I thought maybe it would be nice to get to know the Trent before my Trent. I have coffee made if you wanted to stay and have a cup," I offered.

"I don't like coffee," Trent said.

"What are you talking about? Of course you do. You drank coffee every morning when you were here."

"The fact that I like coffee in the future doesn't hold any bearing on whether I like it right now." Trent must have seen the deflated look on my face, because he suddenly became more empathic. "I wouldn't mind a cup of tea, though, if you have it."

I looked in the cupboard as Trent removed his trench coat and sat down at the table. "Do you prefer an herbal tea or Earl Grey?"

"I love Earl Grey. That's great," he said amicably.

I put the kettle on to boil and then poured myself a cup of coffee. I stood near the stove, leaning against the sink, waiting for the kettle. I was holding my coffee cup, wondering if it would be rude of me to start drinking it before Trent had his tea. What an odd thing to worry about. I set the cup on the counter and folded my arms. I looked at my feet and tried to get my suddenly blank mind to think of something to say.

"So we just have to wait for Time Thief Trent to show up again, and then we can save him?" I asked.

Trent made an uncertain face. "Perhaps. Or it could take several appearances. Those messages might come through in fragments, like the one today, and I might have to piece them together over time. I just don't know at this point. Also, can we please stop calling my future self 'Time Thief Trent'? It sounds weird."

"What do you want me to call him?" I asked, annoyed.

"I don't care. Future Trent. Swoopy-Haired Trent. Literally anything else would be better."

"My Trent," I suggested.

Trent looked at me. "You seem to like the future me. Are you my companion?"

"What do you mean by companion? He's my friend, but that's it."

"Future me is lucky to have someone care so much about what happens to me. That doesn't happen very often. Ever, really. I'm a bit of a lone wolf."

The tea kettle started to whistle. "You must have someone," I said as I prepared his tea. I set the cup down in front of him, fetched my coffee from the counter by the sink, and sat down at the table across from him.

"Nope. There are only a handful of people who truly know what I am, and we don't keep in contact." Trent took a sip of his tea and leaned back in his chair. "No, the only people who give me more than just a passing thought are the members of SABER, and that's because they want to imprison me and steal my device."

"That's so sad. In all this time, hasn't there been anyone?"

"Eh, I try to keep to myself. It's just better that way."

"How is that better?"

Trent looked at me, and then looked around my house. "You look like you're keeping to yourself, too. That's not by choice?"

I frowned at him. "It's complicated."

"Isn't everything?"

He had me there. "Look, it isn't like I enjoy living by myself all the time. I would love to have someone around. It would just be nice if that 'someone' didn't up and disappear on me with nothing but a damn note on the table." I looked across the table at the other Trent, who was sitting in the same spot where my Trent used to sit, and he looked back at me blankly. He had no idea I was talking about his future self and that I was feeling angry with him for something he hadn't even done yet.

"That's unfortunate, but you should probably move on. If someone doesn't want to stay, you can't make them. And if you do, it isn't really fair to either of you, now is it?"

Trent was telling me to move on from my Trent without even knowing he was talking about his future self. It was an unusual conversation to be having. "I suppose you're right," I admitted.

"I usually am."

There was a lull in the conversation, so I blurted out the first thought that came into my head. "So what's it like to change?"

Trent's expression grew solemn. "A lot like dying, I suppose. I lose consciousness, and the person I was and many of the memories I made are lost."

"But you still have some memories. You continue on with your life when you wake up," I said.

"It's a lot more like starting over than it is like continuing. You might better understand it this way: imagine you spend your life building a house, a career, and start a family. Then, one day, your house burns down, your spouse leaves you and takes the children, and you get fired from your job. Yes, you continue on with your life, but you're basically starting over. It's a rough analogy, I know, but I want you to get the point that it isn't a wonderful, magical rejuvenation. It's hard, and scary, and no one else in the entire world can understand the way it feels but me."

"I'm sorry," I said. "I didn't know."

"Of course you didn't. How could you know? It's an unknowable thing for you." Trent sighed. "You know what the worst part of it is? It's in not knowing when it's going to happen. There is no warning. No time to say goodbye or to grieve what I am about to lose or accept that the change is coming. No time to warn those around you that they won't be seeing the 'you' they know anymore. It leaves you afraid to get close to people. It fills your life with a sense of uncertainty and impermanence, and it makes it damn near impossible to build an attachment to anyone or anything."

"How old are you, Trent?"

"It's hard to say. If I had to venture a guess, I'd say I'm probably somewhere in the ballpark of four hundred."

I couldn't imagine what it would be like to live for four hundred years. "Are you saying that in four hundred years, you've never fallen in love?"

"Who would put up with this?" he asked, raising his hands dramatically. "Who would be able to love a man who doesn't grow old with them? Who would be able to live twenty or thirty years with a man that never much ages, then be completely prepared and accepting when he becomes someone else?"

"It would be an unusual situation, I'll admit, but it isn't impossible."

"Isn't it? Look at you, for example. You care about Trent – quite a great deal, it would seem. You know that the man sitting before you is Trent. Yet you look at me as 'other.' I am not *your* Trent. I am just *a* Trent to you. Your brain and your heart aren't connecting us as one person. He is your friend and I am a stranger. I can tell by the look on your face that I'm right," Trent said as he looked away. "I usually am, aren't I?"

I was at a loss for words.

Trent stood up and hastily slipped on his coat. "Thank you for the cupper," he said curtly. "I'll be seeing you." With that, he pressed a button on his watch and disappeared.

Chapter 7

I sat at the table and stared at the empty chair across from me. He had been right. He usually was, wasn't he? I did have a hard time seeing him as the same person as the Trent I knew. It bothered me to admit that to myself. But my Trent and this new Trent (or should I say old Trent?) seemed like two very different people. They were similar enough for me to truly believe that the Trent to whom I served tea today was indeed a past version of the Trent I knew. However, they had strikingly different personalities. The two seemed more like brothers – similar, but not the same.

I thought about how much a person must change in four hundred years just from life experiences. Hell, I am a drastically different person now than I was ten years ago. How old was the Trent I knew? Obviously older than four hundred, but how much older? How many changes did he go through to become who he was? Now that I knew more about him, I couldn't fault him for forgetting me – especially if he'd gone through several changes since first meeting me today. If he'd so easily forgotten me, was it possible that he had fallen in love before and has since forgotten? Is there a woman out there somewhere in time who had his heart?

I was surprised at the jealousy that quickened my heart with that thought. I had no right to be jealous. I didn't even know if a woman like that existed, but even if she did, what was it to me? Perhaps I was just one in a long line of ladies whose hearts had been stolen by the mysterious Trent Morgan.

And, just like that, I was angry with him all over again.

Three days passed with no sign from either Trent. I had spent most of that time worrying and wondering and over-thinking things. So, on this rainy Saturday, I decided to turn up the music on my phone and give the house a proper cleaning in order to get my mind off of Trent. Cattiel was of little help, as he hid under the bed in my room all day while I vacuumed and sang terribly at the top of my lungs. I couldn't really blame him. I mopped the kitchen, did the laundry, and even got dinner in the slow cooker right on schedule. I was on a roll.

As I stood at the sink, washing up the dishes that didn't fit into the dishwasher, I sang all the wrong words to the song on my phone and danced cheerfully. I hadn't felt this carefree in a long time, and I realized that living by myself definitely had its perks. I grabbed a large pan from the strainer and spun around, intending to do an electric slide across the kitchen floor to the towel drawer near the stove. Unfortunately, as I started the slide, my eyes suddenly locked with a very amused Trent, standing near the table with his hands in the pockets of his trench coat and a wide grin on his face. I dropped the pan with a resonating clang, and I came to a stumbling halt, cutting off the note I was so vociferously belting. I stood staring at him, mortified, while the dropped pan settled noisily to the floor. His face bore an expression of utter delight.

I quickly grabbed my phone and shut off the music. "How long have you been here?!" I demanded as I hurriedly fixed my ponytail and pulled my flannel shirt closed over the tank top I was wearing underneath.

Trent picked up the pan I had dropped and set it on the stovetop. "Long enough to hear you sing 'turtle on my knee' instead of 'dirt all on my name.' But don't worry, I won't tell anyone."

I could feel my cheeks burning in embarrassment, but Trent's smile just grew wider as I blushed.

"Why are you here?"

He held up his watch and pointed at it. "Distress signal. Did you see future me around anywhere?"

"Oh! No, I haven't seen anything today."

"That's all right. I'll find it," Trent said, looking down at his watch.

"I'm going to go change quickly while you look for the message," I said uncomfortably, my cheeks still burning. I wished I hadn't chosen to wear the "Bootylicious" sweatpants I'd had since college.

"Don't bother," Trent said as he started to walk away. "I've already seen the outfit. There's no point in trying to pretend I didn't." He headed toward the stairs to the second floor.

"Yeah, but I shouldn't subject you to that torture any longer than necessary."

Trent was halfway up the stairs, and he stopped and leaned over the railing to look at me. "Oh, I don't know," he grinned. "I kind of like it." He then continued up the stairs.

I desperately wished my cheeks would quit burning. I grabbed Cattiel, who had finally emerged from his hiding place in my room, and sat down on the couch, waiting for Trent to find the message from my Trent.

"I think I'm trying to send us coordinates," I heard him yell down to me. He dashed down the stairs and then hurtled the bottom rail athletically.

"You're way too springy for four hundred," I stated dryly.

"At least I'm not wearing trousers that say 'Bootylicious' across the rear." He stopped and put his hand to his chin thoughtfully. "Although, maybe I should be."

"What were you saying about coordinates?"

"Ah, yes! Look," he said as he brought up the holographic display on his watch. "Normal coordinates should look like this." He pointed at a set of numbers separated by commas. "But there are too many sets in the coordinates I sent."

"What does that mean?"

"I'm somewhere I definitely shouldn't be," Trent said ominously. "But I still have to wait. There's more to this message that I haven't received yet."

"Why is it coming through all broken up like this?" I asked. "Why wouldn't he just send it all at once?"

"Well, maybe I did send it all at once. There could be a delay due to traveling from wherever it is I sent it from. Or perhaps I only get fixed amounts of time to transmit information. Or perhaps I've sent the information multiple times, but only some of it makes it to us each time. It's hard to say. It could be any number of reasons."

"He hasn't indicated that he's in danger?"

"No, nothing of the sort. I'm trapped and obviously need help to get out, but there's been no indication of urgency or immediate danger."

"I wonder how he did it. He got the time changing to stop, but then he went and trapped himself. I just can't put together how he managed that."

"Time changing?"

I looked at him with a wry smile. "No spoilers, remember? Besides, you'll enjoy figuring it out…and I'll enjoy helping you figure it out."

I deposited Cattiel onto the couch next to me and stood up. "So, we're back to the waiting game, hey?"

"It appears so."

"The story of my life," I said. I went into the kitchen and started to fill the kettle with water.

"Are you making tea?" Trent asked.

"I am."

"Might I bother you for a cup?"

I turned to him with a grin. "Who did you think I was making it for? I'm having a glass of wine."

When the tea was ready, I poured Trent a cup and brought it to him. I grabbed my glass of wine and sat down at the table across from him.

"So here we are again," I said. "Last time I had to practically beg you to stay for a while."

"People don't usually want me to stay."

"I can't imagine why," I remarked sarcastically.

"Post hoc ergo propter hoc," Trent said and took a sip of his tea.

"Beg pardon?"

"It's Latin for 'after this, therefore because of this.' People assume that since I show up and weird things start happening that I'm to blame, when in reality I came because something weird was going to happen and I was only there to fix it. People don't want me to stick around because they're afraid I'll bring more mayhem down on their little world."

"Have you ever considered your personality might have something to do with it?" I smirked.

"Oi! I'm delightful, thank you very much!"

"Yeah, after someone gets to know you. But you are terrible at first impressions."

"I don't care what people think of me, especially if I'm not going to have to deal with them for long. I don't need people to like me."

"Then why did you stay for tea yesterday instead of just leaving?"

"You were making a sad face. I'm a sucker for a sad face."

"So you must care somewhat, then."

"I didn't mean I didn't *care*. I said I didn't care what people *think* of me. I still care about their well-being, though. I'm not a sociopath."

I smiled and couldn't help but mutter, "I do wonder." I knew he wouldn't get the call back to the conversation I'd had with my Trent outside the retirement home, but saying it brought a smile to my own face in remembering the exchange.

Then it struck me. From Trent's perspective, I was the first one to ever reply to "I'm not a sociopath" with "I do wonder." From my perspective, however, it was him. He was the one who said that to me, and that was why I was saying it now. But was it possible that the reason *he* had said it in the first place was because somewhere in his memory he remembered *me* saying it right now? Who said it first? Was "first" even an appropriate term for it, or was it just an impossible loop of cause and effect with no beginning and no end? More importantly, though, did it mean that my Trent actually *had* remembered me?

Trent's voice snapped me from my thoughts. "Are you literally wondering right now? Are you still with me?" He waved his hand in front of my face.

I blinked. "Yeah, sorry. I was just thinking about something."

"How dare you think of me that way while I'm sitting right here." Trent grinned at me playfully.

"You didn't smile much the first time you were here. I have to admit it's nice when you do."

"Dazzling, isn't it?"

I laughed. "You seem to be in a much better mood today than you were last time."

"Yeah, it turns out I'm rubbish at first impressions," Trent said.

"It's true. But you've redeemed yourself."

Trent and I sat and talked for almost an hour before he left. It was a lot more comfortable than it had been yesterday, but it still didn't feel like he and my Trent were truly the same person. I still couldn't see them as one and the same. I tried to avoid talking about it, though, because it seemed to bother Trent that I felt that way.

The next morning, I awoke to the sound of someone knocking on my front door. I looked over at the clock. Who was knocking on my door at 7:30AM on a Sunday morning? I rolled over and pulled my blankets up over my ear and ignored it, assuming it must be a solicitor.

"Roselyn?" Trent called. It sounded like he was in the living room.

I climbed out of bed and shuffled out into the living room, yawning. Trent was standing there in his trench coat and suit, holding a disposable cup of coffee or tea with foreign writing on it.

"Did you get another signal?" I asked, rubbing my eyes and likely flaking yesterday's mascara all over my face.

Trent was cringing at me. "Do you…need a moment?"

I frowned at him. "No. Why, is something wrong?"

"Did you just wake up?"

"What was your first clue, Sherlock?"

He pointed at my hair with a grimace, and then slowly ran his finger all the way down until he was pointing at my feet, indicating *all of me.*

"I know, I know. My hair is almost as perfectly chaotic as yours," I said, pointing to his spikey-styled hairdo, "but it doesn't look quite the same on me. Ugh, I'll at least go brush my teeth, ok? Thanks for the confidence booster, though."

Trent chortled. "You don't seem like the kind of person who needs confidence boosters."

"Everybody could use one now and again," I said as I went into the bathroom and grabbed my toothbrush. When I saw myself in the mirror, I was almost as mortified as I was yesterday. I quickly brushed my teeth and ran a brush through my hair. When I came out, Trent was still standing in the entryway of the living room, leaning against the couch.

"Trent, why are you here?"

He thrust the cup of coffee toward me. "I brought you coffee. It's from a shop in France that I remember I used to like in a previous life."

"My Trent forgets me, yet you remember a coffee shop from a previous phase?"

"I've told you, I don't get to choose what I remember and what I forget. Do you want the coffee or not?" Trent said, suddenly seeming agitated.

"Sorry. Yes, please." I took the cup from his hand. "Thank you. I can't say anyone has ever brought me hot coffee from France before."

"Not even *your* Trent?" he asked snidely.

"Wait, are we fighting? When did this happen? Did I nod off for a second? I blinked and you were mad," I sassed as I walked away from him to go look in the fridge.

"We're not having a row. It just frustrates me when you call my future self '*your*' Trent."

I grabbed the carton of eggs out of the fridge and walked to the stove. "Why? Why on Earth would that bother you? You didn't want me to call him Time Thief Trent."

Trent was silent. I turned to see if he was still there. He was just standing in the living room with his hands in his coat pockets, his eyes distant.

"Cool. Great talk. Do you want some eggs?" I asked.

"Oh, uh, no thanks. I'm not hungry."

"Where's your drink?" I asked as I started cracking eggs into a bowl.

"What drink?"

"You brought me a coffee. Didn't you get a drink for yourself?"

"No. How is it, by the way? The coffee."

"It's actually quite amazing. Thank you. So why are you really here, Trent? It can't just be to bring me coffee."

"Why can't it just be that?"

I stopped whisking the eggs as the blood rushed to my cheeks. Cattiel took the ensuing silence as an opportunity to remind me with a noisy *purrrrrt* that he needed his food bowl filled.

"Oh, yes, Cattiel. You need breakfast too, don't you?" I said, avoiding Trent's question. I fed the cat and returned to my eggs.

I heard Trent walk into the kitchen behind me as I grabbed a pan and set it on the stove. "Are you sure you aren't hungry?" I asked, turning on the burner. "I can make some more—"

My words caught in my throat when I felt Trent's body come close to me and saw his hand reach across in front of me and turn the burner off. I looked up at him, and he was looking down at me with intense eyes that were as deep and blue as the Pacific itself. He cupped my face with his hands and brought his mouth to mine. It wasn't hesitant or inhibited. He kissed me with everything he had, holding nothing back. It made my head swim.

When our lips parted, he didn't let go of me or step back. He just looked into my eyes, searching for my reaction.

I wanted him to do it again. I wanted to taste his tongue and feel his lips crushing against mine again. But instead, I felt my lip tremble and I asked crossly, "Is this what you do with every woman you help out? Is this your go-to move?"

Trent furrowed his brow in confusion. "What are you talking about?"

I wrapped my hands around his wrists and pulled his hands away from my face. "I'm not going to lie – it's a great move. A really, really great move. But I've fallen for it before. I don't know what kind of game this is to you, but I don't want to play."

"Roselyn, what do you mean? I just…I like you!" he blurted as he took a step back. "Ok? I like you. Why is that a problem? Is it because of something I do in the future? Help me understand here, because I'm lost!" he demanded in frustration.

"How many women have fallen for it?" I asked as I turned the stovetop burner on again and slammed the pan onto it.

"What, you think I just run around snogging random women every chance I get?"

I dumped my eggs into the pan and started stirring them around with a spatula. "Yeah, I think maybe you do."

He brought his fingertips to his temples. "Why the bloody hell would you think that?!"

"Because my Trent did the same thing to me – exactly the same damn thing – and then he just ran off with nothing but a stupid note!"

Trent stood there, breathing heavily, nostrils flared, but I could see the irritation slowly dissipating from his features. His expression became disheartened. "It was me," he realized. "It was me you were talking about that first night." He gave a short, cynical laugh. "And I told you to move on. I thought it was just some bloke." He sat down at the kitchen table and rested his chin in his hand. "If you are so obviously angry with me, then why do you care so much about rescuing me?"

"You can be mad at someone and still care what happens to them."

"Don't I know it."

I cooked my eggs while Trent sat quietly at the table. I tried to ignore the pleasant lingering taste of his mouth on my tongue and the tingle in my belly. Why did it matter so much to me if he had done this with other women? I was a divorced woman who hadn't been with a man in almost a year. My body was on fire for the man sitting only a few feet away from me – a man who obviously had carnal feelings for me – and I was standing here acting like I couldn't stand him.

It was because I cared about him. That was my hang up. I wanted to be more than just another woman to *him*. I wanted him to be more than just a warm body in my bed. It didn't help that I was still sorting through my feelings for my Trent. I still wanted my Trent to come back. Even though this Trent was right here laying his cards on the table, I still missed *my* Trent, and this Trent knew it. And I knew it bothered him. This was the strangest love triangle of which I'd ever been part.

I scooped the scrambled eggs onto a plate and stood at the counter to eat them.

Trent looked at me and sighed. "Are we going to talk about this or am I going to go?"

"I don't have anything to say."

"Yeah, you do."

"You should've had some eggs. They're good."

Trent's shoulders slumped in defeat. "Listen, I just want you to know that this is not something I ever do. All these 'other women' you speak of just don't exist. I don't have a 'go-to move.' I just like you. That's it. No secret motive or devious plot."

I stood there, trying to think of something to say. My feelings were all jumbled up, so what hope did I ever have of trying to articulate them to him?

All I could think to say was, "I don't know how I feel about any of this."

Trent gave me a tight smile. "I understand. Well, I suppose there's no point in me staying and making this any more uncomfortable than it already is. I'll be around."

And just like that, he stood up and teleported out of the house.

I couldn't eat all of the eggs I'd made, as my appetite had vanished just as quickly as Trent had. I sat down on the couch with the coffee he'd brought me and stared out the window. I shouldn't have pushed Trent away like that. I should've at least allowed myself to explore the possibility of him. And, good lord, why couldn't I have let him take it just a little bit further? My body was admonishing my heart for being such a sensitive fool.

I didn't see or hear from Trent for several days. I was grateful for the time to myself, however, because it gave me time to cool off and think with a level head. I thought about how everything that is happening between Past Trent and I right now has already happened from my Trent's perspective. If I was supposed to fall in love with Past Trent, wouldn't I have been an important enough part in his life for my future Trent to have remembered at least *some* of it? And if I was supposed to be with Past Trent, then my future Trent shouldn't have gotten so suddenly weird about kissing me, should he? None of what has already happened made sense unless I wasn't meant to be with Past Trent. As much as my body thought I had made the wrong decision, I knew in my head that no other choice was possible. This was always where I was going to end up because this has already happened before for Trent – and once an outcome is observed, it becomes reality, doesn't it?

As I dug through my closet, looking for a clean pair of athletic leggings to wear to the fitness center for work the next day, I pondered how much of my life for the next few weeks was already predetermined simply because someone else has lived it already and wondered if it applied to the rest of my life as well. The choices I made felt like free will, but were they? Were fate and destiny actually real things? Was it fate that had made me keep putting off laundry so I now had no leggings to wear for work tomorrow? Was it my destiny to find an old pair I had forgotten about buried beneath a pile of oversized t-shirts?

I turned around to toss what clothing I'd found onto the dresser, but as I did, the strangest thing happened. The clothes stopped and floated in midair, hanging as though frozen in time.

Chapter 8

I stared, dumbfounded, and it took my brain several seconds to piece together what was happening. Time was being altered again for the first time since my Trent left, but I was outside the bubble. Time was passing normally for me, but for my clothes, which were now in the bubble, time had slowed down relative to the rest of the world.

I stood in the closet, unsure of what to do. I thought of calling Trent, but I'd left my phone sitting on the nightstand. Would his watch pick up that something weird was going on here right now? Was my Trent any part of what was going on, and if so, was he sending a distress signal? Even if that was the case, Past Trent would probably teleport into the house and end up inside the bubble anyway, leaving me still trapped in the closet like R. Kelly to watch events unfold painfully slowly for the next three to five hours.

But what if I stepped into the bubble? Would it hurt me to make such a transition? It didn't seem to affect my clothes, but then again, they were just clothes – not living tissue. If I didn't make the transition all at once – if part of my body was on the inside, and part was on the outside – what would that do to me? It had the potential to be a biological disaster. I wished I had shown more interest in the closet when Trent had first shown it to me. Perhaps he would've had some insight into what one should do if they found themselves trapped in the closet during an event.

Suddenly, I saw a blinding flash of light, and from that flash, Time Thief Trent appeared. Even though everything else inside the bubble seemed to be moving at a snail's pace, that one particular incident seemed to be instantaneous. Once Trent had appeared and the flash was gone, however, his movements were almost too slow to be perceived. I sat in the closet and watched him, wondering what message Trent was going to leave this time and if it would be the final message needed to bring him back.

The longer I sat and waited, the more I speculated about why there was a time event around Trent's appearance this time when it hadn't happened the last couple of times. There was something odd about Trent's movements, too, aside from seeing them in slow motion. It looked like he was raising his arms, and the longer I watched, I saw it looked like he going to wave them as though he was attempting to get somebody's attention. Was he trying to tell me something? Was he trying to warn me? Was the Big Bad on its way?! What would happen if it showed up while I was outside of the bubble? I reached up and felt reassured when my fingers touched the small metal device on the chain around my neck that my Trent had left me what seemed like ages ago. Even if it did materialize, I was safe.

I tried to occupy myself by sorting through the clothes in my closet. I had several items that I never wore anymore, and I knew I never would even though I kept trying to tell myself that I might. I started making a stack of garments that I was going to donate to the local thrift store. When I got to the formal gowns, I found the beautiful dress I had worn to my senior homecoming event. I held it up and gazed at it, memories of a time full of possibilities and hopes for the future flooding my brain. I remembered how I'd felt when I wore that dress. I'd been overjoyed to be a part of something so important (as a high school senior), but I also remembered knowing that I wasn't *quite* special enough to actually win the vote for homecoming queen. I had been best at many things academically and athletically, but I was never best at being popular. As I stared at the dress I hadn't worn in almost twelve years, I wondered if my life would have turned out any differently if I had won the vote for homecoming queen.

I glanced over at the shadowy figure of Trent. If I had been homecoming queen twelve years ago, would I still have ended up here, in this house? Would I have ever met Trent? I tried to decide if it had been a good thing to meet him, or if I'd have been better off if I hadn't. He sure had made life a lot more interesting. He'd shown me things in the short time he was with me that had opened my eyes to a universe of incomprehensible complexity and a deeper perception of reality than I ever could have imagined before. And he'd made me believe that it isn't impossible for me to fall in love and trust a man again, even after what I had been through. He had hurt me, of course, but I was realizing that there was more to the story than I understood at first. So, I supposed I had been better off having met Trent. Perhaps it was a good thing I hadn't won homecoming queen after all.

All of a sudden, the trench-coat-clad Trent materialized in the bedroom near the doorway. He was just suddenly *there*. I waved my arms at him and yelled to him stupidly as if he were a plane flying over a deserted island I had been marooned on. He was inside the bubble, though, and he was stuck in the "time sap." He might be able to see me, especially if I stood in the same spot for a while, but there wasn't anything he could do to help me unless he teleported out of the bubble to the closet. By the time he figured it out, the time event would be over.

I threw my hands in the air in exasperation and started pacing. I had no idea what time it was getting to be, but I was getting a little stir-crazy just hanging out in my damn closet. I returned my attention to my formal gowns and proceeded to talk to myself to pass the time.

"Why do I even still have these?" I asked myself. "I'll never wear them again. I'm just clinging to a time that's long gone. Oh, but what a time it was, wasn't it? What I wouldn't give to feel the way I felt when I was wearing these dresses, just for a little while." I started to put the dresses onto the stack for donation, but I couldn't bring myself to go through with it. I hung them back on the rack. "I'm not ready to leave it behind. Not just yet."

I turned to the Trents moving slower than sloths in my bedroom. "Is that what you're going to end up being to me?" I asked them rhetorically, knowing that my voice would be talking so quickly to Trent from outside the bubble that he wouldn't be able to hear me at all. "Are you going to be like these gowns – a beautiful memory that I just can't seem to let go of even long after you've gone and left me behind? A feeling that I keep chasing even though I know nothing will ever quite replicate it?" I barely got the last words out before Time Thief Trent disappeared and trench coat Trent started moving at a normal pace. He looked down at his watch, his face bearing a look of bewilderment.

"What the hell just happened to time?!" he asked to no one in particular. He suddenly glanced over at me, looking surprised to see me there. "You weren't there a second ago," he said, baffled. "What just happened?"

"You'll find out some day," I said as I stepped out of the closet. Trent started to open his mouth to speak, but I interrupted him. "Hold that thought. I'll be right back." Not being able to leave the closet meant I also hadn't been able to use the bathroom that whole time.

When I returned to my room, Trent was peering through his glasses at the holographic interface on his watch. He turned to me, and he looked shaken. "Something's happened. My future self needs out. Now."

My heart was gripped by dread. "What do you mean? What's happened?!"

"I don't know exactly, but he's basically sent me an S.O.S. this time."

"Can we get him out?"

"I think so. It seems I have what I need now." After Trent looked through the information on his display for another minute or so, he turned to me. "I need to make sure to be right here in…" Trent glanced down at his watch again before continuing, "exactly 26 minutes, 32.46758 seconds – or thereabouts."

"Why?"

"Because that's when we'll be opening the wormhole."

I raised my eyebrows. "Excuse me?"

"Just a small one. He needs the energy from my watch to keep it open on our end, but it has to be at exactly the same time he opens it on his end or it won't work at all."

"Let me get this straight: you're going to open up a wormhole in my *bedroom*?!"

"Yes. Brilliant, isn't it?" Trent said with excited, sparkling eyes.

"Is it going to be dangerous?"

"Quite possibly. You might want to step out for a bit."

"Not a chance."

Trent smiled slightly. There was a hint of sadness in his expression, though. "That's awfully brave of you."

"It's easier to be brave when you have someone to be brave for," I said. When Trent looked at me like I was some kind of oddity, I asked, "What? What's wrong with that?"

"Forgive me. It's just that I'm not used to the idea of anyone being brave for *me*."

"Well, you don't exactly seem like the kind of guy who regularly needs people to be brave for you."

Trent's smile faded a little, but he didn't say anything.

"Do you want a cup of tea while we wait?" I offered.

Trent nodded. "That would be lovely."

I put the kettle on and sat at the table while I waited for it to boil. I perched my elbows on the table and rested my chin in my hands.

"Am I going to see you after this?" I asked.

Trent folded his hands and rested them on the table in front of him. He looked down at his hands instead of at me when he replied with, "Probably not."

"Why not?"

"I imagine *your* Trent will be planning to hang around, which leaves very little room for me. I can't spend much time around myself, remember?"

"What makes you think he's going to hang around?"

"Because I'm quite certain he has feelings for you."

I gave him a doubtful look. "You don't know that."

"I do, actually."

"How?" I challenged him.

"Because he fell for you when he was me." He looked at me with sorrowful blue eyes.

I felt my cheeks getting flushed. "But…he didn't even remember me."

"Are you quite sure of that?"

I hesitated. Was I? Now that I stopped to think about it, he had made some odd comments in that short while that he'd lived with me – comments that had indicated he knew more than he was letting on. But if he truly remembered me, there were so many things that didn't make sense about his behavior, too. Was it possible that he remembered just bits and pieces about me? Had he remembered this conversation Trent and I were having right now?

The kettle started to whistle, and I jumped up to get Trent his tea. I could feel his eyes following me as I poured the water over the teabag in his cup. When I brought him his tea, he looked at me regretfully.

"I'm sorry I upset you the other day. I knew this wasn't going to work. I knew I'd have to leave once I brought my future self back, but I just…I thought maybe you could feel the same way for me that you do for my future self. I thought maybe you could see us as the same person. I understand now that it was wrong of me to expect that of you."

I sat down across from him. "It's ok. I felt bad about snapping at you. It's not that I *don't* feel anything for you…it's just…complicated."

"To you, I'm not *him*. And I get it. In many ways, I'm not." He was trying to the hide the dejection in his voice, but he couldn't hide it on his face.

We sat quietly for a little while. It seemed that there should've been so much more to say, but when something is coming to an end, you can never think of what those things should be. It probably didn't help that I wasn't sad. Yes, I liked this Trent, and I probably would miss seeing him. But I was so looking forward to seeing my Trent again that it was hard to be properly upset about losing this one. I didn't want him to know I was feeling that way, but I was quite certain he did.

Trent stood up from the table, looking down at his watch. "It's time."

My heart leapt into my throat.

I followed Trent into the bedroom, my heart racing. Trent instructed me to stay back as he manipulated the display on his watch briefly. I stepped back to the doorway and observed as he stared at the watch in silence, his finger poised over a button on it. When the time came, I didn't even see Trent press the button because there was a sudden flash of light so bright that I had to close my eyes. When I opened them again, my Trent was standing in the room. Not a shadow of him – the real him.

When I saw his face, it was the strangest feeling. It was akin to the feeling you get when you walk into your home after being away for a while. There was a comforting familiarity and fondness. He may have looked a bit windswept and unkempt, but he still had that spark of mischief in his eyes and that smile that made his whole face light up.

His jovial laugh filled the room as he clapped his hands together once. "Ha! We did it! I'm back, baby!" He quickly patted himself down. "And I'm still in one piece! Brilliant!" He pointed to his past self enthusiastically. "Hey, I remember you! Or, I should say I remember when I was you! Things get a bit mixed up, don't they?"

"What was all of this? How did you end up in a parallel universe?" Past Trent asked.

My Trent winked at him. "You'll see. Besides, you know you wouldn't remember even if I told you." Trent's gaze moved beyond his past self and his eyes finally met mine. He grinned so widely it made my heart soar. "Roselyn!" He held his arms wide and started toward me.

I met him halfway and did my best to fight the urge to leap into his arms. He squeezed me tightly, lifting me off the floor slightly. I didn't want him to let me go.

"I have so much to tell you!" he exclaimed as he released me. "But first, I need a snack." He walked past me and left the room, heading toward the kitchen.

I looked over at the Trent from the past. He looked stunned. "That's who I become? I'm so…"

"Eccentric? Scattered? Ridiculous?" I filled in for him. "I know. Isn't it great?" I said with a grin. I turned and left the room, and Trent from the past followed me to the kitchen.

We found my Trent rummaging through the fridge, and it was almost like he'd never been gone.

"Roselyn, where's the kale? You seem to be out." My Trent stood up and looked at the other Trent and me. "I'm a bit shocked. She's obsessed with the stuff," he said to his past self as he quickly turned his attention to the cupboards.

I had almost forgotten how annoying he was.

"Listen," Trent from the past spoke up, "I should be going. Roselyn, I look forward to meeting you again." He held out his hand.

"A handshake?" My Trent commented around a mouthful of the toaster pastry he had just bitten into. "Ah, you forget how awkward your younger years were," he mused to himself.

I brushed past Trent's outstretched hand and hugged him. "Thank you," I said simply.

He hugged me back briefly, then stepped away. He smiled at me in a way that gave the impression he was holding back words that desperately wanted to escape his lips. Instead of speaking them, however, he gave a casual salute and pressed a button on his watch, disappearing in silence.

"You didn't show him very much gratitude," I said, turning to Trent. "He put a lot of time and effort into getting you home."

Trent laughed. "It was *me*. I don't think I'm obligated to thank myself for helping myself. I know I would've done the same for me," he jested.

I couldn't argue with that.

"So, how was it?" Trent asked me.

"How was what?"

"Everything. How was life while I was out? How was it getting to know my past self? Did anything exciting happen in my absence?"

"Everything was fine, but I suspect you already know that. Why didn't you tell me you'd met me in your past? Things could've gone a lot smoother if you'd warned me about what was going to happen."

"If I had, it would've changed the outcome. It would've changed my past and your future. It had to happen this way. Besides, I didn't really remember much of it anyway."

"But you knew your past self was going to show up, and you knew you were going to be trapped in another world."

"No, actually I didn't remember the part about me being trapped. I didn't know that was going to happen."

"Why did you act like you'd never met me before when you first showed up at my door?"

"You would've thought I was mad if I'd told you the truth."

"I still think you're mad, so your argument is invalid. Why didn't you at least tell me once I got to know you?"

"Like I said, it would've changed everything. It needed to happen this way."

"Why? What would've happened if it changed?"

"Any number of things. You never know the magnitude of damage that can be done when the past is changed, especially when you mess with your own past."

I thought about the conversations I had been having with Trent's past self – namely, the conversations regarding my feelings for him. I asked, "What *do* you remember about your past interactions with me?"

"Not much. I remember that I met you, and I had to help you with something. I remember that you had met a future version of me, but I didn't know the circumstances around that. That's about it."

I recalled something he had said to me back in the beginning. "When you were trying to understand the time events, you once said that you knew you figured this out eventually. Why did you really say that? I know it isn't because you figure everything out eventually."

"I thought I must have figured it out if my future self had been gone when my past self showed up here. I never leave anything unfinished."

"So, you don't remember anything I talked about with your past self?"

Trent gave me a sly smile. "Is there something interesting I should remember?"

"Ugh, never mind."

"How is it that you don't seem to be the least bit curious about where the hell I have been this whole time? All you want to talk about is my past. I'm more interested in talking about what's going on now. Trust me, it is *far* more interesting!"

"Ok, you have my attention."

"I was in a parallel universe!"

"Yes, I gathered that," I said dryly.

Trent looked insulted. "Time travel was a shocking novelty to you, but parallel universes are just humdrum?"

"What can I say, you've desensitized me to the outlandish."

Trent conceded. "I suppose that's reasonable."

"Well, what did you find? What was it like?"

"I found out who the Time Thieves are. They're just people. Scientists, working for SABER. They don't even know you can see or hear them from this side." Trent waited for my reaction.

This time I was surprised. "Really? Just people?! What about the Big Bad?"

"Now that – that was not a person. That's the probe they were trying to send through the wormhole to collect data on the other side. It was incredibly radioactive from the continual attempts at trying to send it through the wormhole, and they had to keep it contained."

"I'm confused. Why is it only my house? How are they doing this? Why were they doing this?"

"Why does anyone do anything? Curiosity! Well, that's why the scientists were working on it. SABER's involvement, though, pointed at some underlying malicious intent. And the reason it was only in your house is because this is the corresponding location for the SABER compound in the parallel world – like two giant membranes coming together and touching at a single point," Trent explained as he held his hands out in front of him, drawing them closer together. "They are able to accomplish this because they have a particle accelerator that is capable of reaching the Planck energy, and when they focus that energy, they're able to create a wormhole. Oh, and guess who was leading the research and experimentation?" Trent smiled proudly.

"...You?"

"Yes! Not *me* me, of course. But a parallel version of me. Of course, I had to have a talk with myself and warn myself about SABER. It turns out that the parallel version of me wasn't working on time travel at all. Just travel between parallel universes."

"How do you remember any of that? I thought you couldn't remember it when you encountered yourself."

"It wasn't me. It was a parallel version of me. Not the same person. Different memories, different life – different being entirely. And oddly, he actually doesn't change. He still looks like me before my first change. I guess they got the nanobot technology right in his world. Oh, and he even picked a different name than I did. He goes by Jaeger Novak."

"Wait, you picked your name?"

"Of course. I couldn't go around as Number Thirty my whole life."

"Number Thirty?"

119

"That was my embryo number. Out of thousands of trials, only embryo number thirty grew successfully. And here I am."

"What made you choose Trent Morgan?" I asked.

"Well, Trent means 'thirty.' It's also been interpreted to mean 'traveler.' I think it's pretty self-explanatory why I chose that. I chose Morgan as my last name because it means 'sea circle.' The waters of the sea flow, as time does, and a circle is never ending, as I am."

"You should've called yourself Justin Tyme."

"Bit on the nose, don't you think?"

"Yeah, but it'd still be funny. What does Jaeger Novak mean, then?"

"Jaeger means 'hunter,' and Novak means 'new.' Get it? Because he hunts for new worlds. It's quite clever, really."

"Can I ask how the hell you ended up over there in the first place?" I inquired. "I mean, if it took this much of a team effort to get you back, how did you make it over there on your own?"

"When looking through all the data I had collected that night the Big Bad came, I realized that we were dealing with a parallel world and an artificially created wormhole. I was trying to send a communication through to them, sort of a 'cease and desist,' but I accidentally ended up sending…well…myself."

"How do you accidentally send yourself?!"

"Hey, it happens! Teleporting is a tricky science," Trent replied defensively.

"But how did you get through and couldn't get back?"

"The technology they were using to create the wormhole was keeping it partially open on their end at all times, but they didn't have enough of an energy source to make the wormhole complete. In other words, some things could get through, but they couldn't send full, solid objects. What happened is I accidentally opened the wormhole fully to our side – and sent myself through it. But then I was stuck there because I needed that extra boost from our world to get me back through. And the only boost that could do that was my watch. Therefore, I recruited the help of my parallel self to program my watch to send information to our world in order to contact my past self."

"So why didn't time slow down when you would show up as a Time Thief? Why did it only do it this last time, right before we rescued you?"

Trent gave me a surprised look. "You saw me more than once?"

"Yeah. You'd show up whenever you left a message."

"Oh. I didn't realize I was visible to your side. That's interesting!"

"Why didn't time slow down?"

"I wasn't trying to transmit anything but the information, therefore the gravity of the parallel world wasn't affecting the time in this world. The reason it did the last time was because I tried to use the artificially created wormhole in the lab to transmit the information because I thought you weren't getting my messages. And I needed to get out of there before SABER figured out what was going on. They were starting to catch on that something was off."

"How did you get them to stop trying to send things through to this world? The time events stopped as soon as you left."

"I explained to my parallel self what kind of damage was being done to this world, and how much more damage would be done if they were successful in the future. He adjusted his wormhole generator to try for another parallel universe, but he was quite interested in time travel after I told him about my watch. It's possible he's now going to end up going down the same path I did, but that's not my concern."

"He adjusted the wormhole generator just because you said so? Just like that?"

"Just like that."

"Why would he listen to you?"

"You'd listen to yourself, wouldn't you?"

I thought about how often I ignored my inner voice. "Not necessarily, no."

"Yeah, but you have trust issues. I guess I was asking the wrong person. My point is *most* people would listen to themselves."

"I don't have trust issues. I'm just cautious."

"Not the point right now, Roselyn. Pay attention, will you?"

I rolled my eyes. "So, is this all over then? Am I safe?"

Trent smiled. "Yes, I believe so. See? I fixed it. I knew I could fix it."

"What happens now?" I asked hesitantly.

"You should be all set to get on with your life. What happens now is up to you," Trent said.

"But…what about you?"

"What about me?"

"Are you going to, you know, still be around?"

"What are you asking, Roselyn?"

"Am I going to see you again?" I blurted.

"…Did you want to?" Trent asked, surprised.

"Maybe. I mean, what if the time events start happening again?"

"You have my number."

I sighed in frustration.

Trent smirked at me. "If you have something you want to say, maybe you should just say it outright."

"Just…never mind. Forget it," I said with a dismissive wave of my hand. "Thanks for all your help. I'm glad you came when you did." I started to turn away, intending to go busy myself with emptying the dishwasher. I didn't want Trent to see my face at the moment because I was afraid it would betray my feelings.

Trent caught my hand as I moved away from him, stopping me. "Is that it?" he asked.

I pulled my hand out of his grasp and looked up at him. "That's it."

"You weren't going to ask if I could take you away on a holiday?"

"No, I wasn't."

"I suppose *I'll* have to ask then. Roselyn, did you want to, oh, I don't know…go somewhere with me?" He smiled invitingly, and there was a twinkle of mischief in his eyes that made my heart skip.

I swallowed hard and turned away from him again. I tried to laugh off his offer as I began to unload the dishwasher. "Very funny."

"It isn't a joke."

"Take a holiday with you? Why would I do that? Where would we go?"

"I think the more appropriate question is *when* would we go."

I forced a laugh. "That's just crazy. I'm not going on holiday with you. I have a life here. A job. Cattiel. No, it's a terrible idea." I almost had myself convinced that I didn't want to do it.

"Just one adventure. I'll take you anywhere or anywhen you want to go."

"Anywhen isn't a real word."

"When you have a time-travel device, anywhen most certainly is a valid word. Come on," Trent pressed, "you name it, and I'll take you there."

"The only place I'd want to go is back to before I met my ex-husband so I could warn myself to avoid Barry Schmidt."

"You know you can't do that."

"I know. Paradox. So what's the point then?"

"Do you really lack such imagination? Forget about *your life* for a minute and think about all the amazing things in the world there are to see. Or all the things there were to see. You know what? I have just the place. Come on, I want to show you something."

I looked at him reluctantly. "Where?"

"When."

Chapter 9

I sighed and walked over to him, taking my place under his left arm. "Only for a minute, and then we come right back here," I stipulated.

"Only for a minute," he agreed.

He pressed a button on his watch and our surroundings changed in an instant. We were no longer in my living room, but rather in what looked like a savannah with a few tall, fern-like trees. The air was warm and dry. I heard an odd birdlike screech off in the distance, but it was an unfamiliar sound.

"What is this place?" I asked, stepping forward and looking around in awe.

"Somewhere in Utah."

"This is Utah?! How far back did you go?!"

Trent looked around. "Oh, about a hundred fifty million years."

My eyes widened. "Are you kidding me?! When you said anywhen, I was thinking, like, Greece. Rome. Ancient Egypt. I wasn't thinking *dinosaurs*!" I heard another strange animal call from somewhere around us, and I moved closer to Trent. "Are we safe? I feel like this isn't very safe."

"Well, I can teleport us out of here in a pinch, but strictly speaking, 'safe' isn't a great descriptor for our current situation. But stay close and we'll be all right," Trent said cheerfully.

"I want to go home now," I whined.

Trent scoffed at me. "Where's your sense of adventure? We are in the land of *dinosaurs* and you want to go home before you've even had a chance to see one?! Look," Trent said, pointing to my right.

I glanced over and saw a large lake. My mouth fell open when I saw a group of six stegosauri ambling down to the water's edge.

"That's...those...those are real dinosaurs..." I stammered, dumbfounded. They were some distance away, but the sight of them was mesmerizing.

Trent chuckled. "Brilliant, isn't it?"

"How did you know?" I asked as I continued to stare, mouth agape.

"How did I know what?"

"It was my favorite." I could see Trent looking at me from the corner of my eye. I glanced at him briefly and elaborated, "As a kid, the stegosaurus was my favorite."

Trent grinned as he looked over at the magnificent animals. "Of course it was. Isn't it every kid's favorite?"

"My brother always favored the velociraptors."

"He wouldn't if he ever met one."

I stopped staring at the stegosauri to take a quick look around. "We aren't going to see any of those here, are we?" I asked nervously.

"Oh, no. They won't be around for another sixty million years or so. And they wouldn't be in this region anyway," Trent assured me. Then he added, "But, I wouldn't be surprised to run into a Utahraptor here in this time period, and that would be even worse." He looked down at his watch. "We should probably be going now. Your minute is almost up."

"Just…just one more minute," I requested.

Trent looked pleased as he nodded in acquiescence.

As I watched the stegosauri drinking peacefully at the water's edge, I understood why Trent had chosen to take me to this particular time and place. He knew it would fascinate and intrigue me. He knew it would be just enough to make me want to go on *one* more little adventure with him. What he didn't know, though, was that he could've taken me just about anywhere and it would've had the same effect simply because I knew deep down inside that I *wanted* to run away with him.

As I turned back to him and let him put his arm around me, a sudden movement over his shoulder caught my eye. I glanced back and saw a man standing about fifty yards away from us. I gasped and opened my mouth to speak, but we were already back in my own kitchen before the words erupted from my mouth. "There's a man over there!"

Trent whirled around, looking around the kitchen. "What? Where?"

"No! Not here! There was a man back there in Utah!"

Trent became very serious, and it was instantly concerning. He put his hands on my shoulders and looked me in the eyes. "Tell me exactly what you saw."

"I don't know, it was a man! I saw him for just a second before we teleported!"

"What did he look like?" Trent's eyes were locked on mine intently.

"I didn't get a good look at him. He just looked like a man!"

"Clothes? Hair color? Skin? Weight? Come on, give me something!" he demanded roughly.

"Trent, you're scaring me."

"You should be scared!" He shouted. He fidgeted with his watch, scowling. He turned around and started pacing. "There shouldn't be a man in Utah a hundred fifty million years in the past. The fact that there was one means that something is very *very* wrong. And when something is very *very* wrong, you can bet SABER is behind it. Or I am."

"What do you mean by that? Why would you be behind that?"

Trent looked at me. "Who was behind the Time Thieves fiasco?" He held up his hand. "Me."

"Yeah, but not *you* you."

"But some version of me. Enough like me to be a possible threat. The last person on Earth I would ever want to contend with is me."

"But you're a reasonable person. You're a good person. Why would any version of you ever be a threat?"

Trent looked at me with pained eyes. "Oh, my dear, you have no idea. There's a reason I am constantly working to stop SABER – and that's not just to keep them from getting their hands on a time-travel device. That's important, of course, but there's a far more essential purpose for my vigilance. I can't allow them to create another one of me."

I furrowed my brow. "Because you could create a time-travel device?"

"No. It's because I could create any kind of device they asked me to make." He pointed at his head. "This is approaches the limits of what human intelligence is capable. My brain. This mushy gray mass I carry around between my ridiculous ears holds keys to doors that should never be opened. We have some wildly clever artificial intelligence in the future, but nothing that's able to surpass the raw creativity and ingenuity of the human mind. And this one is undoubtedly the most imaginative – and most dangerous." Trent stopped his pacing and rested his hand against the wall, his other hand on his hip. He looked down at the floor instead of at me as he said, "Pack a bag and grab your cat. You aren't safe here. We need to go. Now."

"What? Why?"

Trent turned to me with a look of urgency. "For once can you just do what I ask?!"

"Ok!" I cried.

I ran to my room and started tossing clothes in a bag. I had never seen Trent look so rattled, and it scared the hell out of me. This was a man who faced off against the Big Bad and barely batted an eye, so I really didn't want to be around to meet whatever it was that *did* scare him. In my fear, I stuck my .45 in with the rest of my belongings. I threw my bag over my shoulder, rushed back out to the living room and scooped up Cattiel off the couch.

"I'm ready," I said as confidently as I could.

I barely got the words out of my mouth before Trent swept me up in his arms and teleported us out of the house. He released me and abruptly walked away as soon as the transfer was complete. I found myself in a small home library or office. There was a comfortable-looking beige chair sitting next to a window, and two large bookshelves full of novels and texts. The floors were hardwood, but they didn't appear to be well-maintained. There was a large desk near the wall with several half-burned candle sticks sitting upon it.

"When and where are we now?" I asked, following him over to the bookshelves as I tried to calm Cattiel.

"London, 1923. We are in my home." Trent replied distractedly. He began pulling unlabeled leather-bound journals from the shelves and stacking them in his arm.

"Is it ok for me to let Cattiel run around here?"

"Don't put him down yet. We aren't staying."

With that, Trent grabbed me and teleported us into yet a different location. This time, we were in what appeared to be a more modern apartment. We again were in some kind of library or office, as there were shelves of books along the wall and a desk nearby.

"More books? With all this running around, when do you ever have time to read?" I asked.

"There's always time to read," he replied. "You can let the cat down now. We'll be here a while."

Trent went over to the desk and plopped the journals down that he had taken from London.

"We aren't in 1923 anymore, are we?" I asked with a downward inflection as I set Cattiel on the floor.

Trent sat down at the desk and started thumbing through the journals. "No. This is 2361."

"I'm in the *future*?" I said, surprised.

"The future to you, yes."

"Where are we?"

"Vancouver."

"…Oh."

That got Trent's attention. He stopped looking through the journals and glanced up at me. "'Oh'? What, is there something wrong with Vancouver?"

"No, it's great."

"Then why did you say 'oh' like that?"

"Like what?"

"You had a tone."

"No, I didn't."

"You did. Is Vancouver not exotic enough for you?"

"I didn't say that! It's just that Vancouver is kind of…ordinary, you know? It caught me off-guard after all the excitement."

Trent gave me an irritated look. "You're 343 years into your future *and* you saw dinosaurs today, but hey, by all means, complain that I landed us in Vancouver."

"I wasn't complaining! You're the one making a big deal about it!"

"It bugs me! You expect me to give you over-the-top extraordinary all the time, but guess what? Sometimes ordinary is good too!"

"I don't expect anything!" I argued. "As I recall, I tried to turn down your offer of adventure, but *you* were the one who insisted! I didn't ask for dinosaurs! I didn't ask for the future! And I sure as hell didn't ask for you!"

I immediately regretted my words. I wished I could gather them all up and shove them back down my throat before they could reach his ears.

Trent gave me a tight, humorless smile. "I'm sorry I've caused such a disruption."

"I didn't mean that," I apologized.

"People say things they don't 'mean' all the time. The problem is that there is a part of them that does mean it...at least just a little. Otherwise, the words never would've occurred to them. I think when people say 'I didn't mean that,' what they really mean is 'I didn't want you to know I felt that way.'"

"And sometimes," I countered, "people don't realize until after it's been said that they really, truly, don't feel the way they thought they did when they said it. You should know all about that, Trent. You know, like kissing someone because you think you like them, then realizing you don't and running off and leaving only a note. I think that's a pretty good example of what I'm getting at."

Guilt clouded Trent's face.

"What, nothing snarky to say now?" I prodded.

"It was a mistake. I told you I was sorry," Trent said quietly as he looked down at his journals. The word "mistake" shot through my heart like an arrow. I wondered if that was how he had felt when I had spit verbal venom at him only moments ago.

"Mistake or not, you owed me an explanation. A conversation. Not a note saying 'Hey, you're on your own now!'"

"What was I supposed to say? I was sorry. I said it. I meant it. I didn't want to cause any more complications."

"But then you come back and ask me to go on holiday with you? That's one hell of a complication if you ask me!"

"I know!"

I looked at him quizzically. "Then why did you ask?"

"I don't know! I thought maybe it would be fun!" He sighed. "You know, when I left you that note, I didn't know if I would be coming back, and I certainly didn't know you were going to help rescue me from a parallel world. None of those memories were retained from my past self. But I did remember one thing; and that one thing was that I kissed you back then and you did not like it. And I shouldn't have done it that night before I left, and I'm sorry I did. But, when I came back, and I saw you looking at me like…like you actually *missed* me, I thought maybe you had forgiven me. Maybe it would be ok if we were still friends. I thought perhaps you would like to accompany me on some of my journeys and see the things I see. I'm not expecting anything out of this, if that's what you're thinking. I just thought we could have some fun and kill some time – as friends." Trent looked at me earnestly.

"As friends," I repeated, trying the words out.

"That's all I'm asking."

"Trent, why did you kiss me?" I asked.

"Why does anyone do anything?"

"Curiosity?" I responded, puzzled.

Trent gave me a sly grin and tapped the side of his nose in reply.

I didn't understand the gesture, but before I could inquire, Trent's watch made a strange noise. He looked down at it and knitted his brows.

"What's wrong?" I asked.

"There's something going on at your house. Or rather, something is going to go on at your house."

"Wait, how does your watch know that?"

"I put up an alarm system when I was living there. I haven't deactivated it yet."

"So, what, you have cameras up around my house? Have you been watching me?"

"No, nothing like that. Just a couple of sensors to alert me if anything is amiss. I wasn't going to keep it up, I swear. I have alarm systems up at all of my houses in case anyone ever comes after me."

"Who would come after you?"

"SABER, of course."

"Is it someone from SABER at my house right now?"

Trent pulled his glasses from his breast pocket and slipped them on. He turned on the holographic display on his watch and examined the information. "No, it isn't anyone from SABER. The energy signal is all wrong. I think it's just your run of the mill intruder." He turned off the display and took off his glasses.

My heart thumped violently against my ribcage. *He found me,* was the only thought running through my head. *The bastard found me.*

"I should pop in and see if he's finding everything all right," Trent joked nonchalantly.

"No! He can't know about you!"

Trent looked at me with surprise. "Who can't what now?" he asked, confused.

"It's him. It's Barry. I know it is. If he sees a man in my house, he'll lose it." I was on the verge of a panic attack.

Trent stood up from his desk and walked over to me. "Say that last sentence again."

I gave him a puzzled look. "If he sees a man in my house—"

"*Your* house. Exactly," Trent said. "He doesn't have control over you anymore, Roselyn. Besides, we don't even know that it's him."

"It's him."

"All the more reason for me to go have a chat with him," Trent said with a defiant smirk.

"No, Trent. Please. Please just leave it alone."

"Will he stop if I leave it alone?"

"He won't stop if you don't."

"I can be very persuasive."

"Leave it, Trent. We need to focus on finding out who the man from the Jurassic was."

"We have time for a side quest. This is important."

"Important to me. Not to you."

"If it's important to you, it's important to me."

Those words made me pause. "…Even after I said those mean things to you?"

Trent grinned. "If you didn't say mean things to me, I'd think something was wrong."

"You don't know what you're getting into," I said. "You don't know how he is."

Trent gave me a confident look. "I've been around for over six hundred years. Trust me, I've dealt with plenty of people like Barry."

Six hundred years old?!

"You don't understand. If you go in and start something, it's just going to make an even bigger mess out of this situation and I'm going to have to continue dealing with it long after you've left."

"Who said I was going anywhere?"

"Well, eventually you will."

"Roselyn, even if I'm halfway around the globe and a hundred million years from you, I can still be by your side in an instant. I'm never really 'gone' if you don't want me to be."

"You were just in a parallel universe and unreachable for like two months," I pointed out.

Trent paused, tilting his head. "Ok, you got me there. But to be fair, that was a first, and hopefully a last. And hey! A past version of myself showed up to help and I *did* come back eventually!"

I looked at him skeptically.

"My point is," he said, "you're not alone in this. He's going to try to direct his wrath at you. That's what weak men do. Let me take it instead. Trust me, I've had worse."

I took a deep breath. "Fine. But I'm coming with you. Just give me a minute." I quickly dug through my bag and pulled out the .45 I had acquired in anticipation of a situation like this. I hooked the holster inside the back of my jeans and pulled my shirttail out over it to hide it.

"You won't need that," Trent said.

"Let's hope not."

I steeled myself and stepped up next to Trent. He put his arm around me and we were instantly in my kitchen, standing in the dark, facing the back door. The door handle was jiggling as an unseen hand from the other side was attempting to jimmy it.

Trent stepped forward and turned on the kitchen light next to the back door. He opened the door. "Can I help you?" he asked, sounding irritated. His body was blocking my view of whoever was on the back porch.

"Who the hell are you?" The sound of Barry's voice sent a shiver of dread down my spine. I hated that he could still fill me with such incapacitating anxiety.

"Trent. Trent Morgan. What are you doing to the door back here?" Trent demanded.

"Where's Roselyn? Why are you in her house?"

"Why are you trying to get in?"

"I need to talk to Roselyn. Where is she?" Barry asked impatiently.

"You can talk to me."

"I don't want to talk to you. Look, I know she's here. That's her car in the driveway."

"It's a very common model."

"It's her license plate, asshole. I'm not stupid."

"A bit obtuse, though, aren't you?"

"If you think you're going to talk down to me with your accent and your weird words, you've got another thing coming. Just let me talk to Roselyn and I won't have to hurt you."

Trent threw his head back and laughed mockingly. "Oh, dear. You are a bit of a shit, aren't you?"

"Oh, really?! I'm a shit? You know what else I am? I'm a black belt, fucker." That was a boldfaced lie.

"And I think you'll find I'm rather indestructible," Trent said calmly. That was probably true.

"Who the fuck *are* you?" Barry shouted angrily. "Are you her new boyfriend? You know what a whore she is, don't you?"

"I'm not her boyfriend, but I would consider myself a lucky man if I were. I suggest you watch what you say from this point going forward. Or perhaps you could just keep your rubbish to yourself, get back in your vehicle, and leave this place and never come back."

"I ain't going anywhere, you prissy asshole! Do you think I'm afraid of you?" Barry mocked. "I could break you like the little twig you are."

Trent crossed his arms and leaned against the door jamb. "That mouth just doesn't stop, does it? Wow, you do test one's patience!" he marveled.

When Trent shifted to lean against the door jamb, it had created a clear sightline between Barry and myself. I saw him standing there in the dark, and we locked eyes. My heart stopped and I froze like a deer in the headlights.

"You little bitch! Sending someone else to fight your battles for you? You're a spineless—"

Barry was cut off when Trent put his whole hand over Barry's face and pushed him backwards. Trent stepped outside with Barry and shut the door behind him. I could hear Barry yelling terrible things about me and making threats.

I heard Trent calmly say, "You need to leave, and there's no point in ever coming back because you're just going to be dealing with me if you do. And if I have to deal with you again, I'm going to have to relocate you."

"What the fuck does that even mean?" Barry shouted.

"It's what they do with problem animals. They relocate them to somewhere they can't hurt anyone."

"I'm not going anywhere! I'll come back every goddamn day! How the fuck do you think you're going to relocate me, bitch?"

"Like this."

The silence that followed concerned me. I ran to the door to see what had happened. The porch was empty.

"Oh, Trent, did you just do what I think you did?" I asked aloud to the air.

"If you think I relocated him, then yes," I heard Trent say behind me. I turned around to find him standing in the kitchen, straightening the cuffs of his suit jacket.

"Where did you put him?"

"When."

I put my hand over my mouth. "You didn't…"

"No, I didn't. It would've been funny though, wouldn't it? I put him in Wyoming. With a little effort, he'll find his way home. But I told him if he came here or bothered you or anyone you know again, then next time he'd end up in Russia." Trent smiled at me. "Also, I thought it might please you to know that he cried."

That did please me. "We have a small problem though, Trent. What are we going to do with his truck?"

"It's being towed, of course. Already taken care of." Trent swiped his hand through his hair and straightened his tie. "Well, that was fun, but shall we get back to boring old Vancouver now before we get company that isn't quite so easy to be rid of?"

I nodded as I felt tears welling up in my eyes. It was like someone had released a pressure valve in my brain, and twelve different emotions came bursting out all at once.

Trent scrutinized my face. "Are you unhappy?"

"No, I'm...I'm just a weird mix of emotions right now." I waved my hand dismissively. "It's fine, I'll be fine. Let's go."

As I went to Trent to be teleported back to Canada, I realized just how grateful I was to have him in my life. I wrapped my arms around his torso, resting my temple on his shoulder, and whispered, "I'm sorry I said I didn't ask for you. I'm glad to be able to call you my friend."

Trent put his arms around me and squeezed me. "Ditto." He pressed the button on his watch to send us back to Vancouver, but he didn't let go of me immediately after we arrived. I didn't complain, though, because I didn't let go right away either.

When I finally did release him, he went to his desk to pore over his journals. I wanted to know what it was he was looking for within their pages, but at the moment I needed to go sit quietly by myself and find my composure.

"Is there somewhere I can go lie down?" I asked.

"Oh, you're probably tired, aren't you? I forget how much you lot need to sleep."

"I'm too riled to be tired. I just need some time to myself for a bit."

"There's a very comfortable bed in my room that rarely gets used. I'll put some fresh sheets on it for you," he said as he started to stand. "It hasn't been touched in a while."

"No, don't worry about it. Like I said, I'm not going to sleep. I just need a minute."

"Oh. Well, all right. Do you want me to bring you anything? I probably have some crackers or something nonperishable in the cupboard."

"I'm fine, Trent. I'll be out in a little bit."

As I followed Trent's directions to his room, I almost tripped over Cattiel.

"Crap, you need your food, don't you?" I bent down to pet the fluffy feline. "And a litter box. Damn."

I yelled to Trent about Cattiel's supplies.

"On it," he replied. Within moments, he yelled, "There, he's all set. Come here, kitty kitty! Come get your dinner!"

I chuckled to myself as Cattiel's ears perked to attention and he trotted down the narrow hall toward Trent's voice. I went into Trent's room and turned on the light. I was surprised at how…clinical it looked. The walls were bare. The bedding was plain. It was less personal than a hotel room. It was…sad.

I sat down on the bed and took a deep breath. As I exhaled, I let out the feelings I had been holding in. A flood of tears streamed from my eyes. It had been painful and difficult to see Barry again. I had wondered how I would feel when it finally happened, and it had been as bad as I had imagined. That man had tortured me for so long that now all it took was the mere thought of him to send me into a fit of anxiety. Seeing him again just brought all of those vile memories and horrible feelings of dread and despair boiling back to the surface. I had hoped facing him again would help to ease some of the damage he had done – like ripping off a bandage – but it did nothing but reopen the wound.

But Trent – glorious, wonderful Trent – had stood up for me when I couldn't. He had taken on a burden that wasn't his to take for the sake of my sanity. I pulled the holster out of the back of my blue jeans and laid it on the bedside stand. Barry had been the reason I had bought that gun in the first place. He was the reason I had acquired a concealed weapons permit. It wasn't because I was vengeful or trigger happy. It was because I was terrified. But now that I had Trent around, I didn't have to be nearly so afraid. It wasn't because he was a man and I was a woman. It wasn't as simple or sexist as that. It was because I knew I could count on him when I needed him. I knew he would put himself in harm's way in order to keep me safe. He'd already done it on more than one occasion. In just a short period of time, Trent had become the best friend I was never allowed to have.

I awoke to the gentle caress of fingers brushing hair from my forehead. My eyes shot open. I hadn't realized I'd fallen asleep.

"Did you have a good rest, Wyatt Earp?" Trent asked with a grin. He was standing next to the bed, looking down at me. He nodded toward the .45 on the bedside stand.

"Oh, ha ha," I laughed humorlessly. "What time is it? How long was I asleep?"

"About two hours. I got carried away with my research for a while before I realized you still hadn't emerged from my room yet."

"I'm sorry. I didn't mean to take your bed from you."

"No, it's all right. I don't use it."

"Why not? How is it that you never sleep?"

"I do sleep. Just not nearly as much as everyone else. It's absurd to me to think of wasting six hours a day just lying around."

"I need eight."

"Good lord! How do you get anything done?"

"I know. It's pretty inconvenient," I agreed.

"I get a good hour or two of sleep every few days, and I'm good to go. It's amazing how much you can get done in one go when you don't have to go to bed at night."

"Don't you ever just lie down and relax? It seems like you're always running around or pacing or calculating or waving your arms about like a madman. I don't think I've ever seen you lie down just for the sake of relaxation or contemplation."

"I don't need to lie down to contemplate. And yes, I sit in a chair and read to relax. I'm not *always* running around."

I scooted over and patted the bed beside me. "Sit. You're making me nervous looming over me like that," I teased.

Trent looked mildly uncomfortable all of a sudden. He sat down and folded his hands in his lap awkwardly.

"Am I making you uncomfortable?" I asked.

"No. Well, yes. A little."

"Why?"

"Because I feel like you're putting me in a 'sit down, we need to talk' kind of situation. You aren't going to tell me I'm adopted, are you?"

142

I laughed. "Everything is fine. It's just exhausting watching you sometimes because you're always so annoyingly full of energy."

Trent kicked his giant shoes off and swung his legs up onto the bed, leaning back with his hands folded behind his head onto the pillow. "There, relaxed enough for you?" he asked as he turned and smiled at me.

My body suddenly became aware of his closeness to me. I rolled onto my back to look at the ceiling because I was afraid my cheeks were about to turn beet red.

"Is something the matter?" Trent asked.

"No. I just…I can't think of anything to say now. Isn't that funny how that happens?" I sounded like an idiot.

"Am I making *you* uncomfortable?" he asked.

"No, you're fine. It's just that I had things I wanted to say to you. Things to ask you. And suddenly it's all…poof…gone."

"It's probably more relaxing if you aren't talking the whole time anyway," Trent said.

"Damn, you always know the right thing to say," I commented sarcastically.

"I know. It's your favorite thing about me."

"It really isn't."

We sat in silence for a while, and finally, I felt comfortable enough to roll over and face Trent without worrying about blushing. When he turned his head to look at me, it struck me at just how much my eyes enjoyed gazing at that face of his. The longer I knew him, the more handsome he became to me. How could I have ever not noticed how handsome he was? All I saw now was the delightful way he swooped his hair; the dimpled smile that made you feel like he was smiling just for you; the twinkle of mischief in his eye whenever something clever occurred to him; and the strong, masculine squareness of his jawline. The features I used to view as faults, like his big feet, bowed legs, and rather big ears, were now endearing.

It was time to admit it to myself. I was absolutely, unquestionably in love with Trent Morgan.

Chapter 10

"You're looking at me funny," Trent said, ruining the moment per usual.

"No I'm not."

"Yes, you are. You look like you have something you want to say."

"I don't. Oh wait! Yes I do. Why don't you have any pictures on the walls?" I asked, finally remembering one of the things I had wanted to ask him.

He looked up at the ceiling. "I don't have any pictures to hang."

"Six hundred years and countless adventures, but no pictures?"

"Nope. I don't need pictures. If I want to see something, I go see it."

"What about people, though? You don't have any pictures of people you care about?"

"No."

"Why not?"

"I'm not exactly a popular fellow."

"There must be *someone*."

Trent looked over at me with a smile. "There is."

I tried to calm the flutter in my heart. "I mean someone else."

Trent looked back up at the ceiling again and sighed. "Yes, I have had some friends throughout the years. But I don't keep their pictures."

"Why not?"

"Guilt, mostly. I outlive everyone, Roselyn. They die, and I keep going, and then I forget. It's not because I want to forget – I've told you how it works. I used to keep pictures, back when I was younger. But the first time I saw a photo of someone hanging on my wall and I didn't know who it was, I got rid of all of them. It's painful to lose a friend, but it fills you with the worst guilt you can imagine when you see a picture of someone you're sure was a friend of yours, and you have no memories of the time you shared together. That's how the dead live on – in memories – and I can't even provide them that."

"Why don't you keep a journal to help you remember? You obviously already keep some journals."

"I do keep journals, but only for certain subjects – things that help me keep history straight. If I kept a journal for everything, could you imagine the sheer number of journals I would have? I'd never be able to keep up on them. Besides, it doesn't help me remember. Like I said, those memories are gone. It's really no better than keeping photos on the wall at that point. It just becomes another story."

"What's wrong with being a story?"

A saw a sad smile cross Trent's lips. "Because it's always a sad ending."

I reached over and slid my hand into his. I didn't know what else to do to comfort him.

He turned and looked at me. "There is one friend, though, that I just can't seem to forget. Even after two hundred years and four changes, she's still stuck in my head after first meeting her." I started to smile, but then he added, "I think it was the terrible singing. I just can't erase that terrible singing from my memory."

I gasped in feigned horror. "I can't believe you remember that! Why would you remember that, of all things?!"

He laughed. "Good lord, how could I *forget*? And those sweatpants! What did they say? 'Luscious'?"

I giggled. "Bootylicious."

"Yes! Bootylicious. I rather fancied those sweatpants."

"I bet you did," I teased.

"If only you hadn't been all doe-eyed for someone else..." he said, jokingly.

I hesitated. "Do you really not remember?" I asked.

"All I remember is that it wasn't me."

"It was, actually," I confessed quietly.

Trent furrowed his brow at me. "What do you mean?"

I could feel my cheeks reddening. "It *was* you...*this* you," I said, gesturing to him.

It was like Trent suddenly put up a wall between us and closed himself off. "Oh." He swung his legs over the side of the bed and sat up. "No, I don't remember that part."

I sat up. "Where are you going?"

"Those journals aren't going to go through themselves. Work to do!"

"Wait!" I grabbed his arm as he stood up, stopping him from walking away.

"Please let me go," he said sternly, avoiding eye contact with me.

I climbed off the bed and stood next to him, continuing to hold his arm defiantly. "Why? Why are you running off all of a sudden?"

Trent looked at the floor instead of at me. "I don't want to do something we'll both end up regretting." He was breathing heavily.

"Like what?" I demanded.

Trent sighed. A strange look washed over his face – a look of both defeat and relief. It was the look of someone who was finally giving in to something they'd been fighting for a long time.

"Like this." He turned to me and cupped my face with his hands. His mouth was on mine in an instant, his tongue searching out mine.

I felt a surge of lust rush through my body. His kiss was passionate and needful, and it was making my knees feel weak. There was a tingling sensation that started in my chest and shot all the way down to my pelvis. I cast aside my inhibitions and reached up and started unbuttoning his suit jacket, slipping it off over his shoulders. He leaned into me, and I could feel his rigidity pressing against me through his trousers, which sent another surge of desire through my veins. He leaned down and kissed the side of my neck as his hands slid down and around to my backside. He cupped my buttocks and squeezed before running one hand around to the front of my jeans. As I felt his fingertips pulling at the waistband, it finally struck me that this was actually happening. He intended to take it all the way.

I pulled away from him briefly to pull my shirt off over my head, and I climbed back onto the bed. I grabbed his tie and pulled him down to me, and he climbed onto the bed over top of me. His mouth found mine again as he pressed himself between my legs. His hand slid under my bra and explored the soft mounds beneath. Everywhere he touched he left a trail of fire that fueled the burning lust in my loins. His lips left mine and moved to my neck, caressing the tender skin sensually as they made their way to my bosom. He unhooked the clasp of my bra and cast it aside as his hot, wet tongue descended upon my breasts. I arched my back and tossed my head back, submitting to him fully.

He kissed my neck again briefly before sitting back and loosening his tie. As he undressed in front of me, I could see the wild desire burning in his eyes as he looked at me. I'd never felt so wanted in all of my life. After he kicked off his trousers, he tugged at mine. I assisted him as he slid my jeans down over my hips, my panties coming off with them. He tossed the clothes aside and finally lowered his boxers, releasing his manhood. His giant feet made a lot more sense to me now.

He mounted me, his long bangs dangling down against my forehead, and he looked into my eyes intensely. His waist was poised between my legs, but he hesitated.

"Are you ready for me?" he whispered.

I nodded in consent, my anticipation and excitement rising.

That was all he needed. I felt his manhood pressing against my opening, and slowly, little by little, he entered me. It had been so long since I'd been with a man that it took my body a while to accommodate him. But once he was completely sheathed within me, it wasn't long before I felt a pleasant ache in my abdomen. I could feel the sensation growing in intensity, and I urged Trent on. As he quickened his pace, I entwined my fingers in his hair and buried my face in his shoulder. I bucked my hips wildly against his as I felt an explosion of pleasure and a cry of ecstasy escaped my lips. My response to him was enough to put Trent over the tipping point, and a guttural moan emanated from his throat as he found his release.

We lay there for several minutes afterward, panting and shuddering from the pleasant aftershocks, before Trent rolled over onto his back next to me. I turned to look at him, a smile on my face. It quickly faded, though, when I saw him wipe his hand down his face in a gesture he only made when he was feeling stressed.

"I can't believe I did that to you. I shouldn't have done that."

My heart sank. I felt completely rejected. "That bad, hey?" I snapped.

He turned to me. "No! No, not that at all! That was…that was brilliant! Fantastic! Which is why I shouldn't have done that." He sat up and moved to the edge of the bed. He reached for his boxers and slid them on as he stood up. "We can't do this again," he added as he grabbed his pants off the floor.

"Why the hell not? What's wrong?" I demanded angrily.

He turned to me as he zipped up his pants. His face looked troubled. "I knew it back then, and I know it now: you and I won't work. For some reason, though, I just can't seem to let you be. We can't be more than friends. It has to be this way, Roselyn."

"But…what the hell was all of this, then?!" I said, gesturing to the bed in general.

"This was me losing control. This was me not keeping a handle on my feelings. This was me inadvertently hurting you. I didn't mean for this to happen."

"Are we going to need to revisit the discussion we had on what 'I didn't mean it' really means? Because you most certainly did mean for this to happen," I said as I started furiously grabbing my clothes off the floor and getting dressed.

"Wanting something to happen and meaning for it to happen aren't the same thing."

"Then help me understand, will you? You wanted to do this, but you didn't mean to do it? How does that make any sense?"

"I want you, Roselyn! I do! I always have! But this," he said as he pointed between himself and me repeatedly, "wouldn't be fair to either of us."

"Why not?"

"Think about it! What do you want? At the end of the day, who do you want to spend your life with? What does it involve? Kids? I can't have kids. I was specifically designed to be sterile. A husband who climbs into bed and sleeps next to you all night? I can't do that. Someone who grows old with you? I can't do that either. Hell, I might not always be me! I could change at any time – today, or thirty years from now – and neither of us will have any idea who I will be when I wake. Will I be someone you can love, or will I have changed so much that you can't love me anymore? Will you even see me as *me* anymore?

"You know what the worst part is, Roselyn?" he continued. "The worst part is that I will either have to watch you grow old and die while I live on, or I will have to watch you fall out of love with the person I become. Either way, it's a heartache that I don't think I can possibly endure. You and I are so wrong for each other that it's almost funny. So what on Earth makes you think that this would ever be a good idea for either of us? I make a great friend, but I would make a lousy partner. Domestic life

151

suits me ill, and my life would be dangerous for you. It was selfish of me to give in to my desire for you, and for that I deeply apologize. I just…I just wish I could be man you need and deserve."

The heartbroken way he looked at me shattered me. He'd meant everything he said. I was angry and hurt and I wanted to fight with him and argue that he was wrong, but I just couldn't – because he was right. I hated that he was right, but he was. *Damn, here come the tears again.*

I quickly swiped away the tear that rolled down my cheek and hurried from the room without saying a word. I didn't know where everything was in his apartment, so I just went into the nearest nook I could find, which happened to be the kitchen. I saw a teapot sitting near the stove, so I started looking through his cupboards for tea. I needed a hot cup of comfort right about now.

"There isn't much to be found in there, I'm afraid," Trent said from the kitchen entry.

"I'm just looking for tea," I said flatly.

Trent walked into the kitchen and came up next to me. I instantly reacted by assuming he was going to hug me or touch me in some way, but he simply reached up into the cupboard over my head and pulled out a container of teabags. I immediately felt foolish and took a discreet step back.

I reached for the container, but he held it away from me. "Go have a seat in the library. I can make the tea," he said softly without looking at me.

I found my way back to the library through blurry tears and sat down in his chair at his desk. I didn't know how to feel. I had just made love with the man I have so utterly and completely fallen for, and whom I'm certain has feelings for me, yet here I was in tears, knowing that I was never going to be able to hold on to him. I should have let him walk away when he had tried to leave the room. He was right that we shouldn't have done that, because now it was even more painful knowing I could never have him again. But he was wrong about one thing: I didn't truly regret it. Maybe I should, but if I was never going to have him again, I took solace in the fact that he and I had shared that experience – that bond – together. It wasn't going to make things any easier going forward, though.

I dabbed my eyes and looked down at the journals spread open on the desk. The text was hand-written, and the pages were yellowed with age. It was written in a language I didn't recognize. I opened another journal from the stack and found the same handwriting. What did he need these for? How was this going to help him figure out who was following us?

I heard Trent walking down the hall, so I closed the journal. I found my composure and put on a brave face. I didn't want him to see the damage he had done. He walked into the room with a cup of tea in one hand and Cattiel draped over the other arm.

"I bring you offerings," he said as he set the tea in front of me and handed me the ornery cat. He gave me a hesitant smile, as if he wasn't sure if it was ok to smile at me yet.

I squeezed Cattiel and rested my cheek on the top of his head while he growled at me. "Oh, I love you too," I said to the cat, but when I saw Trent visibly tense up, I made sure to add, "kitty."

Trent continued to stand near me, but he didn't speak. There was a tension in the air that neither of us knew how to clear. I decided to do what I always did – ignore the problem and hope it goes away.

"What are these journals for?" I asked, trying to keep my sniffling to a minimum.

"Oh! Those are my notes. I have to keep notes on all of my dealings with SABER so I don't lose any important information and details that might be of use later on. I was looking through them to see if I've ever had anything like this happen before."

"Find anything?"

"Not yet, but I still have the rest of that stack to go through."

"What language is this?" I asked. "I don't recognize it."

"You wouldn't. It's Unilang. It's like the metric system for language, but it doesn't exist in your time yet."

"I thought Latin was like the metric system for language."

"Eh, in a way, I guess. But how many people do you know that actually speak Latin? Everyone speaks Unilang in the time I come from."

"What time is that, exactly?"

"I was created in the year 2886."

"Wow. I never thought the human race would last that long, honestly."

"Things do get a bit dodgy here and there between your time and mine, but humans are a rather persistent lot."

"How far into the future have you gone? Have you seen if we ever do get wiped out?"

"I don't venture past my own time unless my device detects an anomaly that I have to investigate."

"How can it know that something is wrong in the future if you don't go there?"

"The funny thing about time is that cause and effect don't flow in just one direction. The future affects the past, too, so if something in the future is changed from what it is supposed to be, it can cause ripple effects backward through history."

"I still don't understand why you don't go to the future. Aren't you curious?"

"Of course. But that's unknown territory, and there's always a possibility I could end up throwing a monkey wrench into the natural progression of events if I insert myself into the future. You see, time and events aren't necessarily set in stone until they are experienced. It's kind of like Schrodinger's cat. You are both alive and dead until you open your own box. Whatever you see on the inside is what becomes reality for you. However, it's the events that lead up to you opening that box that determine the outcome, and if you open the box too early, out of sequence, well…you never know what outcome you're going to be stuck with, and how it's going to affect the past."

"You insert yourself into the past and change things. How is that any different?"

"I'm a pretty good judge of what kind of changes will be catastrophic and what kind won't be because I have knowledge of what events are supposed to occur. I lose that advantage if I visit the future."

"What about other planets? There must be other habitable planets like this one out there in the universe. Have you ever teleported off Earth?"

"No. I'm not saying I couldn't, but I'd need to know the exact location I was teleporting to, and, as of yet, I have no such information."

"Really? You're from almost nine hundred years in the future, and we still haven't colonized other planets? What about Mars?"

"You lot have a bad habit of getting distracted by war and politics, not to mention the whole global warming catastrophe. Suffice it to say things happened. Mars took a backburner for a while."

"We haven't even made it to Mars yet?"

"Oh, yeah, we did go to Mars. Didn't go well."

"So, we just gave up?"

"No, not exactly. We're just working on making it more…habitable."

"Terraforming?"

"Bingo."

"But doesn't that take, like, forever?"

"Aye. Now you know why we don't have a colony on Mars."

"Couldn't you steal a space suit and go check it out? Just for a little bit?"

"I might alter something that shouldn't be altered."

"You know, for someone who claims to live so dangerously, you sure do set some restrictive limits on yourself."

"I don't play fast and loose with the fate of humankind."

The cat in my lap started to fuss, so I set him on the floor and got up from Trent's chair. As I reached for my tea, intending to take it and move to the chair over by the bookshelves, I bumped the cup and accidentally sloshed some tea onto Trent's opened journal.

"Oh shit!" I exclaimed. I used my shirt sleeve to quickly dab up the tea on the page.

Trent objected to my method. "Not your shirt, Roselyn! It's fine, just leave it!"

"I'm so sorry," I apologized.

"It's fine. It's just a little tea. These journals have seen worse." Trent came over and pulled a handkerchief from his pocket. He stood next to me as he wiped up the mess I had made. His tendency to stand in close proximity to me, I noticed, was becoming a problem for me. I wanted to touch him, and I wanted him to touch me. Images of us together flooded my brain, and I couldn't stop them. I quickly stepped away from him.

He seemed to notice my abrupt retreat, but he didn't comment on it. Instead, he said, "I should probably get back to reading. Are you sure you aren't hungry or tired? You do realize it's the middle of the night, right?"

"I know. I'm fine. Do your reading so you can get this figured out…so I can go home."

"As you wish," he replied with a hint of dejection in his tone.

I browsed the books on his shelves, and found an odd array of titles. He had classics, like *Wuthering Heights* and *Jane Eyre*, but he also had books I'd never heard of and books in different languages. I finally chose *Pride and Prejudice* and settled into the only other chair in the room. It wasn't until I sat in it that I discovered it was a rocking chair. It made a slight creak when it rocked, but it wasn't terribly loud and didn't bother me. I curled one foot under my other leg and left one foot on the floor to rock the chair. It wasn't long before I heard Trent plop his journal onto his desk loudly. I glanced over at him, and found he was staring at me with aggravation.

"Must you?" he asked.

"What?"

"The chair. Don't you hear the creaking?"

"It's not that bad."

"It really is."

"It's not bothering me."

"It's bothering me."

"If it bothers you, then why do you have a chair that creaks?"

"It didn't creak last time I was here."

He and I stared at each other in silence. Finally, he broke eye contact and looked back down at his journal.

Creak.

I couldn't help myself.

Trent exhaled loudly and looked at me from under his eyebrows.

"Oops."

I waited a little longer this time, until he was really starting to get focused.

Creak.

Trent stood up abruptly, startling me. "Ok, we're leaving. Grab the cat…and his box."

"Where are we going?"

"To a house that doesn't have a creaky rocking chair."

Chapter 11

When we arrived at the new place, we were in yet another small library. "How many places do you have?" I asked.

"Several."

"Do they all have a library?"

"Shouldn't every home?"

I put the cat down and stuck his box in the corner temporarily. "So, tell me about this place."

"Alaska – 2515. And this is an actual house, not a flat. You can pick a room," he said as he sat down at his new desk and laid out his stack of journals.

"Why Alaska?"

"It's still fairly remote. I don't like a lot of attention, so I either choose a location that's so busy that no one will notice me, or so remote that no one is around to notice me."

"How do you afford all of these places?" I said as I started browsing through the books on the bookshelves.

"I told you. I have my ways. I'm very clever."

"But how? Do you steal it?"

"Not technically, unless cheating counts. I take advantage of the stock market and I gamble."

"Like in a casino?"

"And the lottery. It's quite easy when you can get the winning numbers whenever you want."

"Oh. Well, that's not so bad. I thought you were hacking bank accounts or something."

Trent shrugged. "I'm not going to say it's never happened."

"So you are a criminal!" I said accusingly.

"Not necessarily. I just don't remember if I've done it or not…and it kind of sounds like something I would do."

As I looked through the books, I found *The Time Machine* by H.G. Wells. "Is this really why you're afraid to go to the future?" I asked, holding the book up to him.

"What, because I'm afraid I'll find a dystopia with underground savages? No, more like I'm afraid that I'll be the one who's set the events into motion that result in a dystopia with underground savages."

I put the book back on the shelf and grabbed *Through the Looking-Glass*. I took it and curled up in the oversized blue chair near Trent's desk.

"Aren't you going to go to bed?" he asked.

"I'm not tired," I lied.

In truth, I was exhausted, but I didn't want to be alone with my thoughts. I knew if I went to bed, I would just lie there feeling homesick and heartbroken. There was an ache in my chest that was being kept at bay as long as I was near Trent, and I was afraid of what it would feel like if I left his side. I knew I was going to have to face these feelings eventually, but not tonight.

I opened the book and started reading while Trent flipped through his journals. I had a hard time keeping my eyes open by the time I got to the second page, and I was out cold before I ever reached page three.

When I awoke, I noticed I was covered with a blanket that I hadn't had before. I looked over and saw Trent was still sitting at his desk, but the journals had been moved aside. He now had papers scattered over the desk in front of him and he was furiously writing and sketching on them.

"What are you doing?" I asked groggily.

"Good morning, 'I'm-Not-Tired,'" he teased. "I'm planning."

"You found something?"

"I did. Apparently, I have acquaintances in SABER who were secretly working with me to bring it all down – moles, if you will. I had forgotten about them. If I can get some materials from them, I can build a cloaking device to install in your house to keep it off of SABER's radar. You'll be safe at home again."

"Why weren't we safe there, but we're safe in all these other places you have?"

"When I time travel, it leaves a brief 'trail' that can be followed if you have the right technology. If SABER has a time-travel device, it's entirely possible that they had the technology to track me from the Jurassic to your house."

"But what about from my house to the other places we went?"

"The 'trail' disappears quite quickly, so I'm fairly certain that if they did follow us to your house, the trail we left when we teleported out of there would've disappeared before they could get there."

"If they were going to follow us, wouldn't they have shown up at my house already?"

"Not necessarily. That's the fun thing about time travel. But this cloaking device should essentially give them a dead-end or a redirection on their 'trail.' You'll be safe to go home."

"I wonder if I'll still have a job when I get back."

"Why wouldn't you?"

"How long have I been gone? I never called in. People get fired for that, Trent."

"You didn't miss anything. Time traveler, remember?" he said as he pointed to himself. "Now, I have to grab a quick shower and get ready for the day. I have places to go, people to see!"

"What about me?"

"You can shower after I do. The water heaters in 2515 are much better than the ones from your time."

"No, I mean what am I going to do? I'm coming with you, right?"

"I'm not taking you anywhere near a SABER compound."

"You're not leaving me behind."

"Yes, I am."

"Hey, you're the one who asked me to go somewhere with you. What fun is that if you leave me behind?"

"This isn't going to be fun. Besides, I'll be right back."

"I'm going."

Trent sighed and ran his hand through his hair. "Why would you want to?"

"Because I don't know if I'm going to see you again after this," I confessed.

"Why wouldn't you see me again?"

I gave him a knowing look. "I'm not stupid. When you get the 'let's just be friends' speech, it never ends in friendship. It just ends. You're going to drop me off and never come back."

"I wouldn't do that," he said defensively as his brows snapped together.

"You're taking me with you, and that's that." I said with finality.

"Fine! Fine. Whatever. I'm going to go shower," he said as he turned to leave the room.

"Leave the watch," I ordered.

"Damn it."

I held his watch hostage while I got ready for the day to ensure he didn't sneakily leave without me. When I had showered and dressed, I returned it to him. He seemed incredibly relieved when I handed it back to him.

"I've never gone this long without my device," he admitted. "I feel a bit helpless without it. You didn't go galivanting around in the future with it, did you?"

"If I knew how to use it, I might've."

"Good thing you don't know how, then," he said. He pulled a small device that resembled a tiny hearing aid out of his pocket and handed it to me. "You'll need this before we go. Put it in your ear."

I grabbed it and did what I was told. "What is it?"

"A translator. Can you understand me?"

"Yes, why wouldn't I?"

"I'm speaking Unilang. Good, you must have it in properly. Are you ready?" he asked, holding his arm out to me.

I hesitated. "Will the teleport still work the same if we just hold hands?"

Trent looked wounded. "Oh. Well, I suppose so, as long as we are making physical contact. You still have to stand near me, though. Is…is that going to be a problem?" he asked.

His expression hurt my heart, but so did being close to him. "I'm sure it'll be fine." I held my hand out to grasp his and stood next to him. Out of the corner of my eye, I saw him give me a questioning sideways glance, but I pretended I didn't see it. He held up the hand I was holding, as it was the one with the watch on it, and pressed the button to teleport us.

We arrived in a cold, dark room with what felt like a concrete floor. My eyes hadn't had time to adjust to the lack of light before Trent started moving. I clutched his hand and stumbled along behind him, unable to see where we were going. Finally, however, I noticed we were moving toward a small red light. I could make out what appeared to be a doorway next to it. By the time we approached the door, my eyes had become accustomed to the darkness, and I could see the light was some kind of indicator for an ID scanner. Trent held up his watch, pressed some buttons, and the light turned green. The door opened and revealed a brightly lit elevator with shiny white, metallic-looking walls.

"How did you do that?" I whispered.

"I have a thing that does a thing," he said, flashing a smile at me.

"Where are we headed?"

"Quit talking," he said with a finger over his lips.

He led me through the door into the elevator. He looked at his watch briefly, then entered a code into the digital display on the inside of the door. The elevator began its descent.

"Down? I thought we—"

The doors opened and Trent quickly cupped his hand over my mouth and backed himself against the wall to our right, pulling me backward against him firmly. He craned his neck and took a quick look out the door before releasing me. He looked at me with a stern expression and put his finger over his lips again. I raised my eyebrows and grimaced to as though to say "oops." Then I pointed to the watch and tried to use my hands ask why we weren't teleporting where we needed to be. Trent looked perplexed by my wild gesturing.

I sighed and looked around before whispering. "Teleport?"

He shook his head but offered no explanation. He grabbed my hand again and led me quickly down a hospital-like corridor, glancing down at his watch often. We zigged and zagged down one corridor to the next, looking through doors and trying to evade detection. It was hard to walk quietly on squeaky-clean floors, and I desperately wished I had worn different sneakers for this mission.

"Hey! Where's your synsuit?" I heard a man yell behind us. Adrenaline instantly shot through my veins.

Trent whirled around, eyes wide.

There was a man standing in the hallway behind us, wearing a weird gray unitard-like outfit. It was a glossy material, and it covered him from head to toe, except his face. He looked rather ridiculous – like a big, shiny Teletubby.

"Please tell me you're Rick Rodriguez," Trent said hopefully.

The man gave us a strange look. "Do I know you?"

"Perhaps. But you probably knew me when I had a different face."

"...Trent?"

"That depends. Are you Rick?"

"I am. Wow, you *really* changed this time, didn't you? You don't remember me?"

"Sorry, mate. It's nothing personal. Listen, I need your help."

Rick ushered us into the hidden door he had emerged from. It was camouflaged to blend in to the wall, and you couldn't see it at all until he waved his hand over a small, barely visible sensor on it. It looked like the wall just opened inward, and we walked into a bright, circular-shaped room.

"Shayla, you won't believe who just showed up," Rick said.

A woman stepped out of a doorway to our left. She was tall and thin, and she was wearing the same ridiculous "synsuit" that Rick was wearing.

"Who are these people? Why aren't they wearing synsuits?" She demanded huffily.

"Shayla, it's Trent! He changed again," Rick marveled.

The look of irritation on Shayla's face drained away. For a moment she looked pleased, but then it faded into a look of sadness. "Trent," she said softly. Then she looked at me. "Who's your friend?" she asked curtly, her face returning to an expression of irritation.

"This is Roselyn Wolff. You must be Shayla Benlock."

"You ask that like you don't already know it."

"I'm afraid I don't," he replied apologetically. He pointed to his head. "Memories don't have the same longevity as I do."

"It's only been three years since we saw you last," Shayla said, sounding offended.

"For you. It's been just a *tad* longer than that for me," he said, holding his thumb and forefinger close together.

Shayla shot daggers at me. "Why did you bring a guest?" she asked Trent tersely.

"She's under my protection. I seem to have gotten her into a bit of a pickle."

"You're good at that," Shayla said reproachfully. "You shouldn't have brought her here."

Rick turned to Trent and tried to alleviate the tension. "So, what brings you here anyway, Trent? What did you need? I can't imagine we have much time for catching up."

"Probably not. I used the watch to scramble the signals from the monitors in the halls so the men upstairs didn't see us, but I'm sure they'll soon figure out something unusual is going on. Listen, I need some supplies. I was wondering if you could help me out," Trent said, looking at Rick hopefully.

Rick, Shayla, and Trent discussed what he needed and how they were going to get it while I stood off to the side feeling useless. I didn't understand any of what they were talking about, and it made me feel dumb. It also reminded me just how out of my depth I was with Trent.

The plan was set, and Trent went in the other room to don a synsuit. I laughed when he walked out and did a little spin.

"How do I look?" he asked.

"Ridiculous," I said. Then I noticed the glare I was getting from Shayla. "Sorry, no offense," I apologized with an inward cringe. "You guys look great. It's just him," I backpedaled. It wasn't working, so I just stopped talking.

"Roselyn," Trent said to me, "I'm going to grab some supplies with Rick, and you're going to stay here and help Shayla. I'll be back in a jiff." He and Rick left the room.

I turned to Shayla and forced a smile. "What can I help you with?"

"Nothing. I'll do it myself," she snapped as she started to turn away. "Besides, your Old American English is annoying to try to understand."

"What is your problem with me?" I blurted. "You don't know anything about me."

"Yeah, I do. You're my replacement."

"Excuse me?"

"I see the way you look at him. You like him, and you think he likes you. Well, I've got news for you, honey. You're dust in the wind to him. A flash in the pan. Temporary. He doesn't love you, and he never will. And apparently, he'll forget you just like that," she said with an angry snap of her fingers.

I felt the sting of jealousy. "You and Trent...?"

"Yeah. And I've put my reputation on the line for him time and time again to help him. And he doesn't even remember me now," Shayla said bitterly. "Do yourself a favor and don't fall in love with that one. He's a waste of your time, and you're a waste of his. He'll only hurt you in the end. He's incapable of anything else."

Shayla walked into the other room and started sorting through drawers. I stood there, feeling like a fool. Jealousy filled my heart, and Shayla's warnings resonated through my brain. Everything kept telling me to run as far away from Trent as I could, as fast as I could, but every ounce of my being wanted to be with him. I already knew that he and I weren't ever going to work out, but there was still one little piece of me that had been holding out hope. However, Shayla had just stomped out that remaining ember. I still loved him, of course, but as I watched the woman in the other room sniffling as she rummaged through

168

drawers, I felt like I was looking into my own future. I had to let him go now so I could move on.

When Trent and Rick returned, I had a hard time pretending everything was all right. Trent noticed – I could tell from the questioning glances he was throwing my way – but he didn't ask. We collected what we needed and off we went, back to 2515.

"That went much more smoothly than expected," Trent said as he deposited his bounty onto his desk. "Well, other than landing in the wrong place inside the compound. How lucky was it that Rick found us?" Trent said with a chuckle.

"Pretty lucky," I said flatly. I removed the translator from my ear and set it on the desk. "Can I go home now?"

Trent gave me a concerned look. "Is everything all right?"

"I just want to go home."

Trent looked at his desk. "I'll have it together in a few hours, and then I can take you home."

"Good." I turned on my heel and walked out of the room.

I found my way to the kitchen and looked through the cupboards. I still wasn't hungry, but I knew I needed to eat something. I found a package of snack cakes and a tin of sardines. I decided the snack cakes were probably a safer bet. I sat down at the table and ripped open the crinkly plastic.

"Ooh! Throw me one!" I heard Trent yell from the library. He must have heard me tearing into the plastic.

I got back up and grabbed one and looked down the hall. Trent was coming up the hallway toward me. He stopped and held out his hands, so I tossed it to him.

"Thanks, love," he said as he turned and walked away.

169

Why did he have to say things like that? Why did he have to add little terms of endearment that weakened my resolve? I don't think he realized that that's what he was doing, but it was frustrating, nonetheless. It wasn't going to be easy to do what I had to do, but it was necessary. He could call me "love" all he wanted but it wasn't going to change the fact that I had to leave him.

I went back into the library when I was done eating and grabbed *Through the Looking-Glass* from the seat where I had left it earlier today. I sat down and started reading to pass the time until Trent could take me home. He tried to strike up conversation with me here and there as he worked, but I limited my responses to one-word answers. After a while, Trent seemed to get the message that I didn't want to talk, and he left me alone. I didn't want to engage with him enough to allow him to change my mind. I was leaving, and that was that. My heart would just have to deal with it.

Finally, he finished his device. "Ta-da! Look at that!" he held up the device and shouted enthusiastically. "One cloaking device for a Miss Roselyn Wolff!"

I got out of my chair and put the book back on the shelf. "Great. Let me get Cattiel and you can take me home."

I gathered up my things and the cat and met Trent in the library. I avoided his eyes as I allowed him to put his arm around me (I had no free hand for holding), letting myself inwardly enjoy that last little feeling of closeness to him. When we arrived at my home, however, I quickly ducked out from under his arm and headed to my room to put away my things. He went to work installing the cloaking device.

After several minutes, I heard him yell, "It's up and running!"

I stepped out of my room and met him in the space where the hallway, living room, and kitchen all connected.

"You are officially off the radar," Trent said with a proud smile.

"Cool. Thanks. I appreciate it."

His smile faded. "You're welcome," he replied.

We stood in silence for a few moments, with him looking at me while I looked at everything but him.

"So, I've brought you back to the night we left…after the Barry incident, of course. Someone is coming to tow the truck, so it should be out of your way before you leave for work in the morning," he said.

"Perfect. Sounds good."

"Roselyn, what's going on?"

I sighed. "It's time to just rip off the band-aid, Trent. Dragging this out isn't going to make it any better."

Trent furrowed his brow. "What are you talking about?"

"You need to go."

"Ok but—"

"And never come back."

Chapter 12

Trent looked absolutely crushed, and it killed me. "Oh. Well, all right. Ok," he said, clasping his hands together. "I…um…I guess…I guess that's it, then?"

"I guess so."

"Can I still—"

"No. Just leave me alone from now on. I appreciate your help, but I didn't sign up for all of this. I like you Trent, I really do. But there's no point to this. I can't be 'just friends' with you. If you're around, I can't move on with my life. So…I need to remove you from it." I tried to keep my voice from shaking and the tears from falling from my eyes.

"I understand," Trent said quietly. He smiled at me sadly. "I'll be on my way then, I suppose. I'll miss you, Roselyn." He opened his arms to me and approached me for a hug.

Even though it shattered my heart to do it, I held my hand up to stop him and took a step back. I then offered my hand to shake his. Trent paused and looked at me like I had just stabbed him in the heart. He took my hand and shook it briefly.

"I'm sorry…for everything. I won't bother you anymore. It was never my intention to cause you grief." Trent stepped back and smiled at me, and it was somehow the most forlorn expression I had ever seen. And then he was gone.

I crumpled to the floor. The tears flowed and my chest heaved as I sobbed. The ache in my chest I had been trying to keep at bay finally consumed me. There was nothing quite like the pain of a broken heart. No, it wasn't the end of the world – but at the moment, it felt like it. I knew it was for the best to get it over with now, though. My feelings for Trent would've only gotten stronger the longer I was with him, and it only would've hurt more if I'd waited.

I turned off all the lights and climbed into my bed. I wasn't expecting to sleep – I just wanted to bury myself in fluffy blankets and cry. I missed him already. Had I made a huge mistake? My heart kept trying to convince me that I had, but my head knew better. No, this was the right thing to do. I needed to just get it all out and get on with it. But good heavens, did I miss him. I thought about our intimate moment together. Our skin slick with sweat, our bodies sliding, pushing, grinding…his breath hot on my ear as I listened to his panting…inhaling the pleasant smell of his skin as I felt him inside of me, as close to me as another person can get…

And I would never have that with him again. I looked over at my phone on the bedside stand, wanting to call him just to hear his voice. I grabbed my phone and opened up his contact information. I stared at it for several minutes, considering the consequences. And then…I deleted it. If only it were that easy to delete him from my heart.

In the morning, I thought about calling in to work. I looked a fright and I felt even worse. However, I knew it wouldn't do me any good to sit at home and mope for the day. The gym would help distract me from my thoughts. I had a cup of coffee, hugged Cattiel, and walked out to my car. Barry's truck was gone already, as promised. I climbed into my car and headed to work, keeping the radio on the rock station to avoid any sappy love songs that might crumble my composure.

After I worked with my first client of the day, I was feeling a little less emotionally fragile. I glanced down at my watch and noticed that I had a good thirty minutes before my next client's appointment, so I decided it was time to blow off some steam. I strapped on a pair of gloves and made a beeline to the heavy bags. I trained on the heavy bag at least twice a week, but today wasn't training. Today was venting. Today was for *me*. I put all of my frustrations and anger and sorrow into that bag, and by the time I was done, I felt a little better. I took off the gloves and reached for my water bottle with shaky hands.

"Somebody must've pissed you off," I heard a man with a rather deep voice say. *Oh great. Here we go.*

I looked up and the first thing I noticed was his striking green eyes. He was incredibly tall, about 6'5", and in excellent shape – broad-shouldered and narrow-waisted. He looked to be in his late-thirties. He smiled at me, and I couldn't help but admire his lovely teeth. He had long brown hair that he wore pulled back in a manbun. He was kind of beautiful, really.

I shrugged my shoulders at him and didn't respond. I usually avoided conversation with strange men at the gym unless they approached me with a specific question or were clients. I turned away from him and went to take a drink of my water. The steadiness of my hands had been temporarily compromised from my time on the bag, and I realized that about half a second too late. The bottle fell from my hands and clattered to the floor, but

174

not before spraying water right in my face and down my chin. I stood there, water dripping off my chin, hoping that the beautiful man hadn't seen that. I glanced over. He had. He definitely had.

He rushed over and picked up my water bottle for me. "Got the shakes, hey?" he asked as he handed it to me.

"Yeah, a little."

"I'm Sam," he said as he held his hand out to me.

"Roselyn," I said as I shook his hand. Firmly. Businesslike. I could tell from the look in his eyes that my grip startled him, and it gave me an odd satisfaction. It always did. "I'm a trainer here."

"I'm new to the area. Just moved from Kansas."

"You're a long way from Kansas, Dorothy," I mused.

"Oh, no, I'm Sam. Sam Collins," he said, the joke obviously going right over his head.

"No, it's a joke. 'Toto, I've a feeling we're not in Kansas anymore,'" I explained. *Trent would've gotten it immediately,* I thought to myself.

"Oh, ok," he said, still clearly not understanding.

"Well, nice to meet you Sam," I said politely. I turned and started to walk away. I had a new client coming in shortly and I needed to get things wiped down.

"Actually, I think I'm supposed to be meeting with you right now," Sam said.

You've got to be shitting me. I turned back to him. "You have an appointment for 9:00?"

"Yes, ma'am."

"Excuse me for being blunt, but you don't look like you need a trainer."

"I've always had a trainer. I just work better under supervision, I guess," he said with a laugh.

We discussed his previous workout plan and what changes, if any, he wanted to make to tweak it specifically to meet his personal goals. I ran him through a routine, but I felt like I was just there to observe rather than to train. He didn't seem to need much assistance or direction or motivation as he plowed through the workout. I wondered why he would waste the extra money on a trainer he clearly didn't need.

As he toweled off, I said, "Sam, I don't think you need a trainer."

"I just like having someone to push me," he said.

"I barely did anything," I replied.

"It's more of a mentality for me. I go harder when I know someone is expecting me to."

I couldn't fault his reasoning. "Well, then, I have a feeling you're going to be a great client," I said with a laugh.

"Actually, I don't think I want to be your client."

"What? Why?" I asked in surprise.

"Because I'd like to ask you out for coffee sometime, but I have a feeling that's probably against the rules between trainers and their clients."

"Oh. Yeah, that's against the rules."

He raised his eyebrows questioningly at me. "So…if I *wasn't* your client, would you want to?"

I sighed. Oh, what the hell. If nothing else, he'd be a good distraction to keep my mind off Trent.

"Are you married?" I asked. I wasn't about to get in the middle of anything like that.

"No. Divorced."

"I'll tell you what – I'll have you transferred to Roy, and when I get off work after 5:00, I'll stop by the coffee shop across the street. If you're there, cool. But it's not a date. Sound good?"

Sam smiled. "Sounds great."

After work, as I walked across the street, I felt strangely guilty. I felt like I was cheating. I knew it was absurd, especially since Trent and I were never "together." I wondered how he would feel if he knew what I was doing right now. Would he be jealous? No, probably not. He didn't seem like the jealous type. He was probably moving on to a new Shayla or Roselyn anyway…which made me feel instantly jealous just thinking about it.

I forced myself to quit thinking about him as I entered the coffee shop. I saw Sam straight away, standing up from a table in the corner. He waved his hand to get my attention. I held my finger up to indicate I'd be over there in a minute, but he was already approaching.

"I wasn't sure if you were serious or not," he admitted.

"Well, here I am."

I ordered a black coffee, and Sam ordered a bulletproof coffee. I had to stop myself from rolling my eyes. When we sat down, I started in on him about his beverage choice.

"You know that's all shit, right?"

"Bulletproof coffee? No way! It's great for your brain and it burns fat!"

"That is horrible for your heart health. Do you have any idea the saturated fat content in that cup? Do you think high cholesterol and clogged arteries are somehow beneficial to your health?"

"It's keto. Eat fat, burn fat."

"It's rubbish."

Sam gave me a funny look. "Rubbish? Do people really say 'rubbish'?"

Trent always said rubbish. I had to admit, it sounded weird coming from my mouth. It wasn't a word I would've used before I met Trent.

"It's garbage. It's bullshit. I mean yeah, keto works great for some people for short periods of time. But bulletproof coffee? Just…no."

"I feel like we've gotten off on the wrong foot," Sam said.

I sighed. "I'm sorry. I just…ugh, I just hate fad diets. Especially the ones with outrageous claims backed by zero evidence of effectiveness, pushed by people who have zero credentials." I paused. "You know, maybe we should talk about something else. What is it you do, Sam?"

Sam looked relieved to have a change of subject. "I'm a bartender."

"What brought you to Michigan?"

"Family. I had moved to Kansas when I got married, but now that I'm divorced, I didn't really see a reason to stay there. I figured I'd be happier if I was closer to my family and where I grew up."

"Are you? Happier, I mean."

"Yeah. I am," he said with a grin. "I don't get to see my kids as often, though, and that's kind of a bummer."

"You have kids?"

"Three daughters. Eighteen, sixteen, and thirteen years old."

"Oh god, *teenage* girls. I remember being one. I pity you."

"Yeah. I remember being a teenage boy. I pity me, too." I laughed.

"Do you have any kids?" he asked.

"Me? No. I have a cat. I don't think I was really cut out for kids. I barely have this being an adult thing mastered, so I can only imagine what a disaster it would be if I were a parent."

"I know the feeling. You want to know a secret, though? Every parent thinks they're a disaster."

Sam and I sat and talked for a good half hour at the coffee shop. We exchanged numbers before we went our separate ways, though I expected nothing to ever come of it. I had been entirely too unpleasant, I was sure of it. I hadn't meant to be so disagreeable at first, but what was done was done. Besides, I didn't really care if I saw him again. He and I were a mismatch. He was attractive, for sure, but that was the only thing I found appealing about him. I needed more than a pretty face to look at. I needed witty. I needed forgiving. I needed logical. I needed funny – I *really* needed funny. I didn't see those things in Sam. Not yet, anyway.

That was when I realized I was comparing him to Trent. If I was using Trent as my gold standard, no one would ever be good enough, would they? There wasn't anyone else like Trent in all the world and time, of that I was certain. No one could compare to him. I needed to reevaluate my standards, it seemed.

As I climbed into my car and drove home, I felt all the feelings I had been avoiding all day. Now that I was alone, I was overwhelmed with loneliness. I let it overtake me this time, though. Rather than trying to avoid the sad songs on the radio, I sought them out. No amount of male distraction was going to remedy my broken heart. These were feelings I needed to feel.

When I got home, I took a hot shower and put on a pair of sweatpants and my most comfortable ratty sweatshirt. I turned on a sappy movie, grabbed a bottle of wine, and flopped onto the couch next to Cattiel. I was just settling in for a long night of crying when I heard my text notification tone on my phone. I glanced over at it, and was surprised to see it was from Sam. I hesitated before opening the text. What could he possibly have to say to me after our awkward engagement at the coffee shop? I sighed and snatched up the phone.

"Hey there pretty lady."

I rolled my eyes and simply responded with, *"Hey."* If he wanted more than that, he would have to do better than that.

He was quick to reply. *"I had a good time today. Want to do it again?"*

I didn't. Not really. *"Not sure we really clicked."*

"Maybe not yet. One more try? I swear I won't order bulletproof coffee."

I considered it. It wouldn't *hurt* anything, surely. And he *was* handsome. Ugh. *"Fine. Coffee?"* I looked back over my texts. God, I sounded rude. Why couldn't I stop doing that? Why couldn't I just be pleasant?

"Sounds great! Tomorrow after work?"

"Ok."

When the texts stopped, the ache in my chest returned. It was almost unbearable. I drank down a glass of wine in several gulps and poured myself another. By the time I was halfway through my movie and all the way through my bottle of Sangria, I was ready for the pain to stop. I grabbed my phone. It was unscrupulous to take advantage of someone else's interest in me in order to distract myself from my own heartache, I know, but I texted Sam anyway.

"What are you doing right now?" I asked.

"Work."

That's right - he was a bartender. *"Oh ok."*

"You can still text me. Slow night."

"I've been awful to you. I apologize. I'd like to make it up to you. Maybe tomorrow we can do dinner?" I offered.

"That would be fantastic, but are you sure? You didn't even seem all that into coffee a little bit ago."

"I've had time to drink."

"Time to drink?" Sam questioned.

"Think! I've had time to think! Stupid phone! Sorry. Anyway, I think dinner would be a better way to get to know you."

"LOL. Ok! I'm in."

The next day, as I stepped into the quiet restaurant where I was meeting Sam, I swore to myself that I wasn't going to allow my opinion of Sam to be influenced by my feelings for Trent. I was wiping the slate clean and starting over. I was going to be pleasant, and I was going to give the poor guy a chance. He might not be what I was looking for, but he was what I needed at the moment.

The hostess led me to a booth next to a window where he was waiting for me. When I saw him, I had to admit that my pupils may have dilated just a bit. He looked *good*. He flashed a smile and stood up to help me take off my coat.

"You look beautiful," he complimented me.

"Thanks. You do too. Look handsome, I mean."

He laughed as he sat back down. "Thanks for giving me a second chance. I know we were a little out of sync last time."

"It was my fault. I've just been out of sorts and more bitter than usual lately."

"Is that why you were going so hard on the heavy bag yesterday?"

I laughed and nodded. "I hope I'm not as unpleasant tonight."

181

The waiter came and took our orders. When he left, Sam asked, "So, what's had you out of sorts lately?"

"Oh, you don't want to hear about my problems. I'll get over it."

He gave me a knowing look. "Is it an ex-boyfriend problem?"

"He wasn't my boyfriend. Just a friend. Things got weird. That's all."

"Sorry to hear that. But not too sorry, because it means I get a chance now," Sam said with a smile.

"Mm-hmm." I was trying not to be unpleasant, but those cheesy lines just killed it for me. I looked out the window.

"So, how long have you been a trainer?" he asked.

I looked back at him. "About five years. I was going to get into physical therapy, but I found I enjoyed training better. I haven't been at this gym long, though. I moved up here after my divorce and basically had to start all over again."

"You're divorced too?"

"Sure am."

"You know, I'm kind of glad to hear that. I've tried dating women who've never been married before, and all they want to do is get married right away and have kids. They don't really get it."

"Get what?"

"What a damn nightmare marriage is. You get it though, I bet."

I looked out the window again. "Oh, I don't know. It was a nightmare for me, but I think it could be great with the right person. I'm not opposed to getting married again."

"I don't think I could go through it again. I was with my ex-wife for fourteen years, married for twelve. This December

I'll have been separated from her for four years, and in that time, I still haven't found someone that could change my mind on remarrying."

"It's not for everyone, I suppose." I immediately thought of Trent, and I immediately chastised myself inwardly for it. *He has no place in my head on this date.*

"How long have you been divorced?" Sam wanted to know.

"Six months or so," I said.

"Oh, so it's been more recent for you."

"It's fine, though," I said. "You won't find me pining away for my ex. It was a relief to be done with him."

"I actually didn't want my divorce," Sam confided. "She was the one who filed. I'm glad for it now, but I was still in a bad place only six months after the divorce. What was the reason for your divorce, if you don't mind me asking?"

"He was abusive."

Sam looked taken aback. "I've seen the damage you can do to a heavy bag. Who would be stupid enough to lay a hand on you?"

"There are other forms of abuse. Can we talk about something else now?" I asked, feeling uncomfortable. I looked out the window again at the light snow that was starting to fall.

That was when I saw him. My heart stopped. Across the street, looking down at his watch, I saw Trent walk by.

Chapter 13

I jumped up from my chair and rushed to the entrance. I flung the door open and ran outside, adrenaline surging through my veins.

"Trent!" I yelled. I looked around, but he wasn't anywhere to be seen. "Trent!"

Sam came rushing out behind me. "What's wrong?!" he asked. "Who's Trent?" He looked around.

I craned my neck and looked around one more time, but he just wasn't there. Had he ever really been there, or had it been my imagination?

"Roselyn, are you ok?" Sam asked, touching my shoulder.

"Sorry, I just…I thought I saw someone I knew. Sorry," I apologized. I turned to walk back into the restaurant, glancing back one last time. What had I seen?

I got a lot of strange stares as I walked back to my seat with Sam. I felt idiotic. My cheeks were on fire when I sat down.

"What was that all about?" Sam asked, concerned.

"I thought I saw a friend I haven't seen in a long time. I guess I was mistaken," I said, gazing out the window.

I had a hard time giving Sam my full attention after that. I did my best to fake it, and apparently, I faked it well. On my way home, I got a text from Sam asking if he could see me again. I acquiesced.

I started seeing Sam fairly regularly after that. It wasn't love – far from it – but it was nice having someone to talk to and spend time with. The best part was that he kept my mind off Trent when he was around. He hadn't *replaced* Trent, because no one could do that, but he did a great job of making me forget that fact for short periods of time.

The first time I invited Sam to my house, however, we hit a major bump in the road. It was about a month after we had first met, and I had invited him over for dinner. Afterward, I was washing up the pans and loading the dishwasher as he picked out a movie to stream on the television.

I suddenly felt two big hands on my waist and hot breath on the back of my neck. Sam's lips caressed the back of my neck tenderly. I stiffened at his touch. It wasn't because I didn't like it. It wasn't because I was repulsed by him. It was because the last time I was touched so intimately, it had been by Trent's hands and Trent's lips, and this wasn't Trent. Memories flooded my mind, and I tried to get past my apprehension by allowing myself to concentrate on those memories with Trent.

Sam turned me around to face him, and he kissed me. It wasn't bad, but it wasn't great. It was almost mechanical and lacked passion. He then grabbed underneath my buttocks and lifted me up, and I wrapped my legs around his waist.

"Shall we take this to the bedroom?" he mumbled against my lips.

I nodded. What the hell – why not?

He carried me back to my room and laid me on the bed. He quickly took off his shirt and climbed onto the bed. He started kissing down my neck, and that was when it happened. With closed eyes and parted lips, the name "Trent" rolled involuntarily off my tongue.

He stopped immediately and sat back on his haunches. "What did you say?" he asked, his face angry.

"I'm so, so sorry," I apologized profusely. "It just popped out of my mouth."

"Who the hell is this Trent? Is it your ex? Jesus." Sam climbed off the bed huffily and snatched his shirt off the floor. He looked at me, waiting for an explanation.

"It's not my ex. Trent was just a friend. He's not even around anymore. I don't know why I said that. I'm sorry."

"Just a friend, hey? Why are you lying to me?" Sam slipped his shirt back on over his head. "Listen, if you can't be honest with me, I don't know what hope we have of this going any further."

"Sam, wait. Ok. Let me explain. Trent was a friend, that part is true. But we…well…had *relations*. Once. He was the last man I had been with. That's all."

"Where is Trent now?" Sam wanted to know.

"I have no idea. I sent him away and told him not to come back."

"How long ago was that?" When I hesitated, Sam said, "Let me guess – right before you and I met?"

I nodded.

"Christ. You know, Roselyn, I can deal with someone who is working through getting over someone. We've all been there. But I can't deal with someone who is lying to me about it.

When you're ready to be open and honest with me, give me a call." Sam stormed out of my room.

I didn't follow him. I heard him putting on his coat and shoes, and I heard the front door slam. I didn't blame him for being angry. I would've been angry too if I were him. I felt bad for what had happened, but there was nothing I could do now to change it. I just sat on the bed and felt sort of…numb. I liked Sam, but it wasn't the end of the world if he didn't come back. I would be a little sad, but I wouldn't cry. There were other Sams out there. Plenty of fish in the sea, plenty of Sams in the gym.

I was just getting up to head back out to the kitchen to tidy up and finish the dishes when there was a sudden burst of blinding white light. It flooded the entire room, and I shrieked and threw my hands up over my face to protect my eyes. Just as quickly as it had appeared, however, it was gone. I blinked, my eyes still trying to adjust, and I reached for the bed behind me, intending to sit down. The bed wasn't there anymore, though, and I fell onto the floor. Startled, I rubbed my eyes, trying to force them to focus. I suddenly felt a hand grasp my upper arm and roughly lift me to my feet. My eyes were finally starting to recover, and I could tell that I was in a large room. I could see several shapes walking around – people? I didn't have much time to look, though, because I was being dragged backwards.

"What the hell is going on?!" I demanded. "Where am I?"

I received no reply.

I turned and looked at the person pulling on my arm. It was a man in a suit that resembled the ugly synsuits from SABER, but the color was more of a blue and the design was slightly different.

"Let go of me!" I shouted, yanking my arm from the man's grasp.

"Hey!" he yelled in surprise.

I started throwing punches. I felt his nose crack under my knuckles, and I followed the jab with a quick left hook. I kicked him away from me and turned to run.

I didn't make it far before I felt like someone had hit me in the back with a cattle prod. I went down hard, my body convulsing painfully. I faded in and out of consciousness for a while after that, but I remembered being dragged briefly. I woke up in some kind of tiny containment cell, about ten feet long by ten feet wide. The only furnishings in the cell with me were a small cot and a weird looking toilet. Three of the walls were solid and smooth, painted in a glossy gray color. The fourth wall was transparent, like plexiglass, and it looked out into what appeared to be a huge laboratory full of people working in matching synsuit uniforms. There was a large piece of machinery hanging from the middle of the ceiling, like a giant mechanical stalactite.

"Hey!" I shouted. I started banging on the glass. "Where am I?! Why am I here?! Somebody help me!" The people in the laboratory ignored me.

"Did you have a nice rest?" I heard an eerie effeminate male voice say. It sounded like it was coming from somewhere inside the cell.

I whirled around, but no one was there. "Who said that?"

"I did. You can't see me, silly. Wow, you primitives are daft, aren't you? It's called remote communication."

"Where am I? Who are you? Why did you take me?"

"You haven't figured that out yet? Oh, that's right. Primitive! You're in a world parallel to your own, obviously. Where is the Traveler?"

"What traveler?"

"Your companion. Where is he?"

"I have no idea what you're talking about. Why don't you tell me just who the hell you are?"

"I have no reason to tell you that."

"You have no reason not to tell me that."

"You wouldn't understand anyway. Primitives never do."

"Why did you take me?"

"Isn't it obvious? You're the cheese in the trap. The worm on the hook. The damsel in distress. He will come for you."

"Who will come for me?"

"Pay attention! The Traveler, of course!"

They must mean Trent. Am I in the place he was in when he went missing? Is this the SABER from the parallel universe? Why would they take me to get to Trent?

"I don't know who you're talking about!" I lied.

"Lying won't make a difference. We sent him a message. He knows we took you. He will come."

I forced a mocking laugh even though I was completely terrified. "No one's coming! Who's the daft one now?"

The voice stopped talking.

"So what's your plan? None of this makes any sense!"

Nothing.

I sat down on the cot and tried to sort through what I knew. I knew I was in a parallel world, likely the one that was trying to open a wormhole into my house and the one Trent was trapped in for a while. I knew they wanted Trent, and they were trying to use me to get to him. How did they know about me, though? And what the hell made them think that Trent was going to come for me? I sent him away and told him never to come

189

back. I probably meant nothing to him by now. Dust in the wind. He was probably busy solving the man in the Jurassic mystery anyway.

"Wait," I said as I realized something. "Was it you? Were you the one I saw a hundred fifty million years ago?"

"One hundred fifty million years ago? You admit it, then?" the voice said. "You must know the Traveler."

"Obviously you have a Traveler of your own, so why do you want one from a parallel world?"

"How would you know if we have a Traveler?"

"I saw him, stupid."

"Impossible."

"I just told you I saw him in our world, during the Jurassic period."

"You are mistaken."

"I don't care if you admit it or not. I know what I saw. What do you want with Trent?"

"It matters not to you. You will die with your beloved Traveler."

"He can't die," I said insolently.

"Oh, he can die."

I felt ice shoot through my veins. "But why? What is the purpose of all of this?"

Silence.

My brain buzzed with questions. Why would they want to kill Trent? What was their goal? How did they get a "traveler" through to our world without me or Trent noticing, and why were they even bothering to deny it? What were they going to do with me when they realized Trent wasn't coming? I wasn't ever going back to my world, was I? I was going to die here, scared and alone. My family wasn't going to know what happened to me.

Sam would become a suspect in my "missing person" case. Was he going to go to prison over my disappearance? And what about Cattiel? Who was going to take care of him? Was he going to end up in an animal shelter, or worse?

All of this was happening because I allowed Trent in my life. No, it wasn't as simple as that, though, was it? That wasn't it. It was happening because I kicked Trent *out* of my life. If he had been with me, he probably would've had this taken care of and had us home by now. Yes, I was a target because I was Trent's companion for a while, but I was a victim because I chose to walk away from him. Why couldn't I have just *tried* to stay friends with him? Why did I have to throw him away like that?

I lay down on the cot and stared despondently at the dotted gray ceiling of my cell. I had reached my emotional limit. I was just…numb. My thoughts stopped racing, and I started counting the tiny holes all over the ceiling that I assumed must have been there for air exchange. One, two, three, four, five…

…Two hundred thirty-two, two hundred thirty-three, two hundred thirty-four. There were two-hundred thirty-four holes in the ceiling. As I stared at them, I wondered if they were only for air exchange or if there was a more sinister purpose for those tiny, innocuous-looking holes. I sat up and looked back out at the scientists working in the laboratory. There was an abundance of computers and giant screens, large machinery, and work benches filled with lots of shiny appliances and high-tech devices – none of which I recognized as anything familiar from my world.

As my eyes scanned the room, though, I did find one familiar item. Off in the corner, at the far end of the room, there was another containment cell that looked a little like the one I was in. There were brightly colored warning stickers all over the unit. It didn't contain a prisoner, however. Through the plexiglass-like wall or door, I could see the Big Bad inside. It didn't seem nearly as scary now. It just looked like an old, run-down machine that someone had stowed away in a closet like an unused bread maker.

Did that mean that this was the room with the device that opened wormholes? Is that what the giant metallic stalactite on the ceiling was? Is this the room I had arrived in? It had been such a blur that I couldn't be sure.

Just then, something caught my eye. There was a person in the lab, walking with their back to me, who had a rather distinctive bow-legged gait. It stood out, especially in that ugly, skin-tight synsuit. It couldn't be…could it? I practically pressed my face to the glass trying to get a better look, but the individual never turned around. He continued on through the room and exited out a door at the far end of the room. I watched the room like a hawk for the next hour, but I didn't see that particular figure return. I hated to even think it – hated to even give myself that hope – but could it have been Trent?

If it had been Trent – and I wasn't saying it was – had he seen me? Did he know where I was? If it had been him – again, not saying it was – wouldn't he have rescued me? Maybe not. That's what they were expecting him to do. He wasn't stupid enough to fall into a trap. He was a lot of things, but stupid wasn't one of those things.

At the end of the day, or at least what I assumed must have been the end of the day, everyone left the lab and shut down all of the lights, leaving me there alone in the dark. I waited anxiously, feeling a tiny sliver of hope that perhaps the bow-legged man in the synsuit had been Trent, and that perhaps he was going to suddenly appear in my cell and whisk me away from this hell. I waited. And waited…and waited. I fell asleep waiting, and when I woke up, he still wasn't there. When scientists started arriving and my breakfast (a disgusting "nutrition bar") was shoved through a small slat on the floor, I knew he wasn't coming.

I felt foolish for even allowing myself to hope he was coming.

I saw that same bow-legged man walk through the lab every day for the next several days, but he always kept his face turned away from me. I noticed that he came at almost the exact same time every day, and he only showed up once each day. He followed an exact pattern. The only divergence from day to day was that he seemed to be carrying something different in his hand each time. Who was he? What was he doing? No one else in the lab seemed to follow such a stringent and unvarying schedule. No one else in the lab seemed to notice him, either. The scientists would occasionally stop and chat with each other throughout the day, but I never saw anyone ever stop to talk to him. Was that weird, or was I looking too much into this?

After about a week of imprisonment, I was feeling the effects of my solitude. I hadn't talked to anyone but myself since I had arrived. The effeminate voice that had talked to me on that first day had been completely silent ever since, despite my many attempts to strike up some kind of conversation. I had no idea what was going to happen to me, or how long I was going to be held before they got tired of waiting for Trent. I hadn't eaten anything other than nasty "nutrition bars" the entire time, and I had no source of entertainment other than the daily exercises I forced myself to do. I was starting to feel my sanity slipping, and it was the most terrifying feeling in the world.

And then, when I had lost all hope, he came.

"Well, it appears I'm late to the party," I heard a familiar voice shout out in the laboratory. It was like his voice had breathed the life back into me. I sprang up and looked out the front of my cell, and there was Trent, standing in the middle of the room under the mechanical stalactite, wearing his usual tweed suit. Everyone in the room was just standing there, looking dumbfounded. "I apologize for that, especially considering I'm the guest of honor. I hope you'll forgive me."

I rushed to the plexiglass. "Trent! Watch out! It's a trap!"

Trent smiled at me calmly and walked toward my cell. "Are you all right?"

"Been better," I said with a teary smile. "Please. Help me, Trent," I begged as I held my hand up against the plexiglass.

He held his hand up against mine on the other side of the glass. "I'm not leaving without you."

The voice boomed throughout the room. "You're right about that, Traveler. But that's because you won't be leaving."

Suddenly, several people wearing large, ornate hats and long robes materialized beneath the mechanical stalactite. There were ten of them, and they stood in a row facing Trent with their hands clasped calmly in front of them. All of the scientists quickly filed out of the room, leaving only Trent, the people in robes, and me.

"I'm so glad you could all make it," Trent said.

"You will not make a mockery of this council," I heard one of the people in the robes say. It was the same voice I had heard in my cell.

"This council is a mockery," Trent countered. "Look at you lot with your ridiculous hats and pompous attitudes, thinking you can play games with me. It's utterly laughable."

"We've trapped you, Traveler."

"Have you now? See, there's one small problem with that. You think I'm trapped in here with all of you. Unfortunately

194

for you, it's rather the other way 'round. You all are trapped in here with *me*."

There were hushed whispers among the group.

"Silence!" a woman in a robe yelled. "Traveler, you are being sentenced to death for crimes against the Alliance. Do you acknowledge these charges?"

"Are these crimes I've already committed, or the ones I'm about to commit?"

"The Traveler admits to his crimes," the woman declared to the others.

"Oh yes. I've done terrible things. I don't deny it. But before you attempt to carry out the sentence, I must know – who is it? Who made the time-travel device?"

"You are in no position to ask questions."

"Oh, come now. What's it going to hurt? You're going to kill me anyway, right? Just give me some answers before I go."

The council whispered amongst themselves briefly, nodding to each other.

"Our Traveler. The one who conspired against us and compromised our mission by taking us off-course without authorization. He has been charged and his sentence has been carried out."

"You got him to develop a time traveling, inter-universal device, convinced him to spy on me, pried information out of him – and then you just killed him?"

"You are mistaken. He did not spy on you."

Trent paused. "What do you mean he didn't spy on me? Of course he did. I saw him."

"You are mistaken. He did not spy on you," the robed official repeated. "But he had served his purpose. He had paid his restitution for his treasonous acts, and he was liberated."

"Murdered."

"It is not murder. It is justice."

Trent turned to me. "See? A mockery," he said. He turned his attention back to the council. "You obviously want me out of the way so you can invade my world. I know yours has been decimated by war and depleted of its resources. You've lost most of your people and your world is a wasteland. I learned that last time I was here. But why not use the time-travel device to change the past? That is the point of having it, isn't it? Stop the war before it happens. Why bother going to the effort of invading another world? You do realize we aren't going to give it up without a fight, don't you?"

There were more whispers from the group as they looked at each other uneasily. It looked like Trent had struck a nerve.

"Oh! Oh, I see!" Trent exclaimed. "You killed him before he perfected the device, didn't you?! Or did he do something to it before you killed him? Whatever it is, you *can't* go where you need to go to stop the war, can you? It's basically useless to you, isn't it?"

"We do not need it," a different robed official said. "We have you. We can use your device, or we can invade your world. Once you are out of the way, it won't matter. Your world will be defenseless without you."

"Oh, did I not mention? I'm not the defense. I'm the distraction."

"Explain!" the man with the effeminate voice commanded.

Trent looked down at his watch. "I'd really love to, but it appears my time is up. I'm going to take my companion and be off now. I'd rather not be present when everything blows up in your face."

Everything happened incomprehensibly quickly after that. There were flashes of light, shaking, faint sounds of explosions, and the comforting feeling of Trent's body next to mine. And then, just like that, I was in my house, back in my bedroom, with Trent's arms squeezing me tightly. I clung to him like I was afraid to ever let him go. I knew as long as I was holding on to him, I was safe. He put one hand on the back of my head and held my cheek against his shoulder. I felt him rest his cheek on the top of my head.

"You're safe now," he said. "I'm sorry I ever let you out of my sight. I misjudged the situation and left you in harm's way. I'm a bloody imbecile."

"You came for me," I said in disbelief.

"Of course I did."

"They wanted to kill you."

"I know."

"But you came. You came for me anyway."

"Aye."

"You are a bloody imbecile."

Trent chuckled softly. "I promised to keep you safe. And I'm not entirely certain that they *can* kill me. Regardless, I'd rather die trying to save you than live knowing I couldn't."

He started to loosen his grip on me, intending to end the hug, but I clung more tightly to him. "Please, just a moment longer." I closed my eyes and smiled as he enveloped me in his arms in a bear hug. "Was that you I was seeing every day in the lab?" I asked, my voice muffled by his shoulder.

"It was. I wasn't sure if you had picked up on that. I'm sorry I couldn't get you out sooner, and I'm sorry I couldn't let you know what I was planning. I needed time to build the bomb, and I couldn't use my watch to teleport or time travel without

197

them detecting it. Oh, and I needed to locate and snag this," he said as he held up a watch. "I think its time setting is malfunctioning."

"I don't understand," I said, drawing my brows together.

He pointed at the watch. "See, if they try to enter the coordinates and the universal time, it gets all wonky and—"

"No, not the watch. What bomb?"

"I built and activated a bomb in the basement of their compound. I needed to make sure the council was in that lab at that moment so they would be destroyed along with the wormhole device. I don't know if you figured it out or not, but that big machine in the center of the room was the wormhole generator. I couldn't let that continue to exist in their world, and I couldn't risk any one of the council officials escaping. The annihilation had to be complete."

"Since when can you just come and go from the parallel world?"

"Since I tweaked my watch. But I can't just come and go. I had only enough energy to make one trip there and one back. I've taken a bit of time to work on it."

"…How long? How long has it been since you saw me last?" I asked.

Trent looked down at the watch in his hands. "I don't know. Twelve years?"

It felt like I'd been punched in the gut. "Twelve *years*? What were you doing for twelve years?"

"Trying to save you."

I looked at him in confusion. There was so much I still didn't understand.

Trent sighed. "I never took down the alarm in your house. I had assumed the threat to us was from SABER of this world, and that the cloaking device I had installed would keep you off their radar. But I wanted to be sure you were safe, and I wanted to make sure I would be alerted if you were ever in danger. I hadn't anticipated the threat would come from the parallel world, but when I received the alert, I knew immediately what had happened. So, I got to work on a solution. It took me over twelve years of obsessive tinkering, but I finally figured it out, and I went back in time to rescue you."

"Why didn't you go back in time and stop this from happening in the first place?" I asked.

"Unfortunately, it was something that needed to happen. Some things are just unchangeable because they are the catalyst that sets other events in motion. But the important thing is that you're safe now." Trent smiled at me.

"How long was I gone?"

Trent looked down at his watch and pressed a few buttons. "I hadn't yet figured out how to time travel from the parallel world to here to bring you back to right after you were taken, so you've been gone a little over a week. Time travel between worlds is trickier than I had anticipated."

"Oh no," I started to panic. "Cattiel!"

"Oh! Hold on," Trent said. He adjusted his watch and disappeared. When he returned seconds later, he said, "There, I went back and took care of the cat. But that litter box is going to be nasty. I don't do litter boxes."

"Oh, thank god," I said with a sigh of relief.

"You're welcome."

"Wait, if you can go back in time to feed the cat, why can't you just take me back to the moment before I was taken? I get that you couldn't do it from the other world, but now that we're here, you can."

"I can't. Timelines should not be crossed, and in some situations, they can't be. This is one of them."

"I don't get it. It all seems so arbitrary," I complained.

"Just trust me. I usually know what I'm talking about."

I went out into the living room and scooped up my cat, hugging him tightly. For once, he didn't growl at me, but purred instead. He must have been lonely without me.

"See?" I said to Cattiel. "You think you hate me, but when I'm not here, you miss me. Maybe you do love me after all."

"That's not love. That's attachment," Trent pointed out.

I looked at him crossly and continued to hug the cat. "You love me," I whispered to Cattiel.

"There are things that will need to be taken care of," Trent said hesitantly.

I set the cat down and plopped onto the couch. "I don't think I can handle any of that right now. Hell, I probably don't even have a job anymore."

"It's all right! We can fix that! Where's your phone?"

"I think I left it on the counter before I disappeared."

Trent went into the kitchen and found my phone. He held his watch close to it and started pressing buttons on the watch and the phone.

After about thirty seconds, he said, "There you go. I've temporarily synced your phone with my watch. Now you can call back in time and let people know you're going out of town for the week. I'm sure you can make up something."

I sat up as he brought me my phone and handed it to me. "I don't want to do this right now. I just want to enjoy being home. I just went through a week of hell, and I thought I was going to be murdered. I think the call to work can wait."

"Is there anything I can do?" Trent asked, clasping his hands together nervously. He looked at me with concern. "What do you need?"

"I need a bath," I answered honestly.

"Did you want me to draw you one?" he asked as he jerked his thumb toward the bathroom.

"No, no. I can do it."

"Very well. I suppose I should leave you to it," he said.

"No!" I blurted as my hand shot out to him, grabbing his jacket sleeve. I rose from the couch. "Don't you dare leave me. Not ever again. You'd better still be here when I get out of the bath."

Trent smiled at me, nodding. "As you wish. I'll be right here."

I had intended for my bath to help calm me down and ease my mind. However, as much as I tried to relax in the hot, soothing water of the bathtub, I didn't linger for long. I scrubbed up quickly, realizing once I'd climbed into the tub that I was afraid Trent was going to disappear on me. I should've just taken a shower so I could get back to his side promptly.

When I was out of the tub and dressed, I hurried out into the living room. I didn't care that I didn't have on any makeup, and it didn't bother me that my towel-dried hair was a mess. I just wanted to make sure he was still there.

Trent was sitting on the couch eating a toaster pastry. I was relieved.

"You're out of pastries," he mumbled around a mouthful of food.

"All I've had to eat for the past week is 'nutrition bars' and you come into my house and eat my last toaster pastry?"

"What? It's the only normal food you keep in this house."

"It's the only junk food I keep in this house," I corrected.

"Do you feel any better?" he asked.

I nodded. "A little." I sat down on the couch across from him. "You know, there's something that's bothering me. Why did the SABER council keep denying that they had someone spying on us?"

"Because I don't think they did."

"What? Who was that man, then?"

"I don't know. While you were in the bath, I took a look at that watch. There is no way it is capable of inter-universal travel."

"Should we be worried?"

"Whoever it was, they don't seem to be trying to find us or trying to change history. I just wonder if perhaps…if it's me. Me from another time."

"Wouldn't you know?"

"Not necessarily. Whatever he was using to travel with wasn't my watch that I have now, but it doesn't mean it wasn't me."

"So, you're saying we don't need to worry about it?"

"You don't need to. I'm going to keep my ear to the ground, though."

I heard my text alert go off on my phone.

"I suppose I should make those calls now," I said with a heavy sigh.

I looked at my phone. I deleted the junk text I had just received and opened my contacts list. It had a new option in the call settings in which I could select a date and time. I chose the morning after I had disappeared, and I called work and made up an excuse about a family emergency out of town. Thankfully, I have a pretty lenient boss, and she had no problem with me taking the week off. I hung up the phone and set it down on the end table.

"That's it? Just work? What about your family?"

"It's not so unusual for me to not talk to them for a week. They won't think anything of it." Then I remembered Sam. "Oh, shoot. I should probably call Sam."

That caught Trent's attention. He gave me a questioning look.

"Sam? Who's Sam?"

Chapter 14

I felt like I had been caught cheating. I *knew* I hadn't done anything wrong, but my heart had a guilty conscience. I needed to just be upfront and honest with him. He wasn't going to care, was he? After all, he was the one who first said that he and I would never work, wasn't he?

"Sam is the guy I've been seeing." I rose from the couch and started pacing the living room.

I saw Trent's nostrils flare as he also stood up. "Oh. You've been seeing someone? That's good. That's…good."

"Yeah."

We stood in awkward silence for a moment.

"So…where'd you meet?" Trent asked, breaking the silence.

"The gym. He's a divorcee, like me."

"The gym. He works out, then? That's cool. Cool. Is it…is it serious?" Trent asked as he picked at his fingernails a little too nonchalantly.

"I don't know. I'm not even sure if we're still dating. We kind of had a falling out right before I was kidnapped."

"Oh. Darn. Well, that's too bad."

"Maybe," I said as I pulled my phone back out.

I set the call date and time for close to the same time I called into work. I figured it would give Sam the night to cool down.

"Hello?" Sam answered after several rings.

"Hey."

There was a long silence.

"Listen," I said finally, "I'm sorry about last night. I wasn't ready to talk about it."

"Are you ready to talk about it now?" Sam asked.

"No. But I wanted to apologize for what happened, anyway."

Just then, Trent yelled to me from the kitchen, "Oh dear lord! You'll want to toss this shrimp. It's definitely turned!"

"Who is that?" Sam asked suspiciously.

"An old friend."

"*The* old friend?"

I hesitated. "Yes."

I heard Sam sigh heavily. "This is just too much drama for me. I'm sorry. I don't do drama."

"I understand. I don't do drama either, if I can avoid it. Unfortunately, sometimes it just happens. I'll see you around, Sam."

"That's it? That's all you have to say?"

"What else am I supposed to say?"

"I don't know. Usually people have excuses or explanations."

"Sorry, I'm not even going to try to explain all of this."

"You really don't care, do you?"

"Sure I do. But I'm not going to beg you to forgive me. I'm not going to beg for you to give us another chance. If you're done, you're done. It's ok. I get it," I said unremorsefully.

"I never said I was ready to be done," Sam said.

"You didn't? I thought you said you didn't do drama."

"I don't. I hate it. But it doesn't mean I'm ready to be *done*. It just means we have some things to work on."

"You seemed pretty done with things last night."

"I was upset. And rightfully so, I think. But I'm not an idiot. I know you're a woman worth working things out with."

"Oh." I didn't know what to say.

"Can I see you today?"

"Uh, no. No, I'm heading out of town today. I'm taking a little vacation to visit my brother for the week. But I'll call you when I get home."

"Oh. Really? You hadn't mentioned it before."

"It was kind of a last-minute thing. You know, after last night I realized I needed some time away to clear my head," I lied.

"I understand," Sam said. "I'll talk to you when you get back."

I hung up the phone and turned around. Trent was watching me expectantly.

"Well?" he raised his eyebrows.

"I guess we're still seeing each other," I said with a shrug.

"I see. So, when do I get to meet him?" Trent asked, crossing his arms and leaning his shoulder against the wall. "I need to make sure he is good enough for you."

"That's not your decision to make."

Trent's face became serious. "You are the most important person to me in all of the world and time. You better believe I'm going to make damn sure the man you end up with is worthy of you."

I felt my breath catch in my throat and I swallowed hard.

"Why do you have to say things like that?" I asked.

Trent's forehead creased. "Because it's true."

"I can't possibly be the *most* important person to you."

"Why not?"

"I'm not that important."

"No one is unimportant. And you, Roselyn, mean the most to me," he said with a smile. "I spent almost twelve years working to save you – and I would've spent a thousand if I had to. How can you think you aren't important to me?"

"Why? What does an immortal genius time traveler from the future find so important about me?"

"Have you met you?" Trent said with a chuckle. "You are my favorite person! You love hard. You live fiercely. You find the humor in life. You keep me on my toes. You forgive me even when I don't deserve it. You irritate the hell out of me and frustrate me, then you find some little thing to do or say to make me wonder why I was cross in the first place. You are never cruel. You are always so, so brave. You are everything. Everything I don't deserve…and I'll be damned if I let another man have you if he doesn't deserve you either."

I had to wipe my eye. "If you think so highly of me, how could you walk away from me so easily?"

"You thought that was easy for me? That was the hardest thing I've ever had to do! But I had to do it."

"Why? Why didn't you even try to change my mind?"

"Because that's what love is! Real love isn't trying to change each other or change each other's mind. Real love isn't clinging to someone and trying make them love you back. Real love is letting someone go if they want to go. It's letting someone have an opportunity to find happiness, even if it isn't with you, and finding happiness in their happiness. Real love isn't bitter and angry and forceful. It isn't holding on to someone at all costs to make yourself feel good. If you truly love someone, you let them do what is best for them. You let them be free to find the happiness they deserve. Real love is understanding that sometimes you just aren't what they need – and not being angry about it. I might not be perfect, and I know I've made some grievous mistakes, but I'm trying to do my best by you because you deserve the very best." Trent looked at me soulfully.

"You need to stop talking. Just stop." I said, frowning.

"What's the matter?"

"This…*thing* you always do!"

"What thing?" Trent said, looking bewildered.

I gestured wildly at him. "*This!* I convince myself, after a long internal debate, that I am indeed better off without you, and then you come swooping in with your hair and your suit and say the most eloquent, beautiful thing anyone has ever said to me and you make me fall in love with you all over again and I *hate it*! Hate it!"

Trent turned his head and looked out the window quietly.

"Well?" I demanded a response.

He turned to me, looked me in the eye, and said, "You're awful, your hair is messy and you smell like cabbage. And don't get me started on the damn kale."

I was flabbergasted. "Excuse me?"

"Is that better? Would you rather me say things like that?"

"I…I smell like cabbage?" I said as I took a test sniff.

Trent bit back a grin. "No, of course not. None of that is true, obviously." After he took a second to think about it, he added, "Really? That's the part you were worried about? Not the part about being awful?"

"Everybody is awful once in a while, but nobody ever wants to smell like cabbage."

"I suppose you're not wrong," he granted.

"God, it's like I can smell it now."

"You don't smell like cabbage."

"Why would you say that, anyway? I do smell like cabbage, don't I?!"

"You don't smell like cabbage."

"I feel like I need another bath now."

"You don't smell like cabbage, Roselyn."

"Ugh. I'm going to go change."

"Oh, good heavens, what have I done?" I heard Trent say in exasperation as I headed to my room.

As I changed my clothes, I remembered what we were talking about before I got distracted by the cabbage comment. How did he do that? Instant situation diffusion. Deflection. Redirection. He was like a goddamn magician.

When I returned to the living room in a fresh shirt, I found Trent kicked back on the couch again. He immediately started grilling me. "So, are we going to go hang out with Sam soon? Can I meet him?"

"I don't know how I feel about that yet," I said.

"Why not?"

"Because I don't know how I feel about Sam yet."

"Perhaps my opinion would help."

"I really don't think it will," I said. "Besides, I don't think he's going to be very excited to meet *you*."

"But I'm delightful!"

"He knows about…us," I said, wagging my finger between him and me and raising my eyebrows for emphasis.

"Ah, I see…but you weren't dating him then," Trent pointed out.

"I know, but…well, it's complicated."

"It's all complicated. Avoiding it isn't going to make it less so."

I sighed. "I know. But I just don't think this is the right time to put you two in the same room together."

"I'll be charming. I promise."

"No."

Trent grunted. "Fine. But you can't stop me from accidentally running into him."

"You wouldn't."

"I totally would."

"I prohibit it!"

Trent raised his eyebrows at me. "Well now you just went and made it more interesting! What is it you don't want me to know? You're definitely hiding something about him."

"I'm not hiding anything. Just leave it alone, Trent."

He leaned his head back against the back of the couch with a pouty sigh. "I get it. You're embarrassed by me."

I went over to the couch and sat down next to him. "You were bound to find out some day," I teased.

He draped his arm over my shoulder and pulled me closer to him. I rested my temple on his shoulder. "You must be tired," he remarked.

"I am. I feel like I haven't slept for more than an hour all week. Damn, I'm turning into you," I joked.

"Heaven forbid," Trent said with a short chuckle.

He was right. I was tired. I closed my eyes and just enjoyed being close to him again.

After a few minutes of relaxing silence, he mumbled, "I missed you."

Without opening my eyes, I smiled and replied, "I missed you, too. Don't let me run you off ever again, ok?"

"I was still here when you needed me," he said.

"No, you weren't. I needed you long before I was abducted by SABER."

"But you've got Sam now, though, right?"

"He isn't you. I still need *you*."

Trent was quiet for a while, so I let the conversation die there.

I woke up in a mild state of confusion. It was dark in the living room now, and I was lying on the couch. One of my legs was wedged between the back of the couch cushion and…someone else's leg? My body was partially on top of another warm body and my head was on his chest. I could hear a slow, steady heartbeat. It took me a moment to remember Trent was here. I lifted my head up and blinked, my eyes adjusting to the dark living room.

"Did you have a good nap?" Trent asked as he smiled at me in the dark.

"You stayed this whole time? How did we end up like this?" I asked, surprised.

"Every time I moved, you just leaned on me more. I didn't want to disturb you."

"How long was I out?"

"About three hours."

"Seriously?! You didn't turn on the TV or anything?"

He looked over and pointed at the end table about three feet out of reach. "The remote was over there."

I laughed. "I'm sorry! Weren't you bored?" I asked apologetically.

"No. Well, a little. But it was fine. Did you know you talk in your sleep? And you twitch. *A lot.*"

"Did I say anything good?"

"Oh yes. I'm still blushing."

I laughed and laid my head on his chest again.

"You should go to bed and get some rest," he suggested.

I felt my heartbeat quicken as a question came to my lips. I opened my mouth to speak, but the words wouldn't come out at first. I had to clear my throat and try again. "Would you…would you come with me?" I felt my cheeks flush once the words were out.

Trent's silence hung in the air, weighing on my heart with every passing moment. Finally, he replied softly, "What are you asking of me, Roselyn?"

My heart was in my throat. What was I doing? There was no way he was going to go for this. "Do I really have to come out and say it?"

"I think you'd better be clear with me, yes," he said. I could hear his heartbeat accelerating in his chest. It thumped thunderously against my ear.

"I can tell by the way your heart is beating that you understand my meaning," I disclosed.

He hesitated. "We shouldn't do that again."

"But you want to, don't you?" I asked.

"Of course I want to! But that doesn't make it a good idea." He sounded conflicted, but I could feel his anticipation growing against my hip.

I lifted my head off of his chest and looked at him. It was dark, but I could see the desire burning in his eyes as he looked into mine. He just needed a little push. One tiny, little push – and he'd forget his objections. I ran my fingers gently through his hair and pressed my lips to his. That was all it took.

A soft groan rumbled in his throat as he gave in. His kiss was ravenous as he raked his fingers into my hair. I slid my leg over him and straddled his hips, feeling the hardness within his trousers between my legs. He ran his hands down to my waist as he pressed himself against me, his kiss becoming even more demanding. The heat between my legs yearned for him. God, how I needed him...

I pulled away from his mouth and sat up, looking at him beneath me. His hair was chaotic and his eyes were wild. I climbed off of him and stood up.

"Let's take this back to the bedroom," I said, my chest heaving.

Trent rose from the couch and stood in front of me. He kissed me, biting my lip gently, before smiling mischievously at me. I grabbed his tie and started to lead him back to my room, but he snatched me halfway to the bedroom and pressed my back against the wall in the hallway, his body pressed firmly against mine. He took my hand and pressed it back against the wall. His mouth devoured mine, his other hand caressing the side of my face.

When our lips parted briefly, he murmured, "Why do you do this to me?"

I just smiled against his lips. "Did you want to stop?"

He glanced down at my lips hungrily before looking up into my eyes. "You couldn't drag me away with a freight train."

I kissed him again and led him back to my room. I was already tossing my shirt aside when we crossed the threshold, but that was as far as I got before Trent overtook me. He scooped me up and dropped me onto the bed. I got up on my knees and started unbuttoning his shirt while he loosened his tie, and when he had dropped his tie and was shrugging off his shirt, I started on his trousers.

He pushed me back onto the bed once I had his pants undone, and he reached for the button on my jeans. He unzipped my pants and slid them down over my thighs. I slipped my underwear off as he tossed my jeans onto the floor. I started to scoot up to lay my head on the pillows, but Trent reached out and hooked his hand under my knee, pulling me toward him to the edge of the bed. In the darkness, I felt his mouth on my inner thigh. He trailed light kisses up my thigh until he reached my most intimate folds. His warm, soft tongue explored me gently, and I threw my head back and closed my eyes, my breath catching in my throat. As I felt my pleasure quickly growing, I stopped him. I needed all of him.

"Take me now, Trent. Please," I begged.

He kicked off his trousers and climbed onto the bed on top of me. He kissed me passionately, the taste of my desire still lingering on his tongue. He pressed himself against my wetness, and I wrapped my legs around his waist and urged him on. Feeling Trent's body pressed against mine, our bare, slick skin sliding against each other; his heavy breaths in my ear and his moans making my entire body tingle; his lips brushing against my neck; his tongue dancing with mine; my fingers in his hair; hips pushing, grinding, bucking against him – it was ecstasy. I felt my pleasure rising, and my moans grew louder as I clung more tightly to Trent and rocked my hips against his. He thrust hard and deep, sensing that I was close, and it sent me over the edge. I couldn't contain my cries of pleasure as my body was rocked by the most powerful orgasm I'd ever experienced. I buried my face in his neck and clung to him as we rode it out together.

Afterward, as we lay next to each other, catching our breath, Trent said, "We can't keep doing this."

"I know," I replied. I turned onto my side and threw my arm over his bare chest, sidling my sweaty, naked body up next to his.

"You aren't mine to do this with," Trent said guiltily. He suddenly threw his hand over his mouth and looked over at me, giving me a scandalized look. "What about Sam?! Oh, dear, I've done a very very bad thing!"

I put my hand on his cheek. "Sam isn't my boyfriend. Relax."

Trent was quiet for a moment. "Are you going to tell him?"

"No."

"Have you and him…?"

"No."

"Why does it seem like you don't fancy him all that much?"

"I don't know. I like him, I do. But…I keep holding him to impossible standards, knowing he'll never measure up. He's a perfectly all right guy, don't get me wrong. I just…I'm looking for 'wow,' and I'm not sure if he can give me that."

"You deserve 'wow,' and you shouldn't settle for less."

"I don't think I have much of a choice. It might be time to settle for 'good enough.' The great thing about 'good enough,' though, is that it doesn't hurt so badly when it doesn't work out."

"That's a terrible way to look at it," Trent admonished.

"It's the only way to look at it."

"Don't you want to be happy?"

"Of course I do. And I am happy – right now. With you. That'll do for now. You are my 'wow.'"

"You know we can't be together," Trent said quietly.

"I know. But it's nice to pretend for a while."

"I want you to have someone who gives you 'wow' every day for the rest of your life. I give you grief and trouble. I'm not your 'wow.'"

"You don't get to tell me that. You don't get to tell me how to feel."

"No, of course not. I was just observing."

"Obviously not through my eyes," I replied.

Trent gathered me up in his arms and held me tightly. "I wish I could actually be the man you see when you look at me through your eyes. I dread the day you take off those rose-colored spectacles."

"I don't think I've ever met anyone who hates himself as much as you do. What reason could you possibly have to be so hard on yourself? Why do you feel so undeserving?"

"We all have our secrets. We all have moments we aren't proud of. I have over 600 years' worth of those moments. I've had to do things no one should have to do. I've had to make decisions no one should have to make. And I've made mistakes – mistakes that cost people their lives. It didn't happen once or twice, either. This is something that happens time and time again. When you are burdened with the task I have been burdened with

– when you have to keep history from being unraveled, humanity from being corrupted – the line between good and evil gets blurred. Sometimes you have to do bad things to keep others safe. Someone has to get their hands dirty…unfortunately, I'm that someone. I don't deserve your admiration, Roselyn."

"I don't know what you've done, Trent, and I'm not going to ask. Not right now, anyway. But I know that you are a good man. You have a good heart. Anything bad you've ever done had to have been done for good reason, I'm sure of it. I refuse to believe that you'd ever be malicious or evil."

"I'm not a good man. I try to do what is right, but it doesn't make me a good man. I've lived too long and fought too many battles to still be good."

"After all this time, you fight because you still care about what happens to the human race. You fight even though no one is making you. You do it because it's the right thing to do. If that isn't a good man, I don't know what is. The real evil in this world isn't in the actions of bad men, but in the indifference of otherwise good men. You refuse to be indifferent, and that tells me everything I need to know."

"You romanticize it. You make it sound noble. But you don't really understand. It's grotesque and heart-wrenching and sullying…and I write every single line of it down. Every unspeakable horror I've witnessed or had to commit, I record it. I might not have the memory of every act, but I know everything I've done or have allowed to happen. I write it down lest I ever forget who I truly am and for what purpose I am here to serve. And unfortunately, Roselyn Wolff, being your 'wow' isn't part of that purpose, as much as I wish it were."

"I don't care. I still—"

Trent interrupted me. "I had to kill someone working for SABER because they were developing technology to go back and kill Hitler. I had to *protect* Hitler. Do you know how that feels? Knowing that you *could* go back and stop the Holocaust, but you won't? You won't because it's not the way it's *supposed* to go? Knowing I *can* change something but *not* changing it – that kind of makes me responsible, doesn't it? If you really think about it, it does. Millions of people suffer and die horribly in an unimaginable hell because I won't allow history to change. Because I know it's how it *has* to go. Yes, my hands are tied, but ultimately it is *my* decision. And it's a horrible decision to make."

"You have no real choice, Trent. You can't blame yourself for having to let history run its course."

"I killed all of the people in that SABER compound when I came to save you. Did you realize that? That bomb was intended to take out the entire building, and everyone in it. Even the scientists. Even the cafeteria workers. The security guards. The custodians. I couldn't warn anyone, because it might've compromised my mission. I walked beside many of them every day for a week, knowing what was going to happen to them. I even learned some of their names. Some of them were good people. Hell, a lot of them were good people, just working for a corrupt authority. They're all dead now because of me. But I couldn't let them come to our world and decimate our Earth, now could I? I couldn't let them murder you. I had to destroy them before they destroyed us. Again, my hands were tied, but it was still *my* decision to make."

I didn't know what to say to him, so I simply said, "I'm sorry."

"That's just the tip of the iceberg. There's so, so much more…so much that I can't even tell you about. I don't think you'd ever look me in the eyes again if I tried."

"Then let's not talk about it. I didn't mean to dredge up anything."

"You didn't dredge. It's always simmering just beneath the surface. It's not something you find respite from for very long." After an extended silence, Trent looked down at me and said, "Do you still think I'm a good man?"

"I'm certain of it."

Chapter 15

I woke up in the morning still naked and tangled in my bed sheets, but Trent wasn't beside me. I looked over to see if any of his clothes were still on the floor, but they weren't. I felt a creeping anxiety rising in my chest. If he'd left, I didn't know if it was going to be for a day, a month, or forever. I didn't expect him to *never* leave my side, but I was terrified of him disappearing without saying goodbye and never coming back. I threw on a pair of pajama pants and a t-shirt and hurried out to the living room.

"Ah, you're up!" Trent said from the kitchen.

An overwhelming sense of relief washed over me. "Jesus, I thought you'd run out on me again," I confessed.

"We're in the wrong millennium for Jesus, aren't we? I met him once, you know. Nice chap…just don't give him a whip." Trent had his back to me, and he was busy doing something over the stove. I noticed he was wearing a different suit from yesterday.

"What are you doing?" I asked.

"Getting breakfast ready." He turned around with two plates in his hands and brought them to the table.

"Did you make omelets?" I asked, raising my eyebrows.

He nodded with a proud look on his face. "I did."

"I thought you didn't cook."

"I learned."

"When?"

"While you were sleeping."

"I see you changed your clothes, too."

He looked down at his suit. "Oh, yes. Can't take a cooking class in dirty, crumpled clothes."

"Wait, you took a whole class? To learn how to make eggs?"

"Omelets. Quit grilling me and just eat."

"Was that a cooking joke?"

Trent smirked at me. "You know it was."

I sat down at the table and looked at the large omelet in front of me. I didn't have the heart to tell him that I don't have the stomach for a big breakfast in the mornings. I was going to do my best to eat every last bite of that damn omelet, even if it was terrible. Trent brought me a cup of coffee and sat down across from me. He watched me, waiting for me to take the first bite.

"I can't eat with you watching me," I said.

"Sorry." He dropped his gaze to his own plate, but I could tell he was still observing me.

I cut off a corner of the omelet and took a bite. "Oh my god. This is actually really good!"

"I know!" he said excitedly. "I went through two cartons of eggs before I got it right, but I finally nailed it!"

"What's in it? I've never had anything like this before."

"Black truffle and robiola."

"Seriously?! Where the hell did you get black truffles around here— wait, don't answer that. Dumb question to ask a man with teleportation capabilities. What was that second thing? Rebola?"

Trent laughed. "Robiola. It's an Italian cheese."

"This is amazing. Thank you. You've ruined me for omelets now, though. Mine will taste like crap after this."

"You're welcome." Trent was beaming.

After breakfast, Trent insisted upon loading the dishwasher because I "do it wrong." I went into the living room, grabbed Cattiel off the couch, and sat down with him in my arms. I turned on the TV and channel surfed with an overfull belly and a contented heart.

"Well, I suppose I should be off now," Trent said as he dried his hands on the hand towel in the kitchen.

I dreaded those words. "You're coming back, right?"

"Well, not right back. You have your life to live, right? You have some things to talk to Sam about too, I suspect. I'll be around, though. Don't worry, I'm not disappearing forever."

I dropped the cat onto the couch and jumped up before Trent could leave. I hurried to him and threw my arms around his neck, forcing him to bend down slightly. He hugged me back tightly.

"You better not disappear forever. I'll never forgive you."

"Well, we can't have that, now can we?"

As I dropped my arms to my sides and released him, I suddenly remembered something. "Oh! Wait!" I grabbed my phone quickly and handed it to him. "I need you to put your number back in my phone."

"I thought you had my number," Trent said as he drew his brows together.

"I did. But I…erased it."

Trent entered his number and handed my phone back to me. "Why would you erase my number?"

"Because that's what you do, you know? When you try to erase someone from your life, that's the first thing you do – delete their number."

"I take it you've decided to keep me after all?"

"I'll never try to delete you again."

"I'm going to hold you to that," he teased.

"You know, there's something that's been bothering me. When you left last time, and I told you not to come back, I saw you. I was at a restaurant with Sam, and I saw you outside walking down the street. Why were you there?"

Trent gave me a doubtful look. "No, I wasn't around here. Are you sure?"

"Yes. It was you. At least I thought it was…"

Trent shrugged his shoulders. "Maybe it was me. All I can tell you is I haven't done it *yet*, at least."

"Oh."

"You sound disappointed."

I shook my head. "No, nothing of the sort. Anyway, I'll see you soon, right? Don't be gone too long. I'll worry."

Trent laughed. "I don't think I've ever had anyone worry about *me* before."

"Well, get used to it."

Trent smiled at me, and then he was gone.

I sat back down on the couch with Cattiel again. He had been right when he detected disappointment in my voice. There had been a little part of me that had secretly hoped that it had been him that day at the restaurant – that he was checking in on me to make sure I was all right. But it wasn't. What was it I had seen, then? Had it just been my imagination manufacturing a Trent that wasn't really there because I had yearned to see him so badly? It was entirely possible. It wasn't nearly as satisfying of an answer, but it was entirely possible.

After getting ready for the day, I went into the kitchen to look at what I needed to throw out and what I needed to get from the store. As I started sorting through the fridge, I pulled out my phone to call Sam. When I went to place the call, I noticed the time and date option was no longer available. My phone must no longer be synced with Trent's watch. I dialed Sam and sat in front of the fridge with the garbage can.

He answered on the third ring. "There you are," he said. "I was beginning to think you were never going to call."

"Here I am," I said. Ugh, the melon in the fridge had turned to mush. "Did you miss me?"

"I did. You didn't think I would, did you?"

"You didn't think you would." Oh my god, where did that avocado come from?

"I knew I would. So, when do I get to see you? Can I come over?" Sam asked.

"I actually need to go out. I have some grocery shopping to do today."

"Oh, perfect! Did you want to maybe meet for coffee when you get into town? I can accompany you to the store afterward if you wanted."

"Sure, that sounds good." I smelled the cottage cheese. It seemed ok, but did I trust it?

"I'll see you in, what, half an hour?" Sam asked.

I opened my vegetable drawer and saw a brown-tinted liquid covering the bottom of it. "Let's make that an hour. I've got a couple of things I need to take care of first."

Once my fridge had been purged and cleansed and exorcised, I bundled up and headed to town in the snow. It was a miserably blustery day, and as I walked from the curb to the coffee shop, I wished I had just stayed in. I'm sure I could've found something in the freezer to eat for dinner. But alas, here I was. I was just going to have to make the best of it.

I had arrived early to the coffee shop, so I got a tall black coffee and sat in the corner and waited for Sam. When he walked in the door a few minutes later, he looked out of breath. He was dressed for jogging. His face lit up when he saw me waiting for him and he waved. I grinned, despite myself, and waved back. I mean, he *was* cute. He got a coffee at the counter and joined me at the table. He leaned over and kissed me on the cheek before sitting down across from me.

"Sorry if I'm a little sweaty," he said. "I ran here."

"I see that. I didn't realize you were completely insane when I agreed to meet you for coffee."

Sam laughed. "It's not that bad. You warm up pretty quickly."

"You and I have very different opinions of 'not that bad.'"

Sam took a drink of his coffee. "So, how was your week at your brother's?

"Hm? Oh! Uh, yeah, that was nice. It's always good to see him."

"Did you have a chance to clear your head?"

I nodded. "A little bit, yeah."

"So…are we ok? Are we going to give this another shot?"

"Sure."

"That was a very noncommittal response."

"Yes, we are going to give this another shot," I tried again.

There was a brief pause in the conversation as we both sipped our coffee and looked at each other, waiting for the other to say something.

Sam broke the awkward pause with, "So, how's Trent?" There was a bitter tone to his voice.

My heart was instantly in my throat and I was flooded with guilt. "He's good. Things are better now."

"What does that mean for me?" he asked. "I mean, I hate to sound selfish, but is he going to be a problem for me?"

"No, he won't be a problem. He actually…well, he wants to meet you."

"So he knows about me, then?"

"Of course. He just can't wait to see me settled with someone, I think."

"…Really? Is this the same Trent…?"

"Yep. There's only one Trent. It's all good, Sam. Don't worry, I told him it probably wasn't a good idea if you two met right now."

"No, actually I'd like to meet him. Put a face to the name. It'd be nice to know what exactly I'm up against."

"It isn't a competition," I said with a sigh. "He's just a friend."

"That's not a reassuring line. 'He's just a friend.' In my experience, he's never 'just a friend.'"

"I don't know what you want me to tell you."

"The truth would be nice."

"The truth is that he and I would never work. Ok? He wants to see me with someone else."

"And what do you want?"

"'Wow.'"

Sam looked at me strangely. "Wow what?"

I sighed. "Nothing. I just want to be happy."

"What's it going to take to make you happy?" Sam wanted to know.

I looked across the room at nothing in particular. "I don't know. I'm still working that out."

"Am I wasting your time, Roselyn?" Sam asked bluntly.

I looked back at him. He looked to be on the verge of defeat. "No, you aren't wasting anybody's time. I'm sorry. I don't mean to be so cynical. I'm just trying to figure out what I want out of life, I suppose."

"I can get behind that. Hell, I'm thirty-seven and I'm still trying to figure out what I want to do when I grow up," Sam chuckled.

I smiled. "I'm still wondering when I'm going to start feeling like a grown up."

Sam laughed. "I know what you mean. I swear I'm still the same guy who was getting my old Chevy stuck in the mud somewhere out in the woods on the way to a bonfire in high school. The only thing that's changed is the truck is newer, the 'night moves' aren't as awkward, and now I'm the one kicking people out of the bar instead of the one getting kicked out."

"Did you and I go to the same high school or what?" I joked. "Man, it feels like just yesterday. I can't believe how long it's actually been. It's scary how fast the time flies by."

"Yeah. I'm creeping closer to forty now, and I'm still not sure how I feel about that."

"They say forty is the new twenty."

"Well, let's hope 'they' are right. I do what I can to turn back the clock, but when your hair is more gray than brown, it's hard to deny that time is indeed marching forward."

I looked at his brown manbun. "Your hair isn't gray."

"Oh, it is. Thankfully, though, they make this awesome product called hair dye. Could be worse, I suppose. At least I'm not going bald."

"I bet you'd look good if you let the gray show."

"You'd be wrong," Sam laughed. "The woman who used to cut my hair would laugh every time she got the clippers into it because all the gray would pop out as soon as the hair over it was trimmed. She said I looked twenty years older after my haircut. That's why I decided to grow it out."

"You grew your hair out because your hair stylist was making fun of you?" I asked.

"No, I grew it out so I wouldn't have to dye it after every cut. It looks good like this, though, right?" Sam asked with a wink.

I laughed. "It does. I can't argue with that."

Sam accompanied me to the grocery store up the road. It wasn't terribly exciting, but I was surprised by what a pleasant day it turned out to be. I noticed as we walked through the aisles, there were a couple of women who quite openly checked out Sam as we passed. He didn't seem to notice. It was kind of satisfying.

After we went through the checkout, he helped me carry my groceries to my car. "You are a very efficient shopper," he said as he put the bags in the trunk.

"How so?"

"In and out without a fuss. I like it."

"I hate grocery shopping. I like to get it over with as quickly as possible."

"You were so focused you didn't even notice the guy at the deli checking you out."

I laughed. "He did not."

"He did. Don't worry, though. I threw some shade his way." He demonstrated a stern look for me.

"Very intimidating. I'm sure you really showed him," I jested.

"I did. He was scared."

I chuckled. I looked up at the sky, watching the heavy snow starting to fall. "So, did you want a ride home?"

"Nah, I'll run it. But I would like to see you for dinner soon."

"Smooth transition," I said.

"It was, wasn't it? So what do you say?"

I nodded. "Yeah, we can do that. I think I'm pretty much open all week after work."

"Perfect. I'll text you."

Sam leaned down and kissed me casually on the lips. It was light and brief, just a peck, if you will, but it surprised me.

It surprised me because I didn't like it.

He waved as he put his earphones in and jogged off across the road. I climbed into my car and headed home. I spent the ride wondering what the hell was wrong with me. Sam looked good on paper. He was charming and handsome, was built like an athlete, made an absurd amount of money as a bartender, drove a nice vehicle, and had his own house. He seemed like a genuinely nice guy and I enjoyed myself when I was around him.

Best of all, he really liked me. Why couldn't I just let myself fall for him? It shouldn't be this hard.

I just needed time. Maybe he would grow on me, like Trent did. I didn't like Trent all that much when I first met him, did I? Granted, I had warmed up to Trent immensely quicker than I was warming up to Sam, but it could happen. Trent was what I wanted, but Sam was what I needed. It was time I accepted it and quit fighting it.

The next few days were the epitome of normalcy, and it bored the hell out of me. I went back to work and made up some story about a dead grandmother to explain my week off. Well, I didn't make the story up, exactly, because my grandmother had died just as I said she did. It had just happened several years earlier. My boss and my clients were glad to have me back, though. Since I didn't really have friends, it felt good to know I was missed by someone other than just Sam.

On Friday after work, I'd made plans to get dinner with Sam. I met him at the same restaurant we had been at before. When living in a small town, variety is, unfortunately, severely lacking. When I arrived, he was waiting for me at the entrance, looking dashing in dark gray slacks and a matching suit vest. His burgundy tie was neatly tucked under the vest and contrasted nicely with his light gray oxford shirt.

He held the door open for me. "You look absolutely stunning," he said with a charming smile.

I laughed. "I feel a bit out of place in this dress." I looked around at the patrons eating dinner in their jeans and t-shirts. I was wearing a long-sleeved, somewhat form-fitting pink and black midthigh-length dress with tall black boots. I could feel the eyes on me as we were led to our seat. "I feel like everyone is staring at me," I whispered.

"There's nothing wrong with that," he replied. "I can't really blame them. You're gorgeous."

I smiled uncomfortably and sat down at the table. Compliments always made me feel awkward. "You look great, too," I said.

After we ordered our food and handed our menus back to the waiter, Sam looked me in the eye and said, "I'd like for you to meet my parents."

I almost choked on my own saliva. "What?! Why?"

He scrunched his face. "What do you mean 'why?' Isn't that what people do?"

"Yeah, but not until things get serious."

"You don't feel like this is getting serious?" Sam sounded surprised.

I didn't know how to respond. "Well, I'm not saying that, exactly…I just…I don't know, it's only been a few weeks, you know? And it hasn't all been smooth sailing, either."

Sam raised his eyebrow and leaned forward. "It's been over a month. And I've been happier with you over the past month than I've been in a long time. I know it isn't perfect all the time, but that's part of getting to know each other. Don't you feel the same? Aren't you ready to take the next step and make our relationship official?"

"You're asking me to be your girlfriend?"

Sam nodded hopefully.

I felt put on the spot. "Oh. Um. Yeah, sure. I mean yes, of course. That would be…great."

Sam looked unconvinced. "If you want to wait, that's ok, too. I'm ok with that. If we aren't both in the same place yet, I don't want to force it."

I waved my hands. "No, no, I didn't mean to sound so noncommittal. I'm ok with it. We can take the next step. I just wasn't prepared for the whole parents thing," I said with a nervous laugh.

Sam smiled. "That's ok, we can wait to meet the parents if you want." Then I saw Sam's gaze shift as his face took on a puzzled look. "Wow. And you thought you were out of place in your outfit. Get a load of that guy," Sam said as he subtly nodded in the direction behind me.

I turned and looked behind me just in time to catch eyes with Trent.

Chapter 16

Trent raised his eyebrows and smiled, raising his hand enthusiastically at me to indicate that he had found me. I gave him an embarrassed smile and turned back to Sam as Trent approached the table.

"Why is he coming toward us? Do you know him?" Sam asked, looking confused.

Before I had a chance to answer, Trent was at the table. "Hello!" he said, barely glancing at me as he focused his attention on Sam.

Sam stood up from his scat. "What do you want?" he asked curtly.

Trent held his hand out and smiled amicably. "You must be Sam. You're much…larger than I had imagined," Trent said as he looked up at Sam, who had a good six inches and at least five stones on him. Trent looked over at me with a quick frown. "You didn't tell me he was so annoyingly handsome."

Sam looked to me for an explanation, his face contorted in puzzlement.

"Sam, this is Trent. Trent, this is Sam." *Dear lord, this isn't happening right now.*

Sam looked at Trent's hand hesitantly before shaking it. "I've, uh…I've heard about you," Sam said.

"So I am to understand," Trent said, wringing his hands uneasily. He suddenly turned to me with his finger in the air. "Oh! Before I forget! It turns out that it *was* me! When you asked if I had been here and I said no – it just hadn't happened yet! I got the time wrong on my first attempt at getting here. Kind of funny, isn't it?"

"What the hell is he talking about?" Sam asked. I could tell his patience was running thin.

"Nothing, it was just some stupid thing we were talking about the other day," I said to Sam. To Trent, I asked, "What are you doing here?"

"You weren't answering your phone," Trent said.

"I shut it off because I'm on a date! It couldn't wait?"

"I seem to have misplaced a rather important item," Trent said sheepishly. "Have you seen the watch?"

I looked down at his wrist. "It's right there," I said flatly.

"Don't be daft. Obviously I'm not talking about this one. The other one."

"Oh, the faulty one? No. I don't have it."

"Bollocks," Trent said, biting his knuckle. "This never happens. How could I lose it? I don't *lose* things."

"Trent?" I said, trying to get his attention.

He looked at me like he suddenly remembered I was still there. "Yes?"

"Can we maybe talk about this later?"

"Oh!" Trent pointed at Sam. "Yes! Sorry! My apologies! You two have fun!" Trent winked at me as he left in as much of a whirlwind as he had arrived.

I looked at Sam apologetically. "I am *so* sorry about that."

"Is he always like that?" Sam asked.

"Yeah, pretty much."

"Did he call me 'annoyingly handsome'?"

I pressed my lips together and nodded. "Yes, yes he did."

"I don't…what the hell just happened?"

"Yeah, he has that effect on people. I'm so sorry."

"Are all of your friends like that?"

"No. Well, I don't really have other friends. He was actually the first friend I made after my divorce. I wasn't allowed to have friends when I was married."

"How on Earth did you become friends with that guy? I mean, that must be one hell of a story."

"He, um…he helped me find a solution for a pest problem when I first moved into my new house. We just kind of stayed friends after that."

"He's an exterminator?"

I raised my eyebrows. "I suppose you could say that. Just don't call him that to his face."

It took a while to get the date back on track after that. By the end of the night, however, Sam was at ease again. When he walked me out to my car, he lingered by my door as I unlocked it. When I opened it and turned to tell him goodnight, he slipped his hand around my waist and pulled me to him. His lips bumped against mine and his tongue invaded my mouth. I kissed him back with as much enthusiasm as I could muster, but I knew I was probably giving a lackluster performance.

When he finished the kiss, he looked down at me. "Is everything all right?"

"Yes. I'm just sorry about having our date interrupted. I feel badly about that."

"It wasn't your fault. It's not like it was ruined. Don't worry about it," Sam said reassuringly.

"I'll make sure he doesn't do that next time."

"Speaking of next time, I have tomorrow night off. I was wondering if maybe you wanted to try a do-over of the night things went a little sideways – see if we can get it right this time."

I knew this moment was going to come eventually. I nodded. "Yeah, we can do that. If you want to come to my house again, I can do up those ribeyes we picked out at the store."

"That'd be fantastic. I'll see you tomorrow, beautiful." Sam leaned down and kissed me again before we parted ways.

When I got home, I called Trent at that wonky number he had. Instead of answering, however, he just appeared in my living room.

"Did you find it?" he asked eagerly.

"No. It's not here. I don't know what you did with it. Did you check the pockets of your suits?"

"Yes! All of them! I've looked everywhere. I'm beginning to worry that perhaps I didn't just misplace it. What if someone took it?"

"Who would take it?"

"I don't know, but it wouldn't be anyone we'd *want* to have it," he said.

"Can't you use your watch to locate it?"

"Not unless someone uses it to time travel or teleport. I didn't have a chance to sync it with my watch."

"Well, at least you know no one is using it."

Trent tilted his head to the side. "There is that, I suppose."

"I'm sure it'll turn up."

"I don't do things like this. I can't believe this happened," Trent said, starting to pace. He looked unusually bothered.

"You said that at the restaurant. You've never misplaced anything? Surely in six hundred years you must have lost something."

"This is different. It's important. I don't lose important things."

"It's ok, Trent."

"It's not ok. What if I've forgotten? What if I did something with it and I've forgotten? What if that means I'm getting ready to change again?" Trent looked at me with panic in his eyes.

My heart stopped at the thought of him changing. "But…I thought you didn't have any warning before you changed."

"Not that I've ever noticed, but it doesn't mean there aren't subtle warning signs that I've just been missing."

"Don't panic. Please, just sit down."

"I don't want to change. I don't want to do it again," Trent said, distress etched deeply into his features. He looked at me with his eyebrows curved upwards. "I don't want to leave you yet. I'm not ready."

He was filling me with anxiety, but I put on the bravest face I could compose. I stepped up to him and put my hands on either side of his face. "Stop. Stop it right now. You aren't going anywhere. You don't have my permission to change yet."

Trent gave a short laugh and smiled at me with sad eyes. "If anyone could stop the inevitable, it would be you."

"Then stop worrying about it, ok?"

"I'm sorry. I'm ruining your night yet again, aren't I?" Trent sat down on the couch and rested his giant foot on his narrow knee, exhaling heavily.

"It's all right. Everything's fine. You know, Sam really didn't know what to think of you tonight."

"He wasn't what I was expecting, either. He's a bit older than you, isn't he?"

"…Says the six-hundred-year-old man."

"And he's big! I think he could beat me up. I don't say that often, but I'm fairly certain he could do it. And I'd probably cut my hand on that chiseled jawline if I tried to hit him back. Are you sure he isn't genetically engineered, too?"

"I know. He's uncommonly perfect, isn't he?" I said with a downward inflection.

"You make it sound like that's a bad thing."

"It's not a bad thing. I'm just having a hard time convincing myself to fall in love with him."

"Who says you have to fall in love with him? There are other men out there."

"Yeah, there are, but not a lot of good ones."

"Did you want me to steal you one from another time? Another region?" Trent teased.

I laughed. "No. I'm sure he'll do. I just need time to get used to him."

Trent looked at me hesitantly. "Can I raise a little flag of warning here?"

"What is it?"

"Falling in love is supposed to be the easy part. Staying in love is where it gets tough. If you're having a hard time with the first step, what makes you think it's going to work at all? And, I hate to be the one to say it, but...what about Sam's feelings? How would he feel if he knew how you really felt?"

"I know. Nobody wants to be the silver medal. The only thing worse than settling is finding out *you* were the one they settled for. I know all of this. Trust me, I've thought about it and felt guilty for it. But what am I supposed to do? When you can't be with the one you love, love the one you're with, right? Fake it 'til you make it."

Trent looked at me with disappointment. "That isn't the Roselyn I know."

I gave him a humorless smile. "We all do things we aren't proud of, don't we?"

Trent broke eye contact with me and looked down at his hands. "You're thinking that this isn't any of my business, aren't you?"

"Yes."

"I see. Well, I do wish you all the best, Roselyn. I just want you to be happy."

"I know. But maybe you should focus on finding that watch for now and let me focus on me."

Trent nodded. "Point taken. Again, I'm sorry about tonight."

"It's all right. But I should warn you that Sam is coming over for dinner and a movie tomorrow. You probably shouldn't pop in tomorrow evening...or the morning after."

Trent's jaw visibly clenched as he stood up from the couch. He avoided my eyes. "Oh. Yes, I understand. I'll stay out of your hair. I wouldn't want to…interrupt," he said with a hint of disdain.

"You want me to love someone else, Trent. You know that involves other activities too."

"Except you *don't* love him."

"Someday I will."

"If you say so," Trent said cynically.

"Jesus, Trent. Isn't this what you wanted?" I confronted him.

"Not this!" he shouted suddenly. "Not for you to go through the motions of love with someone that doesn't make you happy. Not for you to pretend. I want you to find the real thing."

"I did! Remember? But that didn't work out, now did it? So you don't get a say anymore!"

Trent's nostrils flared and he threw his hands in the air dramatically as he started pacing about the room. "Yes, of course, throw it in my face yet again why don't you? Everything is my fault, isn't it? I ruined you – is that it?!"

"Yes! That is *exactly* it!" I shouted.

Trent rubbed both hands down his face in frustration. He took a deep breath. "And what, exactly, do you think you've done to *me*?" he asked between clenched teeth.

I was taken aback. I stared at him with my mouth slightly agape.

"Oh, you never considered that, did you?" he continued. "Maybe if you'd pull your head out of your own perfect arse for five bloody minutes you'd realize that you aren't the only person in the world who has feelings! This isn't easy for me either! You think I enjoy the thought of another man doing the things to you that I…I can't even say it. I can't! I don't want to even think about it! But you know what? At least I'm *trying*. I'm doing my best for you because that's what you *need me to do*. So don't you dare try to tell me that I don't get a say anymore." Trent stepped in front of me, bending down slightly so that he was at eye level with me. "I gave you up, even though it *kills* me every second of every day, because it was the right thing to do. I *will not* stand here and let you act like I don't care!" he said, pointing to the ground.

I didn't know what to say. I fumbled for the words. "No, I...I never...I didn't say you didn't care. Not for one second did I ever think you didn't care. I just...I thought you were having an easier time letting me go because..." my voice trailed off.

"Because I don't feel as deeply as you do?"

"I don't know. Maybe."

"After everything we've been through? After all the times I've expressed how important you are to me? I don't know how you can possibly believe that."

"When you've spent the last several years of your life being manipulated to feel like no one could ever love you, you tend to fall back on the notion that people don't care all that much about you. It's just what I do. I don't want to feel that way. I'm not trying to use it as an excuse to be difficult. As much as I hate it, it's just who I am now."

Trent grasped his chin, resting his elbow on the wrist of his other folded arm. "You know, you and I are like sodium and water. Put us together and *boom*!" Trent threw his arms around wildly to imitate an explosion. "Instant, intense reaction! Sometimes it's a good intense, sometimes a not so good intense. It's both exhilarating and exhausting."

I couldn't deny it was true. In an effort to slow the current "reaction," I said, "So, I guess the real question is: which one of us is the sodium?"

241

Trent looked at me and grinned, and the tension in the room was instantly lifted. "If only we had a little chlorine, we could have the *solution*," he joked.

"Let's try not to be so *salty*," I laughed.

Trent clapped his hands together and pointed at me with a chuckle. "Nice."

If there was one thing I could say for Trent and me, it was that we didn't stay angry with each other for long. We always found a way out of it. One of us always relented. We knew when the flash of anger had run its course, and we let it die before too many hurtful things were said. It was why we could still be friends despite all the tension that had built up between us. And to be honest, I think we both kind of enjoyed the occasional explosion.

"Well, I should probably go before we find something else to argue about," Trent said. I saw his eyes quickly look me up and down. "You look fetching tonight, by the way. I couldn't tell you that earlier because Sam probably would've punched me, but I wanted to."

I felt my cheeks getting hot. "Thank you. I don't think you've ever seen me in a dress."

"I haven't. It's quite breathtaking," he said with a warm smile.

I blushed so hard my ears were on fire.

"Sorry, I didn't mean to embarrass you," Trent said. "I'll be off, now. See you in a while, Roselyn."

I gave him a little wave as he teleported out of the house. I didn't see him again before my date with Sam the following night.

When Sam showed up at my house for dinner, he was dressed a little more casually than he had been the night before. I was glad for that, because I was, too. But he looked handsome in his jeans and black polo shirt. He handed me a bouquet of red roses as I invited him into the house, and he kissed me lightly on the lips as he stepped inside. I turned away to go get a vase for the roses he'd brought while he was slipping his shoes off. As I turned, I unconsciously ran the back of my hand over my mouth.

"Did you just wipe off my kiss?" Sam asked.

"What? No. Did I? I didn't mean to!"

"Relax, I'm just kidding," Sam said.

I laughed uncomfortably. We weren't off to a great start.

"The steaks are ready," I said as I looked at the clock on the stove. "Your timing couldn't have been more perfect." I reached up into the cupboard above the fridge to grab a vase, but I couldn't quite reach it. As I started to climb onto the counter, I heard Sam laugh behind me.

"What are you doing?" he asked.

"I was getting a vase."

"Here, let me," he said, still chuckling. He reached up and easily grabbed the vase from the cupboard as I slid back down off the counter. He handed it to me with an amused grin.

"I could've gotten it," I said matter-of-factly as I filled it with water.

"I don't doubt it for a second. You're quite acrobatic."

"Um, thanks?" I said as I crinkled my nose. "Have a seat. Let's eat," I ordered.

I put the roses in the vase and set it on the table between our place settings. I then fixed a plate for Sam and brought it to him. I sat down with my plate and looked across the table at him – and all I saw were the roses.

Sam leaned over and peeked around the roses at me. "Mind if I slide these aside?" he asked with a chuckle. He moved the vase to the edge of the table. "There you are," he smiled.

"I hope you like your steak medium rare. It's the only way to eat a ribeye, if you ask me."

"That'll be perfect. It smells great."

I smiled politely and started to cut into my steak. Unfortunately, the sawing motion of our steak knives jostled my small table enough to shake the vase right off the edge. It crashed to the floor, shattering, and water splattered across the kitchen. I just stared at the mess in disbelief.

"I'm so sorry, that was my fault," Sam said as he jumped up to clean up the disaster.

"It's nobody's fault," I said. I grabbed a roll of paper towels and the garbage can and got down on my knees to help him carefully pick up shards of glass.

"No, you go ahead and eat," Sam said as he took the roll of paper towels from me. "Enjoy your steak while it's hot."

"If I help you, we'll get it cleaned up faster and we can *both* enjoy our steak while it's still hot."

"It's ok, I can get it."

I ignored him and kept cleaning. "I'm not about to let my guest clean up a mess while I sit and eat and watch. Don't be silly."

We went back and forth like that until all the glass was collected and the water had been sopped up. When we sat back down to eat, the steaks weren't quite as warm as I had hoped they'd be. Tonight was turning out to be a total catastrophe.

When we finished eating, I put our plates in the sink and looked at the roses I had tossed in the other side of the sink. There were tiny shards of glass interspersed throughout the foliage, so

I had figured I'd take care of them later. The way they sat there, though, looking so cast aside, it was a feeling all too familiar. They were so beautiful and elegant, but all it had taken was one little mishap and they'd wound up tossed carelessly in the damn sink. I left the dishes and the roses in the sink and went into the living room to pick out a movie with Sam.

As Sam and I sat next to each other on the couch, with Cattiel sitting on the couch opposite us, giving us the evil eye, I was keenly aware of Sam's hand on my thigh. Every time he moved, I tensed up. I wasn't even paying much attention to the superhero movie we were watching because I was too worried about what was coming next. I knew what was going to happen tonight. Sam knew what was going to happen tonight. I was just waiting nervously for it to begin. I had tried to prepare myself for it by thinking about it all day, but it hadn't helped at all. I hoped that I would be more into it when it actually happened. Sam was a devastatingly handsome man, and there was no reason I shouldn't be able to enjoy a night with him, right? I just had to relax and not think about Trent.

Except now I was thinking about Trent.

And then it happened. I got up to use the bathroom, and when I came out, Sam was leaned against the back side of the couch waiting for me near the hallway. I froze in the hallway, not sure what to do. Was I ready? He sauntered up to me and pulled me to him, kissing me softly.

"I'm not really into this movie anymore. What about you?" Sam whispered into my ear, then ran the tip of his tongue along the edge of my ear lobe.

I wrapped my arms around his thick neck. "I wasn't really into it from the beginning," I said. I was going for it. It was going to be great, and it was going to change everything. It had to. I just had to ignore the mildly empty feeling in the pit of my stomach.

Sam scooped me up in his arms and carried me back to my room. He reached over and flicked on the light switch as soon as he crossed the threshold. I reached back over and swiped the switch off.

"No lights?" Sam asked.

I didn't think I could handle lights tonight. Not yet. I was nervous enough as it was, and lights just made it worse. "No lights."

"Why?" he asked as he lowered my feet to the floor beside the bed.

"It's too distracting," I said. It wasn't entirely untrue.

"Fine. But next time, I want lights," Sam bargained.

Next time? He was already thinking about next time? "Deal," I said.

Sam leaned into me, and I backed up onto the bed. He climbed over top of me and kissed me. It wasn't the way Trent kissed me. It wasn't urgent, or hungry, or passionate. It was…mechanical. His technique was adequate, but there wasn't any fire behind it. He pulled away from me briefly to take his shirt off, so I took that opportunity to slip mine off as well. When he returned to me, he kissed me once, then wrapped his arm around me and rolled onto his back, pulling me on top of him.

I didn't want to be on top, but I tried to go along with it. I straddled his hips and kissed him again. I felt him pushing me away gently, so I sat back, trying to figure out what he wanted me to do.

"Let me look at you," he whispered. He reached up and lifted my bra, pushing it up awkwardly toward my neck. I quickly reached up and unhooked it, slipping it off. He ran his hand from the center of my chest all the way down my stomach to the waistband of my jeans. "God, your body is so tight. Look at those abs," he admired.

"Oh. Uh, thanks. It is kind of my job," I said with a forced giggle.

Sam unbuttoned my jeans, then sat up. He flipped me around onto my back again. I wasn't used to being moved around like this. It wasn't bad, it was just…different. He slipped my jeans off me and lowered his – but he didn't take them off all the way. He just pulled them down to his thighs. I heard him opening a wrapper, and I waited for him to roll on the prophylactic.

When he climbed on top of me again, I felt his manhood press against me – and it felt so wrong that it made my stomach turn.

"No, wait. No. Jesus, I'm so sorry. I can't do it," I cried as I scooted out from under him. I felt tears welling up in my eyes. *Oh god, don't cry. Don't cry. Don't cry.*

"What? Seriously? What's wrong?" Sam asked, flabbergasted.

"I'm not ready. I'm not ready for this yet. I'm so, so sorry," I apologized profusely.

Sam sighed as he pulled his pants up. "It's him, isn't it?" he asked knowingly. "The skinny weirdo in the hipster suit with the stupid hair. *Trent*," he said mockingly.

"I'm just not ready yet."

"I don't get it, Roselyn. What does he have that I don't? I seriously do *not* get it."

"I just need some time, Sam. I'll get there, I promise."

"No, you won't. As long as he's around, you won't."

Sam got up and stood next to the bed. He bent down and grabbed my jeans and underwear off the floor and handed them to me. I thanked him quietly and pulled them on.

"I'm trying, Sam," I said.

"You shouldn't have to try this hard," he replied sourly. "I never had a chance, did I?"

I chose not to answer him. I climbed off the bed on the opposite side from him and picked up his shirt from the floor. I tossed it across the bed to him and started searching for my bra.

"Hey, is my bra over there?" I asked embarrassedly when I couldn't find it on my side.

"I didn't see it. Get the light. I'll check under the bed over here."

I stepped over to the light switch and flicked it on, then crossed my arms self-consciously over my bare breasts.

"Oh, here it is," I heard Sam say from under the bed. Then, "What the heck is this?"

"What?"

Sam stood up, holding my bra in one hand, and a watch in the other. A look of realization crossed his features. He gave me a knowing look. "This is the watch he was looking for, isn't it? Hm, I wonder how it ended up under your bed," Sam said accusingly. He looked down at it, still holding my bra in his other hand, and wiped his finger over the face of it.

And then he disappeared – with my bra.

Chapter 17

"Sam!" I shrieked. *Oh shit oh shit oh shit oh shit—*

I heard my phone going off in the other room. I didn't even grab a shirt before I ran out to answer it. It was Trent.

"He disappeared!" I shouted into the phone frantically. "He found the watch, and it took him!"

Trent was in my living room instantly. He looked at me, looked down, and slapped his hands over his eyes. "Ah! Sorry! I didn't know you weren't decent!"

I grabbed his hands and pulled them down, all sense of modesty gone out the window. "Forget that! The watch took Sam! He's gone! We need to find him!"

"Yes, I got that! I saw the signal on my watch. Now please, go put a shirt on! I'll find him." Trent looked down at his watch, then back up at me. "I'm kind of relieved, to be honest. I was really starting to worry about what had happened to that wa—"

"You can be relieved after we get him back home!" I shouted down the hall as I ran quickly to my room to snatch my shirt.

"'We'?"

I threw my shirt over my head, running back down the hall while still putting it on, and I bumped blindly into Trent. I grabbed his arms. "Yes, 'we'! Let's go!"

"Hold on a tick! Who said you were going?"

"I did. You're wasting time, come on!"

"I'm not going to talk you out of this, am I?"

"No."

Trent sighed heavily as he walked past me down the hall to the bedroom. I saw him take a sideways glance at the rumpled bedding when he entered the room, but he didn't say anything. He looked down at his watch and moved around the room, like he was following a compass. He walked over to where Sam had disappeared and stopped.

"The trail's still fresh. Come on, we can follow him."

I threw my arms around Trent's torso, and we were teleported to – a familiar savannah-like landscape.

"Are…Are we in the Jurassic again?"

"We are," Trent said, looking down at his watch. "That's odd. This is almost exactly the time that we—OH!" Trent pointed at me with wide eyes.

"Wha—OH! Oh!" I threw my hand over my mouth as I put it together. "It was *him! Sam* was the man in the Jurassic!"

Trent laughed and threw his hands up. "Mystery solved!"

I looked around. "But…where'd he go?"

Trent looked down at his watch. "He teleported again. From over there," Trent said as he pointed off to his right. "We *just* missed him."

I followed him to the location Sam had teleported from, and I found my bra sitting on the ground.

"Oh, thank god. It was my favorite one," I said as I picked it up and shook it off. I then proceeded to put it on under my shirt while Trent looked on with one raised eyebrow. "What?" I asked defensively.

"Nothing. I'm not saying anything," he said, holding his palms up to me.

Trent and I followed Sam's trail and tracked him to a busy sidewalk. A woman wearing a weirdly baggy, pink sweater stopped abruptly and gasped as she almost ran into us.

"Sorry!" Trent said, looking up. "That was a farther drop than I thought it would be!" Trent ushered me away quickly while the woman looked up to where Trent had been looking, trying to figure out where we had jumped from.

"Is that how you explain it when you land in busy places?" I asked as we rounded the street corner.

"Sometimes. Sometimes I just act like it's a part of a magic trick. And sometimes I just run. Why do you think I'm such a matchstick? All the running!"

"Where are we going?" I asked. "Where did we end up?" I noticed everybody was wearing ugly baggy clothing, and a lot of women had shaved heads.

"We are in Germany, 2462. I'm not getting a signal. I don't think Sam has transported out of here yet, but I have no idea where he is. We'll have to find him the good old-fashioned way, I guess."

"He couldn't have gone too far," I reasoned.

"Well, he probably had about a thirty-minute head-start on us."

"Oh. Well, shit."

"Where would he go?" Trent asked me.

"How the hell should I know?"

"You know him."

"Yeah, but not *that* well. Not well enough to be able to guess where he would go."

"Well, you know him well enough to let him carry your bra around."

"Shut it," I said, jutting a finger at him.

"Maybe we should check out the nearest gyms. When people panic, they head for familiar territory," Trent said, half-joking.

"Oh! A bar! Maybe he'd go to a bar!" I suggested.

"Really? A bar is familiar territory for him?"

"He's a bartender! Hell, I think anyone would seek out a place to drink in this situation."

"Oh wait! He's moved again," Trent said, looking down at his watch and holding his finger up to halt me. "Oh, bugger. We'd better hurry. The trail is across town."

With all this running, I was glad I had found my bra.

When we made it to the next trail, Trent said, "It's growing faint. If we fall too far behind him, we'll lose him. Just imagine the kind of damage he could do to Earth's timeline bumbling around with a device he doesn't understand. We need to hurry."

When we teleported this time, we landed in what appeared to be a big aquarium. I looked at the tanks around us, and while there were some familiar creatures, such as sharks and octopi, there were also creatures I had never seen before. Creatures that didn't look of this world. As I turned around to see the tanks behind me, I saw a sight I never thought I would see outside of a movie theater. There were a family admiring the sharks in a tank – but it wasn't an ordinary family. They weren't *people*. They were anthropomorphic, but they weren't human.

They appeared to be...alien. They were quite short, only about four feet tall, and they had blueish colored skin. They had freakishly large, gold-colored eyes, and when they turned those eyes toward me, I quickly looked over at Trent. He was staring at them also, his eyes wide.

I elbowed him. He looked at me and a huge grin spread across his face. "Something new!" he whispered in wonderment. "I love new things!"

"Where the hell are we?!" I asked. "Are we still on Earth?!"

"Yes!" He looked down at his watch. "But we are way beyond where I have ever been. This is 5211!" He rubbed his fingers together and looked around eagerly, as though he were trying to decide what to investigate first.

"Focus, Trent! We need to find Sam. He's probably freaking the hell out right about now."

"Oh! Right!" Trent looked down at his watch again. "Well, he hasn't left yet."

"Why would he stay *here*? Why wouldn't he have tried to teleport out of here right away?"

"He's probably getting scared he's going to end up somewhere even weirder. There are two kinds of panic, Roselyn. The frantic kind, and the shut-down kind. It looks like Sammy may be experiencing the shut-down kind."

"Is that a good thing or a bad thing?"

"That's a good thing. If he starts mashing buttons on that watch in a frantic panic, who knows what will happen. If he just stops and freezes up, we've got a much better chance of finding him. Now, come on. Let's explore – *carefully*. He might still be in here."

I hooked my arm through Trent's and walked alongside him through the aquarium. I marveled at the strange creatures in the tanks and the even stranger creatures walking around the aquarium with us. There were plenty of people in the aquarium too, but they weren't like the people I was used to seeing. Everyone was unusually similar and unusually perfect. Everyone had skin the color of caramel, and everyone had short hair. Men and women both wore similarly styled, extremely form-fitting clothing. They reminded me of the synsuits from Trent's time, except they didn't cover from head to toe, they were more colorful, and made of a thinner material. Trent and I stood out like a sore thumb, and we got a lot of strange looks.

There were almost as many of the little blue people with the gold eyes as there were humans. They dressed like the people did, apparently sharing the same fashion preferences. I wondered how much of the culture was shared between the humans and the little people. I wondered where these little creatures had come from. Were they alien? Were they a species of Earth? Were they some other kind of creation entirely? I wanted to query Trent for his thoughts on the subject, but I noticed that no one in the building was talking. I heard a giggle or a sneeze or a cough here and there, but no one was *talking*. I would catch people nodding and smiling at each other, as though they were having some kind of private conversation, but no words were passing their lips.

Once we made it all the way through the aquarium and determined that Sam wasn't in the building, Trent was ready to see the world outside. He had spent a lot of his time in the aquarium staring at his watch rather than looking at the exhibits and the animals, and he seemed eager to share something with me. When we walked outside, though, we found it to be eerily silent out there, too. Birds weren't singing. People weren't

254

talking. The streets were filled with small, pod-like vehicles that were quietly floating a few inches off the ground on some kind of track. Life was bustling all around us, but it sounded like we were in a monestary. I looked up at Trent for answers.

He raised his eyebrow at me and smiled. He pulled a device out of his pocket, and I recognized it as the translator he had given me when we had gone to his time. He took my hand and opened my palm. He set the device in my hand and then used the watch on it the same way he had used the watch on my phone when he programmed it to call the past. When he was done, he gestured for me to put it in my ear. I placed it in my ear and Trent reached over and tapped it.

My world was suddenly filled with sound. Advertisements blared at me from unseen solicitors while music played in the background, and I could hear a robotic woman's voice notifying me that I had message requests. I looked at Trent with wide eyes. I pulled the device out of my ear, overwhelmed by the sudden sensory overload. Trent took the translator from my hand and stuck it in his own ear. He listened for a moment, then held his watch up to his ear, apparently making programming adjustments.

When he was done, he grinned and whispered, "This is really quite brilliant, but it's only half of the sensory unit. You need the eyepiece, too."

"How do you know all this? Have you been here before?" I asked.

"No. I've been collecting data," Trent answered.

He slipped on his glasses and activated the holographic display on his watch. It showed a screen similar to what you'd see on an internet browser – several tabs open to messenger-like applications, advertisements, sound options, and captions and

255

links displayed over everything we could see through the hologram. It was real-time internet and social media, basically.

I leaned closer to Trent, noticing the people staring at us. It was probably unusual for them to see people actually *talking* to each other. I whispered as quietly and discreetly as I could, "Sam isn't going to have any idea what the hell is going on. He's going to look like a crazy person to these people."

"All the easier for us to find him, then," Trent said. He tapped the device in his ear and started manipulating the display on his watch.

"What are you doing?" I asked.

"Searching."

Trent started walking down the absurdly clean and smooth sidewalk, still focused on his watch. I walked alongside him and tried to keep him from running into the little people that were below his line of vision.

"Aha!" he shouted suddenly.

Everyone around us turned and looked at him. He cringed and held his hand up with an apologetic smile. When everyone turned away again, he took off across the street at a rapid pace, and I had a hard time keeping up with him without running. He weaved through the people on the sidewalk, his eyes darting from his watch display to his surroundings and back again. He reminded me of a bloodhound hot on the trail of a wanted criminal.

Finally, he stopped. So abruptly, in fact, that I ran right into him. I looked up at him, and saw he was pointing. I followed the direction of his finger with my eyes and saw Sam standing among a group of people, trying to talk to them. He waved his hands around, gesturing wildly, apparently assuming that they either couldn't hear him or didn't understand him. They all looked at him curiously, but no one was speaking to him. They just stared. Some of them were smiling in amusement at his behavior. Trent grabbed my hand and we rushed to Sam.

When he saw us approaching, he looked briefly relieved, then angry. "What the hell is going on?!" he demanded.

Trent shushed him as he deactivated the holographic display on his watch. He then snatched up Sam's arm and inspected his wrist, and I saw that Sam was wearing the watch he had found under my bed. He quickly unhooked it and pulled it off Sam's wrist.

"Don't shush me! What are you doing?!"

Without responding, Trent grabbed Sam and me and pulled us in close to him, as though we were going in for a huddle. We were instantly back in my bedroom. Trent turned and walked out of the room without a word, looking down at his watch and the watch he had taken from Sam.

I looked over at Sam hesitantly. "So…the dinosaurs were cool, hey?"

Sam stared at me like I had lost my damn mind. "What was that?! Where was I? What the hell did that watch do?!"

"Ok, calm down. I'll explain. Um…ok…where do I begin? You were time traveling. You went to the Jurassic. You saw Trent and me there, actually. Well, not us from right now, but us from a few weeks ago. It was me before you met me. But that's a whole different story for another time. Anyway, you then went into the future. The last place we were in was…what, like three thousand years from now I think? I don't remember. It was something like that."

"…What?!"

"The watch is a time-travel device. Trent has one that he created a long time ago – well, in the future, but a long time ago

257

to him – oh! And it's also a teleportation device. He can go anywhere or anywhen."

"Anywhen isn't a word!" Sam shouted, extending his arms dramatically. "None of this makes any sense!"

"Anywhen most certainly is a word," Trent said from the doorway. I turned and saw him leaning casually against the door jamb. He slid his glasses off and stuck them in his breast pocket. "And it all makes perfect sense."

"You just aren't quite there yet," I added.

Sam pointed at Trent and me. "You're both completely insane. I don't want any part of this!" He brushed past me and bumped Trent's shoulder roughly on his way out of the bedroom.

"Wait!" I shouted, following after him. "Don't you have questions?"

Sam stopped and turned. "Yeah, I do have a question: can I leave now?!"

I knitted my brow. "That's it? Really? You aren't even the slightest bit curious about what just happened?"

"I don't need to know! I just want to forget it, ok? And I never want to see you again. This has been the absolute worst day I've ever had, and that's saying a lot. Goodbye, Roselyn."

"Sam!" I said, reaching for him.

Trent grabbed my arm and stopped me. "Let him go," he said calmly.

Sam looked at us. "Yeah, listen to your boyfriend," he said snidely. He slipped his coat on, and as he walked out the door into the night, he added, "And lose my number."

I couldn't say I blamed him. I didn't understand how he couldn't be curious about what he'd just experienced, but I couldn't blame him for not wanting to have any part of it. I couldn't blame him for not wanting to see me again, especially after what had happened between us before he had found the watch under the bed. I wouldn't want to see me again either. I wasn't particularly upset about it, but I would be lying if I said it didn't hurt my feelings just a little bit. Sam wasn't a bad guy. He just wasn't the right guy for me, and that was now more obvious than ever. I couldn't be with someone who lacked imagination and curiosity. I couldn't be with someone who wouldn't be able to eventually accept that my life was a little bit…exciting.

"I'm sorry," Trent said softly.

"Sorry for what? You didn't do anything."

"I was careless. If I hadn't lost the watch under the bed, none of this would've happened."

"Yeah, well, the watch wouldn't have gotten lost under the bed if I hadn't invited you into my room that night, but I don't regret doing that."

"So…did Sam find the watch in the same manner that I lost it?" Trent asked.

"Um…"

"Sorry, that's none of my business," Trent said, holding a palm up to stop me from responding.

"It didn't happen," I blurted.

"Beg pardon?"

"I didn't…I didn't go through with it. I couldn't do it."

"Oh." Trent sounded almost pleased.

"It just didn't feel right. I'm beginning to think that maybe you *have* ruined me," I said, trying to make it sound like a joke, but finding a great deal of truth in those words.

Trent didn't laugh. He smiled dryly and said, "You'll find someone. He just wasn't right for you."

"Evidently. If he can't handle a little bit of unexpected time travel, then obviously he just can't hang with us."

"Am I a problem, Roselyn?" Trent asked suddenly.

"What do you mean?"

"Am I screwing up your life?"

I scowled at him. "Don't you dare. Don't even think about it. If you care about me, you won't even think about leaving again."

"Just because you care about someone doesn't mean you should stick around and screw up their life."

"Too late for that. That ship has sailed. I can't go back to a time before you shattered my narrow view of the world. I can't go back to a time before you showed me what real passion felt like. You've already destroyed any chance I have at being happy with a normal life. You have already planted yourself firmly in my heart, whether either of us intended for it to happen or not. So, yeah, if you care about me, you will stick around and continue to screw up my life – because I kind of love it."

Trent laughed softly.

"Ok?" I asked, looking for an indication that he understood me.

"Ok," he said with a smile.

"Guess what?" I asked in a playful tone, trying to lighten the mood.

"What?"

"I bought toaster pastries," I said with a big grin as I rushed into the kitchen and threw open the cupboard. I pulled out one of the noisy, crinkly packages and tossed it to Trent. "And wine! But that's for me," I added as I grabbed a goblet. When I passed the sink on the way to the fridge, I noticed the dirty dishes I had left in the sink. Then I saw the roses still sitting there. Tossed aside. Abandoned. Forgotten. All of this before they had even begun to wilt.

Like Sam.

I felt immediately guilty. I should be more upset about losing him, but all I felt was relief. I had thought I could make it work with him, but as soon as he had walked out that door, all I could think about was how much more time I could spend with Trent now. I knew I'd have to find someone eventually, but…not just yet. That could wait. I grabbed the roses and tossed them into the trash.

I poured myself a huge, brimming goblet of wine and sat down on the couch across from the chair where Trent was sitting with his toaster pastries. I brought the bottle with me.

"That place we visited – the one way into the future – that was absolutely wild," I said.

Trent raised his eyebrows. "I know!" he exclaimed, a few crumbs of pastry flying from his mouth in his enthusiasm.

"What were those little blue people?" I asked.

"I don't know! They weren't like anything I've ever seen before! I tried to scan one of them discreetly when we were in the aquarium, but they were far too wary of us. All I was able to pick up was that they aren't DNA-based life forms. Whether they were synthetically created life or alien life is still unclear."

"Why did all the human people look the way they did? Why was everybody so…similar?"

"I'm not sure. People don't look like that in my time. I'm guessing maybe they've created synthetic bodies and that just happens to be the 'style' they chose. In my time, they regrow tissue that becomes damaged or old, but maybe they've replaced that system with synthetic bodies. They would be much more durable, I imagine, and it would make it easier to link them all together through a common network."

"It was like they were living in Facebook."

"Basically, yes."

I took a big gulp of wine and looked at the smile on Trent's face. "You had fun in the future, didn't you?"

"It was wildly exciting!"

"Are you going to go back?"

"Oh, no, I can't do that. I had to go to retrieve Sam, and that was the only reason I went."

"The world didn't fall into chaos. Don't you think you could venture into the future just a little bit? Just occasionally?"

"It's a bad idea. We've discussed this."

"I know. But some of the best ideas are bad ones," I said. "You've obviously never been a rebellious teenager."

"No, not really. Not in the way you were. But I do know plenty about rebellion and bad ideas – I'd even venture to say I've had more experience with bad ideas than you have."

"Oh yeah?" I challenged. I finished my glass of wine and poured another while Trent looked on.

"Yeah. And hanging out with you is on the top of that list," Trent teased.

I laughed. "If you're waiting for me to contradict you, you're going to be waiting a while." I took a drink. "But you like it."

"Yeah, I kind of do," he admitted with a grin.

"Seriously, though, Trent. You should really start thinking about the future."

He laughed out loud. "I feel like you're about to give me a talk about savings accounts."

I laughed. "I'm just trying to point out that you've already been to the year 5000-something, so you already know what's going to happen then. What's wrong with going back and sight-seeing?"

"I don't know what happens. I just got a small snippet of it. There's still a whole lot of damage that could be done if I went back."

"If you do, then change it! If you have to actively stop SABER from going back in time and changing things, then obviously it's something that can be done. The past can be changed, and so can the future."

"Yes, it can be changed. But you never know what you are changing. You never know what the outcome will be…and I shouldn't be the one to decide what to change."

"You decide to stop SABER. Doesn't the very act of stopping them from changing things change things?"

"Yes, in a way, but it's a corrective change – like if someone nudges a steering wheel and you nudge it back. I'm not actively picking out the route."

"Then who is?"

"Humankind. Not SABER, and certainly not Trent Morgan," he said. "No one person should have that power. I think that's what scares me most – seeing a future that I want to change, knowing I have the capability to change it, but also knowing that I shouldn't. It's hard enough wrestling with the moral ambiguity of keeping the past unchanged. I don't need to have the future on my conscience, too."

"You're kind of like a god," I said.

"No, I'm not. I don't want to be a god."

"I want to be a god."

"I think you should slow down on the wine."

"…I think you're right."

Chapter 18

Trent got up and coaxed the glass from my hand, but not before I downed the rest of its contents. He grabbed the bottle off the floor next to the couch and took it into the kitchen.

"This bottle is almost empty," he chided.

"I only had two glasses," I said defensively.

"Two fish bowls is more like it," he mumbled.

A few moments later I heard dishes clanking. I craned my neck and looked over into the kitchen.

"What are you doing?"

"Nothing." I could see him putting dishes in the dishwasher.

"I was going to do that," I said.

"You do it wrong. How do you always do this wrong?" He was pulling things out and rearranging everything I had in the dishwasher.

"Dude, just leave it," I said.

He stopped and looked at me indignantly. "Did you just call me *dude*?!"

I laughed. "Sorry. *Kind sir*, please leave it."

Trent nodded his head approvingly. "That's better. But no. I must remedy this atrocity."

"You're cleaning up dishes I dirtied while having a date with someone else. Doesn't that bother you? Even a little?"

"I'm not your boyfriend."

"I know, but...don't you ever think about it? What it would be like if you were my boyfriend?" I leaned my head back against the couch and closed my eyes as I talked. My eyelids were suddenly heavy.

"I try not to."

"Why?"

"There's no point to it. It isn't going to happen, so why think about it?"

"You know what I think? I think it would be a lot like it already is. I think you and I are already bound to each other. It masquerades as friendship, but we both know what it really is. We're just trying to put off the inevitable."

The silence in the kitchen lasted so long that I had actually started to drift off to sleep. I was startled awake when I heard Trent say, "When you find someone, it won't feel this way anymore."

"Hm? Feel what way?" I was trying to remember what we had been talking about before I fell asleep. The wine was fogging my memory.

I heard Trent sigh. "Never mind. You should go to bed."

"I should."

Trent came into the living room and handed me a large glass of water. "Drink this first, though."

"Why?"

"It'll keep you from getting dehydrated and having a headache in the morning."

"I'm not going to get a hangover from two glasses of wine."

"Just drink it. Doctor's orders."

I grabbed the glass from him and chugged it. I wiped my mouth on my sleeve and handed him back the empty glass. "Happy?"

"You can thank me later," he said as he took the glass back to the kitchen.

I stood up and stretched my arms, yawning. "I'm going to bed. I'm beat."

"Goodnight," Trent said as he shut off the lights in the kitchen and stepped back into the living room. He stood there with his hands in his pockets, looking at me. I could tell something was on his mind.

"Did I say something?" I asked. "You look like I killed your kitten."

"Eh, don't worry about it. I'll check in tomorrow and maybe we'll talk then."

I felt a sudden tightness in my chest. "What do you mean we'll talk then? Is there something we need to talk about?"

Trent looked down at the floor instead of at me. "I think maybe. But this isn't the time."

"No, don't do that. Don't do that shit," I said angrily. "Now I'm worried and I won't be able to sleep and I'll sit up all night fretting over what you want to talk about with me. You might as well just spill it now."

"I can't yet."

"Why?"

"Because I'm not sure what it is I want to say yet."

"Give me something, Trent," I begged with watery eyes.

"I'd rather have this conversation when you have a clear head. I'll see you tomorrow. Goodnight." Trent held up his watch.

"Trent, wait!"

It was too late, though. He was already gone.

"Damn it!" I shouted. "Goddamn it, Trent!"

I lay awake in bed for what felt like hours, my mind coming up with all kinds of heartbreaking scenarios. He was going to leave me, wasn't he? That had to be it. What else could it be? What had I said to him that had changed his demeanor so drastically tonight? I couldn't remember. It couldn't have been *that* bad, could it? If I'd said anything too outrageous it seems like I would've remembered it, even if I had been tired and tipsy. But obviously something had struck a nerve.

I spent my entire Sunday morning waiting. Every time the floor creaked or the cat jumped off the furniture, my heart leapt into my throat and I whirled around, expecting to see him standing there. But he didn't come. By lunchtime, I was starting worry. Was he coming at all today? I tried to call him, but he didn't answer. He was a time traveler – he had no excuse to keep me waiting. But I waited, and he didn't come. I ate dinner and paced around the house all evening. But he didn't come. I watched the clock on the wall tick over to midnight. He was officially a day late. Something was wrong. Something had to be wrong.

I hardly slept at all that night, and I went into work on Monday morning looking like a train wreck. I was distracted all day by my own thoughts, and I had a hard time focusing on my clients. Where was he? Why hadn't he shown up? Why wasn't he answering his phone? What had happened to him?

On the ride home, a terrible thought occurred to me. What if he'd changed after he left me Saturday night? What if that's where he was – lying on a floor somewhere, unconscious, changing. What if I had lost the Trent I loved? What if he had forgotten me, and I was never going to see him again? Then again, what if he didn't forget me, but he didn't want to come back? What if he thought I wouldn't love him the same? Would he really just leave me out on a ledge like this? Would he deny me closure? Would he deny me the opportunity to try to love the new him? I couldn't bear to think about it.

After my shower, I went into my room to get dressed, but instead I climbed into bed. I was exhausted, and I was a nervous wreck. I just wanted to close my eyes and enjoy the numbing relief sleep provided. I pulled my blankets up over my head to shut out the evening light filtering in through my curtains. I must've been more worn out than I had realized, because it wasn't long before I was teetering on the edge of sleep, my mind halfway dipped into a dream.

I suddenly felt the blankets being pulled down off of my face, and my eyes opened slightly. When I saw a face looking down at me, my fist reflexively shot out at it before I registered who it was that was looking down at me. I punched Trent right between the eyes.

He leapt back with his hands over his face. "Bloody hell!"

I sat up in bed, but quickly remembered that I never did get dressed after my shower. I pulled my covers up over my bare breasts.

"Jesus, Trent! Are you ok?!"

"Damn. I'm usually pretty quick, but you still got me." He walked over and looked in the mirror. "Well, at least there isn't any blood."

"Are you going to have a black eye?"

"No, I don't get black eyes. I heal much more rapidly than the average person." He turned back to me and approached my bedside. "What are you doing in here? You never go to bed this early. Are you feeling all right?"

I ignored his questions. "Where the hell have you been?!" I demanded angrily. I had been so worried about him that now that he was here, it manifested as anger.

"What do you mean? I was only gone for a couple of days."

"You didn't answer when I called!"

"I was busy."

"So busy you couldn't let me know everything was ok?"

"Why are you so cross with me?" Trent asked, bewildered.

"I thought you'd left me!" I cried, my eyes reddening.

"Why would you think that? It was only a couple of days!"

"A couple of days means a lot more to me than it does to you! I think you forget that! I only have so many days – I don't get an endless supply like you do. And I don't want any more of them wasted without you in them, you jerk!"

Trent's expression softened. He reached out and used his thumb to wipe away the tear that had started to roll down my cheek.

"I'm sorry. I didn't realize."

"It didn't help that you left me the other night saying we needed to talk, and everybody knows that 'we need to talk' is never a good thing. So, I've been a jumble of nerves worried about you and worried about us and I haven't been sleeping well and—"

Trent's lips were suddenly against mine, silencing me. I could feel my anger and anxiety melting away. God, how I had missed those lips. I threw my arms around his neck, dropping the covers I had been holding up around me.

When the kiss concluded, Trent glanced down. "You're naked!"

"Don't act so scandalized. It's nothing you haven't seen before." I reached out and tugged gently on his tie, encouraging him to join me on the bed. He sat down on the side of the bed and turned toward me with one foot still on the floor.

He looked down at the bed. "Is it terrible that knowing that I wasn't the last man in this bed fills me with jealousy?"

"No. But don't let it bother you too much. You might not have been the last one to *be* in this bed, but you were the last man for everything else."

Trent looked down at his hands. "Is it terrible that I wish I could be the *only* man?"

I felt my heart flutter.

"I thought you wanted me to find someone else?" I said questioningly.

"I thought I did, too."

I paused. "Trent, what are you saying?"

"I've been thinking about what you said. You were right. The way we're going on right now…there's really no point in denying it, is there?"

"…What did I say?"

Trent gave me a puzzled look. "When you said we were bound to each other, and our friendship isn't really just friendship. You don't remember that?"

"Oh, yes. That. Of course." I didn't remember saying that. I had felt that way for a long time, but I never meant to say it.

"You were right."

"Wait, what are you saying, exactly?"

Trent reached over and took my hand in his, looking at me with soulful eyes. "Roselyn Wolff, I love you. I love you like I've never loved anyone. I've loved you since I first met you two hundred years ago, and you've stuck in my heart through every change ever since. I waited all that time, knowing I would get to be with you again – knowing that someday perhaps you would fall in love with me, when I bore a different face. I never told you this, but as time passed, I checked in on you. I wasn't trying to be creepy. I wasn't stalking you, and I only did it a handful of times. I just…needed to see you. You never noticed me, and that was the way I wanted it to be. I knew eventually I would be called to you and you would notice me this time. But the more I thought about it the older I got, and the more jaded I became – I began to realize that I wasn't what you needed. I decided that if I loved you, I needed to let you go. And I tried to. I really did. But, dammit, my heart has just refused to let you go completely. So now I put it in your hands. What do you want, Roselyn? What do you need from me? Is this a life you can live with? Do you want more? Do you want less? What do *you* want?"

I was speechless. I'd heard Trent talk about love in regard to me before, but this was the first time he'd ever explicitly told me he *loved me.* I looked away and wiped my eyes.

"If this isn't what you want, I understand," Trent said dejectedly.

I turned back to him. "Haven't you been paying even the slightest attention? Jesus, Trent. Yes, this is a life I can live with. I want more. I want everything you have to offer, the good and the bad. I want it all! That's what I've been asking for this entire time!" I leaned over and kissed him. "It's about time you finally asked me what I wanted."

Trent smiled against my lips. "Then I guess there's just one more thing to ask you then." He pulled the watch that he had stolen from the parallel world out of his pocket – the one that had caused all the ruckus with Sam. He held it out to me. "Roselyn…run away with me."

I threw my hand over my mouth. "You…you're giving it to me?"

"I am giving you everything I have. All of time and all of me. Now you will always be able to find me no matter where or when I am. No force on Earth will be able to keep us apart."

"But…what if I screw something up?"

"Don't worry. I've repaired it and reprogrammed it. It's basically got 'training wheels' programmed into it right now, and I'll work with you on it."

I gently took the watch from him. "I don't know what to say."

"Say yes."

My heart soared. I touched my forehead to his and nodded. "Yes. Of course, yes."

Trent grinned happily at me. "So, is there anywhere or anywhen you want to go first?"

I started to unknot his tie. "I just want to be right here, right now – with you."

As Trent leaned over me and kissed me, his hands exploring the body that now belonged to him and him alone, the watch he had given me slipped unnoticed from my hand and clattered under the bed.

I've never looked back.

THE END

About the Author

I was born and raised in Michigan. I have spent most of my life in the Upper Peninsula, where I currently reside with my husband and our two children. I earned my Bachelors of Science degree from Grand Valley State University in 2008 and started my first book in early 2010. When I'm not writing, I teach painting classes, read, and enjoy being active.

I have been inspired by the works of a variety of both fiction and nonfiction authors, including Brian Greene, Michio Kaku, Carl Sagan, Stephen King, and Dean Koontz.

If you enjoyed *The Time Thief,* look for the sequel, *The Time Thief: A Change of Face.*

Special thanks to my family and friends who have been so supportive and given me constructive criticism and ideas along the way. I couldn't have done it without you.

84133459R00168

Made in the USA
San Bernardino, CA
03 August 2018